PRAISE FOR R_

"It would be fair to assume that most literature has its genesis in verisimilitude—after all, don't creative writing teachers always say, "Write about what you know," and Sally Fernandez knows a lot about what's happening today. *Redemption*, with its excellent analysis of our current economic situation and disastrous government policies, has all the qualities and experiences to merit the term. It "fits the bill" as the saying goes. Lively economics/political discussions among the characters are fascinating to follow and the setting is most intriguing. Once again, a work that merits the accolade, 'A good read!'"

—Alfredo S. Vedro, Media Production Consultant, Florida

PRAISE FOR "THE SIMON TRILOGY"

The Ultimate Revenge (Book 3)
"If you love conspiracy theories, whether those that are factual or imagined... if you delight in a storyteller who mixes real-world contemporary people and events into her fictional venues... if you enjoy connecting the dots... whether you are a believer or are just fascinated by all the possibilities...then *The Ultimate Revenge* has to be the choice for your 'best read' this season. Intrigue and suspense dominate throughout this compelling final episode in "The Simon Trilogy." A real page-turner."

—Alfredo S. Vedro, Media Production Consultant, Florida

"A blockbuster! I thoroughly enjoyed and recommend this latest in Ms. Fernandez' interrelated novels. It is a real *tour de force*, suspenseful, and compelling—a page-turner. The intricacies of the plot are fascinating and Ms. Fernandez' weaving of its elements is truly impressive. There are politics involved, as Ms. Fernandez explains very clearly in her Afterword, and I learned a lot about the international background of our own nation's political evolution. Fascinating, to say the least. Ms. Fernandez gets better and better with each installment of her tale. I found the characters of Noble, Max, and Stanton come alive in a new and interesting way. I am hoping for more adventures in which they grow and develop. I am also waiting for Amanda to come more out of the shadows. I can't wait for the next volume in the series."

—R. Halpern, B.A. (Honours) Oxford University, M.A. / Ph.D.
Princeton University

"Just finished reading *The Ultimate Revenge*. In a word—phenomenal! Having thoroughly enjoyed the first two books, *Brotherhood Beyond the Yard* and *Noble's Quest*, I was more than anxious to read the final book of "The Simon Trilogy." It is an incredible and fitting finale in the lives of characters created by an author who takes you into a world of intrigue where she expertly weaves a story that has the reader pondering the possibility, or perhaps I should say probability, of fiction being more real than we dare to think. A great read that I would strongly recommend!"

—Donna Post, Banking Consultant (Ret.), Florida

"You do not have to be a political junky to love this book of intrigue. *The Ultimate Revenge* takes you to a place that will make you question— could it happen—and if it did? The recherché and insight that has gone into this book will certainly keep you wondering for a long time."

—Ann E. Howells, Wine Consultant, Florida

"The line between reality and fiction is totally blurred in this well written, well researched novel. I just finished reading *The Ultimate Revenge*. My head is spinning... as Fernandez did an amazing job weaving fact and fiction! More than a few times, I had to stop reading and check the copyright date. Did she write the story *before* it was revealed in the news? Did she write the "facts" *before* it happened in real time? What was/is "real"? What was/is "fiction"? I consider myself fairly knowledgeable when it comes to political news in our country. After reading this book, I am very confused. My confusion, I feel, stems from Fernandez' incredible research...and her imagination—all based in reality. Well done!"

—Beth Littman Quinn, Vice President at
Marketburst, Massachusetts

Noble's Quest (Book 2)
"A captivating second addition to "The Simon Trilogy." Intense rhythmic development woven brilliantly—at times haunting and foreboding—at others a palpable sensation of an unerring power, leaving you to confront your own views of contemporary events. The modern political thriller has a strong advocate in Fernandez."

—Maestro Debra Cheverino, Internationally Recognized
Conductor, Fulbright Scholar (Florence, Italy)

"I was anxiously awaiting the publication of *Noble's Quest* as I had read the prequel, *Brotherhood Beyond the Yard*. I was not disappointed! *Noble's Quest* is everything I was hoping for and more. Along with solid characters development (Noble Bishop really comes alive), Ms. Fernandez has a tight grip on the pulse of the high stakes world we live in today. Her ability to merge political intrigue, international terrorism, and state of the art technology into a swirl of tension-filled events brings to mind the writing of John La Carre. I can't wait for the last installment of the trilogy."
—William Kelley, Artist, Florence, Italy and Sarasota, Florida

"Put it down? *No way*! Simon at his tricks with a sparkling cast! There were new unexpected developments that truly enhanced the *Brotherhood*. So real, it's easy to visualize in real life. Or was it. Making us wait for number three is crazy! Bring it on Sally. I thought it merited six starts."
**—Garrett B. Vonk, President-Keiser Career College &
Southeastern Institute Florida**

"As the sequel it met my expectations for another exciting work of intrigue and adventure. Sally does a fantastic job of keeping three balls in the air while moving each plot along in a well thought out methodical track. Characters are fully developed so you really know them, as this is critical for the story to move along. Max is just what Noble needs to compliment who he is as an investigator and person. Simon is more sinister than ever and his control is more evident as the reader follows his devious mind. I do not want to divulge the ending, but wait! It's not over! Well written and paced…a great read for any season!"
**—Richard Cobello, Director, Information Technology,
Schenectady County Government (New York)**

"I've never been a spy nor an intelligence agent nor a villain, but I would love to be one so I could inhabit the world of *Noble's Quest*, Sally Fernandez' sequel to *Brotherhood Beyond the Yard*, her excellent first novel that took readers through the intricacies of maneuvering a fraud into the office of the President of the United States. Now the intrigue continues as Fernandez brings us into a world where nothing is as it seems at first—places, people, and events morph from one apparent reality to another… Fernandez' writing style is a delightful blend of fast-moving, crisp language presented in a paradoxically unhurried pace that allows the plot to develop slowly and deliberately. We are constantly challenged to think about where she might be going; almost sparring with her to see if we can guess correctly... Finally, the ending caught me by complete surprise. Fernandez won the sparring contest. The clues were there—no obfuscations—just cleverly woven into a very entertaining and thoughtful narrative."

—Alfredo S. Vedro, Media Production Consultant, Florida

Brotherhood Beyond the Yard (Book 1)

"Simon Hall, one of the characters in Sally Fernandez' addictive novel, *Brotherhood Beyond the Yard*, is an ace puppeteer, manipulating the people he encounters, taking them and you on a thrilling political rollercoaster. Timely—could it be paralleled to the current administration?—and masterly crafted, Sally's action prose will have you riveted right up to the last page. I impatiently anticipate a sequel to see Simon's next strategic move."

—Dann Dulin, Senior Editor, *A&U Magazine*

"Unquestionably, this is a book for the thinking reader. The book's combination of intellect, authenticity and believability, led me on several occasions, almost to forget that I was reading fiction. The author's use of language is quite exceptional...I'm still pondering the book's serious dose of reality and am impatient to get my hands on a copy of the sequel!"

— Edwin Chadbourne, Ph.D., Human Resources Professional (Australia)

"A parable for the times in which we live. Fernandez has written a classic fable for our Age of Doubt, just as Kerouac defined the Age of Hippies. Worth reading no matter what side of the political spectrum you inhabit."

—Aladar Gabriel, Florence, Italy

"Fascinating story, intriguing title. It certainly is thought provoking and intellectually stimulating. It easily brings to mind the power of the Pericles quote at the beginning of the book. Kudos to a new and exciting author!"

—Dr. Patricia Ames, Fulbright Scholar, Maine

"Two thumbs up! *Brotherhood Beyond the Yard* is a gripping story of intrigue from beginning to end. The reader is captured by the ingenuity

and daring of the *Brotherhood* and their unprecedented impact (one hopes) on the political and economic future of our country and the world. In its daring exploitation of the national political process with worldwide implications, the reader is left to ponder the possibility of reality and its consequences. Truly a mystery one is left pondering could it really happen. Can't wait for the sequel."
   —Philip Ames, Marketing Director, General Electric (Ret.), Florida

"Excellent read in these interesting times...well-crafted and contemporary with intelligent twists and turns! Had me missing a few nights of sleep..."
   —Roland Marcz, Owner, Shanghai Malong Construction
   (Shanghai, China)

"I have finished reading *Brotherhood Beyond the Yard*. I commend the author for her imagination and for her use of her expertise and knowledge of politics, finance, academe, and electronics. The plot is a natural for a Hollywood film: I can see George Clooney in several of the roles. *Complimenti*!! I eagerly await the sequel."
   —Horace W. Gibson, Co-Founder of the International School of
   Florence, Italy

"Amazed and Amused. *Brotherhood Beyond the Yard* far exceeded my expectations from a new writer on the scene. I was pleasantly drawn into the plot, and as it developed, I was often amazed and amused at how well the author manipulated my curiosity and intrigue regarding the characters as they intertwined their lives in order to devise and undertake a 'master' plan. Now I am left wanting to read more of what I hope will the first part of an epic story to come. Did someone say the future is now...?"
   —Philip Claypool, Acclaimed Country Western Singer/Songwriter

"The *Brotherhood Beyond the Yard* is a wonderful story—compelling and all too believable. It is masterfully plotted, with every episode revealing an increasingly tangled but utterly plausible scheme in which fundamentally decent people perpetrate a despicable fraud, manipulated by a master puppeteer. The fast-paced denouement satisfies all the expectations of a political thriller and yet leaves just enough unfinished business to leave readers anxiously awaiting the next installment...This is a story that unfolds both psychologically and visually, almost begging for a cinematic rendering, and I found myself visualizing many of the individual chapters as scenes in a movie..."
   —Linda Cabe Halpern, Dean of University Studies,
   James Madison University

"...I strongly recommend *Brotherhood Beyond the Yard* for those looking for an exciting, pithy read. As you near the conclusion of, I hope, this first book, the pages will jump out of your hands. A great read for either the beach or the fire."
  —John Pearl, Partner, Pearl Associates (Greenwich, Connecticut)

"I highly recommend this book. Mystery thrillers, detective thrillers, even vampire thrillers are really enjoyable read. *Brotherhood Beyond the Yard* is just that...an international political thriller that's timely and provocative, and contains extremely believable characters placed in well researched locations and situations."
  —Baroness Suzanne Pitcher Flaccomio, Founder and Director of Pitcher & Flaccomio (Florence, Italy)

"You'll want to fasten your seat belt to navigate the twists and turns of this global political thriller. Fernandez combines knowledge of banking, technology, and politics to offer a 'back to the future' reading adventure. And, the author's intimate familiarity of Florentine life makes one want to buy a one-way ticket."
  —Donna Davidson, Davidson Associates (San Francisco, California)

"Great read! Unfortunately, all the clichés in English are true and have become so firmly entrenched in our vocabulary that few or no fresh phrases have entered the language. So, when we want to give praise we are stuck with the all-too-familiar 'compelling,' 'page-turner,' 'riveting,' and the like—all appropriate for *Brotherhood*, but I lack the talent to come up with anything more complimentary. So, I hope readers will accept my very simple *wow*! I thoroughly enjoyed *Brotherhood*—plot, characters, setting, and the many subtle little cleverness's and clues the author drops in as the plot progresses—that I can't quote here for fear of giving it away."
  —Alfredo S. Vedro, Media Production Consultant, Florida

Redemption

Redemption

Aftermath of
The Simon Trilogy

A Novel

Sally Fernandez

Redemption
Aftermath of The Simon Trilogy
Copyright © 2015 by Sally Fernandez.

www.dunhamgroupinc.com

Trade Paperback ISBN: 978-1939447654

Ebook ISBN: 978-1939447661

Library of Congress Control Number: 2015931334

Printed in the United States of America

*It seemed more than befitting to dedicate the last novel
in this series to Joe Fernandez, my incredible editor,
greatest supporter, and loving husband. Without him,
I never would have been able to persevere through the
intense writing and research involved to turn
"The Simon Trilogy" into a tetralogy.*

Ti Amo

"The government's view of the economy can be summed up in a few short phrases: If it moves, tax it. If it keeps moving, regulate it. And if it stops moving, subsidize it."
– Ronald Reagan

Simon Hall, a notorious terrorist, also known as Mohammed al-Fadl, jumped to his death off the Peace Bridge in Buffalo, New York on April 3, 2017.

A national disaster of gargantuan proportions had been averted.

Twenty-two years earlier, Simon filled a different role as the self-appointed leader of a group of Harvard scholars calling themselves *La Fratellanza* or *The Brotherhood*. These extraordinarily brilliant men had devised a thesis that began as an intellectual game. Later it morphed into a real-life experience with the presidential election of Abner Baari. Then, five months before the end of his second term, Baari resigned in disgrace and fled the country. No one could have foreseen the consequences or its ramifications, especially this group of literati.

The death of Simon brought no closure—for another crisis loomed with the U.S. government reporting the national debt at a staggering $22 trillion. Although, several economists believed that number to be a gross miscalculation by leaving out certain unfunded liabilities. By factoring in government loan guarantees, deposit insurance, and actions taken by the Federal Reserve, as well as the cost of other government trust funds, the total amount the government owed was, more likely, a staggering $70 trillion. Now, with entitlement programs on the verge of becoming insolvent, foreclosures again on the rise, and social unrest continuing to permeate the airwaves, the U.S. braced herself once again. At the same time, a crisis of confidence in the newly elected president had become problematic; the stagnant unemployment rate and massive debt were about to become unsustainable; the threat of an economic collapse was imminent.

1
HAIL TO THE CHIEF

A dark cloud cast a shadow over Washington, D.C., but it was insignificant when viewed against the massive gray sky that loomed over the country. With April temperatures fluctuating between 85 degrees one day and 50 degrees the next, coupled with torrential downpours, a state of gloom and malaise seized the American public.

Granted, Simon Hall was dead to the relief of many, and the national electric grid remained operational despite the constant threats. But the stagnant economy and a job market with no predictable improvement in sight presented a herculean challenge for President Randall Post in his first few months in office.

The weather was of little consequence.

The country, coming off the heels of a world recession, was destined to head back down that slippery slope. The president needed to act. He had retained a slight majority in the House and in the Senate, but it left the opposition enough muscle to oppose any sweeping legislation. There were no guarantees, but it afforded President Post two years to try to turn the country around before the off-year elections—but the country could not wait two years.

∽

The clock read five minutes of two. Noble Bishop, the director of the States Intelligence Agency, needed only three minutes to walk down the stairs to arrive at the Oval Office. That gave him two minutes to wonder what the president's urgent request entailed.

"Go in; he's waiting," the president's secretary announced as Noble rounded the corridor.

Seconds later, Noble found himself locked in the customary handshake. "Mr. President."

"Thanks for coming down on such short notice," the President greeted him. Then, seeming more officious than usual, he motioned Noble to the sofa on the left. "Have a seat." The president remained standing.

Noble readied himself for the unexpected.

"You're a smart guy," the President continued, offering a slight smile. Then he asked, "What have you found to be the number-one concern of the American people?"

Noble was surprised by the rather simple question, considering it was the topic dominating the national conversation. He offered the logical answer. "Jobs, sir."

"Hmm, I asked my twelve-year-old niece the same question, and she gave that exact answer. Precocious and quite mature for her age, she persisted and asked, 'Uncle Randall, you're the president; can't you fix it?' I promised the sweet child that I would do everything in my power to resolve the problem."

After his pronouncement, the president walked over to the other sofa and sat down opposite Noble. Then, while he maintained unsettling eye contact, the conversation took an even odder twist. He began to deliver what sounded like a State of the Union Address from his seated position.

"Our nation's economy continues to be unstable and a weak economy threatens our national security. In the last two months alone, there have been massive layoffs, witnessed by the streaming picket lines of unemployed workers protesting against their companies. And when they're not railing out against their employers, they're protesting against the newly amnestied immigrants, fearing their own government subsidies are in jeopardy. Social unrest is spreading across the country."

Noble was well aware that the president had inherited an untenable situation, but was saddened that the president spoke as though he was personally responsible. At that moment, for some inexplicable reason, an unattributed quotation popped into Noble's head. "Sir, someone once said, 'War is when the government tells you who the bad guy is;

revolution is when you decide that for yourself.' I hope that's not what we are facing."

The president cocked his head. "Clearly, the citizens have already attributed their woes to the bad guy—their government." He stopped and looked straight at Noble with an unusually painful expression. "The country is divided; her mere existence is in peril. As I told my niece, I would do everything in my power to resolve the problem. There are a multitude of options to consider, but to be utterly honest; I'm not sure where to start. After a brutal election, partisan politics have reached their apex. The past Congress, incapable of stopping the bleeding, perpetuated the problem. And the freshly elected Congress has yet to make the difficult choices." The president paused for a moment and then lamented, "I've become the Commander in Chief of Triage. With all the government resources at my disposal, I still can't see a clear way out of this crisis. And most indeed it can't be resolved with the swipe of a pen!"

"Sir, unfortunately, the crisis doesn't stop at our borders," Noble said, referring to the ongoing crisis in the Middle East and the increase of radicalism throughout the world.

The president seemed not to take note; his focus was on the domestic front for the moment. Then, he abruptly backed away from his earlier self-recrimination and returned to his usual stoic presidential mode.

Noble noticed that the president glanced toward the American flag, positioned behind his desk. He assumed the president was contemplating his next statement. Then without warning, he redirected his eye contact to Noble.

"Our unemployment rate has flatlined at six-point-five percent, notwithstanding the staggering number of people who continue to drop out of the workforce and become dependent on the government. Today, one third of eligible workers have been unemployed for more than a year. That's one of the dynamics that caused the Great Depression." His decisive statement was coupled with great unease. He continued, "People once again are defaulting on their loans, and with energy costs soaring, the middle class is barely able to sustain its lifestyle. As a direct result, the embattled housing market is bracing for another moment of truth—the likes of the 2008 crash."

"If we continue to sashay down this path the economy will become *unsustainable*," Noble stated with emphasis, signaling that he understood the gravity of the situation.

Satisfied at Noble's grasp of the situation, the president nodded and then continued in the same vein, quoting numerous statistics to support his premise. Then, he cited another grave concern. "After three years, the country is still recovering from the influx of one hundred and fifty thousand immigrants arriving from Central America in 2014, increasing pain to the already suffering. Added to the mix was the induction of twenty million more illegal immigrants that needed to be prepared to stand in the so-called *path to citizenship*. The entire process has put a terrible strain on state governments and the taxpayers. The language barrier alone adds to the tension. Noble, we are about to ride the killer wave in a perfect storm. God willing, we'll come out on the other side."

"Sir, we are all grateful that you were able to gain approval to reallocate funds to seal the border at long last."

"We're not home free yet—but we are getting closer. Increased border security will have to suffice in the interim until we find permanent solutions. But the processing and deportation have been an exhaustive administrative nightmare. The costs are untold." The president let out a noticeable sigh before readjusting his seat. Then he confessed, "You'll never hear me speak about this outside these walls, but had Baari gone to the table with comprehensive immigration reform, it would have saved the taxpayers billions of dollars. His end run around Congress, directing the Department of Homeland Security to ignore deportation, was unconscionable. But the final blow was the sweeping amnesty provisions he neatly wrapped up in an executive order. In the final analysis, he chose to abdicate his responsibility for leadership and turned it over to the governors and state taxpayers to bear the burden."

Noble continued to listen intently but felt distraught at the president's even bleaker assessment that followed.

"We are standing on the edge of the precipice and run the risk of falling into a depression. It would create insurmountable damage not only to the country but to the world economy," he stated, as though it were a personal default on a promise. The concern resonated in his voice. "In the eyes of the people, the makeup of the new Congress makes no difference. Confidence in the government as a whole has been lost. The people see the legislative branch and the executive branch as still being polarized, not able to shake off the rhetoric from the last eight years that divided the nation."

The president stopped. The room became eerily silent, adding to Noble's discomfort. Then he redirected the conversation back to the prior administration and alleged, "The information that spewed out of the White House from my predecessor seemed to take a circuitous route, directing the citizens away from the truth." He noted a few scandals to make his point, emphasizing Benghazi, Bergdahl, and NSA, IRS, DOJ, among other jumbled letters. Then, sounding more like his fighting, spirited self, he became most emphatic and announced, "The American citizens deserve better! I must regain their trust!" -

After a few more statements in a similar vein, it appeared that the president was about to wind down the conversation—leaving Noble even more confused as to why he was summoned in the first place. For certain, the sweeping change in the tenor of the conversation had left him flummoxed. But before he departed the Oval Office, the discussion would take another curious route.

"Did you enjoy your prior position as research analyst at the CIA?" the president asked.

Noble, taken aback by the question, responded instinctively. "There are times I miss the simplicity of the role, sir—relatively speaking."

The president offered no reaction to his answer. But then the actual purpose of the meeting unfolded. Over a ten-minute period, the president made a series of requests and then posed the ultimate question. "Can you do this?"

Noble took a deep breath and then replied, "Yes, sir. It can be done!"

It was the only acceptable response.

After a few hurried pleasantries, Noble left the Oval Office, carrying more questions than answers.

It was not an agenda he could have anticipated.

2
CALL TO ARMS

Noble trekked back up the stairs to his office, contemplating the situation along the way. Then he readied himself. As he entered his reception area, he exclaimed, "Fine!" without giving Doris the opportunity to ask the inevitable question.

She was predictable. For years, his secretary had asked the same question each time he returned from the Oval Office. "How did it go with POTUS?" had become her mantra.

In response to his outburst, Doris just rolled her eyes and refocused on the keyboard.

In that particular moment, he was in no mood for chitchat. And truth be known, there was nothing *fine* at all about his conversation with the President of the United States.

"Doris, hold my calls," he ordered as he headed into his office.

Before even reaching his desk, Noble hurriedly opened his famed xPhad, a combination smartphone that transformed into a tablet. Although it was somewhat thicker than an iPhone, when unfolded the tablet became the identical thickness as the iPad; it was a device essential to his day-to-day activities. Now, seated at his desk, he began to use the stylus to doodle on the tablet as he reviewed in his mind the gist of the meeting. Then, after firmly collecting his thoughts, he started to dissect point-by-point the issues the president had addressed. As Noble continued to mull over the series of questions that had been raised, he was overcome by the same trepidation that the president had projected.

One question in particular caused him to reflect on Hamilton Scott, his predecessor. It was a time when Hamilton had plucked him out of the CIA and coaxed him to join the SIA. Fatefully, it had thrust Noble into a case that required him to interrogate his former classmates from Harvard, the infamous members of La Fratellanza. In some ways, he was affected as well, despite the fact that he had refused to become part of the illicit group. Certainly, after the death of Hamilton, he was pulled into a life-changing game of cat and mouse with Simon Hall, challenged to track him down and bring him to justice; three times he had failed. Without foresight, he had been robbed of the opportunity. It all came to an end with Simon's grand leap off the Peace Bridge.

The conversation with the president had also dredged up memories of the years spent in the hunt for Simon and of the final words Simon left in a message on that fateful day. Noble could still picture vividly the last sentence that read, "Act Three has yet to begin—watch out." That statement continued to haunt him to this day. *This is no time to resurrect the past*, he thought fleetingly, until he quickly admonished himself. *The answer will have to wait.* He shrugged.

With stylus once again in hand, he continued to jot down a few more points. Then he reached for the phone and made the first of his calls.

Secret Service Agent Stanton hung up his phone, mildly curious as to the reason for all the secrecy. Although, the SIA director had said that the orders came from the president. It was not his job to question, only to obey orders. Of all people, he understood protocol, having been a major in the U.S. Army's Special Forces. And he trusted Noble. Had it not been for his recommendation, Stanton would not be heading up the president's Secret Service detail. It was then that Major Stanton proudly traded in his medals and uniform for the standard black suit and earpiece.

Stanton first met the director during Operation NOMIS, an operation tasked with entering an underground encampment south of the Dugway Proving Ground in Utah. The mission was to capture Simon inside the encampment where they suspected he was hiding. Noble's deputy director, Maxine Ford, was in charge of the initial operation, at which time she was badly bruised in an explosion that killed two soldiers. The next day Major Stanton met Max. At first, sparks flew as they stepped on each other's turf; then the sparks took on a different meaning. Not surprisingly, Stanton moved to Washington a short time thereafter—and not for purely professional reasons.

From the onset, Stanton and Max recognized that their respective professions could create tension from time to time in their personal relationship. But he was grateful that Max had top-secret security clearance and was familiar with most of the Secret Service assignments. Unquestionably, it made their time together easier and generated many lively discussions. Later that evening, Stanton was scheduled to meet Max at the Blackfinn American Saloon, a watering hole for the politicos inside the beltway. It was their usual go-to spot before deciding where to head for dinner. For the first time, Stanton would not be able to discuss his latest assignment—an assignment that was beyond even Max's purview.

3
STRANGER IN THE NIGHT

Max rushed out of the White House and into the pouring rain. "Shit," she uttered as she retrieved her umbrella. Then she sprinted the typically nine-minute walk to meet Stanton, all the while trying to avoid the taxis that managed to splash through most of the puddles on the street.

Fortunately, Stanton didn't notice her bursting through the front door at the Blackfinn, nor the fact that she was running late. Unaware, he sat at the end of the bar nursing his beer. Without delay, she removed her soggy raincoat and hung it on the last of the empty wall hooks. Then she tiptoed over and playfully slid her arms around him from behind. Stanton jerked his body forward, apparently surprised by her arrival.

"Hey babe, I told you not to do that," he cautioned, and then little by little softened his lips into a smile.

"Sorry. I know!" Max admitted, wrinkling her nose. She hated it when she fell out of character, and it was a trait that was occurring with some frequency as of late. Despite the fact, she was well aware of the pitfalls of their professions and knew to stay vigilant. The whole relationship thing was still very confusing—a concept she would admit only to herself. More often than not she would question her behavior and confess to herself, "If this is what love does to you—I'm not sure I want any part of it." Embarrassed at her *faux pas*, she immediately changed the subject. "You seemed deep in thought. Is everything okay with the big guy?"

"Everything is fine. POTUS has been staying pretty close to home these days. I think, in part, he wants to assure the public that he's at the helm, trying to stem the economic crisis."

"Why does everyone keep bringing up the economic crisis?" she carped, annoyed by the perpetual chant.

Stanton ignored her slight distraction. "On a happy note, it keeps me in Washington close to you." Considerably more at ease, he moved in, but was able to manage only a kiss on the cheek. Without niggling, he asked, "What can I get you?"

"The usual." Max sat up on the bar stool and began to tackle the potato-chip bowl.

"Hungry?"

"Not really. Sorry I'm late; I was wrapping up a few cases. So what are you working on?" she asked, throwing a question back at him.

"You mean other than keeping the president safe?"

"When the rooster is in the roost, you must have other duties?"

"Max, what's going on? You're aware of what I do."

"Nothing. I guess I can't decide what to talk about tonight."

"We could go to your place. I'm sure we can find something to do that doesn't require talking." Stanton reached over to pull Max closer but she jolted backward.

"Now who's pulling away?"

Max had just viewed a figure entering the door at the front end of the bar. "See that guy? The one who just walked in, the one in the hoodie and dark glasses."

"Yeah."

"I saw him a few days ago at the supermarket. Yesterday, he was at the bus stop when I was walking to work. I had this weird sensation that he was following me."

Stanton, without hesitation, stood up.

"Sit down!" she ordered brusquely.

"I'm going over to speak with him," Stanton insisted.

"I can handle this, Agent. Let it go for now—maybe I'm imagining things!"

"Max, this doesn't sound like you. The Max I know would have pinned his face against the wall."

"I'll be on my guard. I promise. Can we change the subject, please?"

"Do you think you could find a subject you would like to discuss?" Stanton was becoming frustrated, and he didn't need a fight at that moment. "Look, you seem tired. Finish your beer and I'll walk you home."

Max glared at him.

"I'll leave as soon as you are safe inside your front door."

"I'm sorry. You're right. Let's call it a night."

Stanton flagged the bartender for the tab.

Max glanced over toward the front door.

The hooded figure was gone.

4
RECOVERER'S REMORSE

The rain didn't stop inside the beltway but persisted as it moved up the coast, blanketing the Northeast with the same gloomy sky. The darkness also lingered heavily over one of the households belonging to a member of La Fratellanza.

Chase Worthington was the campaign finance director for Abner Baari's political campaigns, both for the senatorial and presidential races. However, he chose not to join the White House Administration. Instead, he opted for his dream position as the chief financial officer at the National Depositors Trust Bank in New York.

Chase was always at his finest when tucked away in his office on Park Avenue. And, despite the fact it was Sunday, he longed to be there. Especially at that moment, having unsuccessfully negotiated with his wife over the course of the past hour. Now it was time to try a different tactic. He hoisted his hand in the air and stated sharply, "Enough!" in hopes of bringing the discussion to a final close.

It had no effect.

She adjusted her sails and used a more delicate approach, in hopes of getting through to him. With more composure, she asked, "Darling, are you sure?"

His answer came in the form of a blank stare.

However, she persisted. "You've been doing so well all these months. Spend more time with your therapist if you need to, but you're strong enough to manage this from home." Then she beseeched, "Your children need you here."

Invoking the children brought him back to the fore. "Trust me!" he snapped. "It's happening again. The anxiety is brewing and I need to go back into rehab, please!" It was his turn to supplicate, not his usual demeanor, but he had to win this round. It might be his last chance to put the past behind him.

She softened her approach a tad more, and asked with composure, "What brought it on this time?" As she cocked her head to face him, she happened to glimpse at the newspaper lying on the table next to him. The day's headline read, *DOW TOPS 25K WHILE QE THREATENS A COLLAPSE.*

Chase caught her expression and exclaimed, "The economic outlook is worsening! I can't stop reliving the fact that I helped start the downfall! Dammit, is that what you wanted to hear?"

As CFO, he understood that the persistent QE, or quantitative easing, by the Federal Reserve could force investors to make riskier investments. He believed they were just buying time and not addressing the underlying economic problems.

On impulse, he grabbed the newspaper and thrust it into the air. "This is a formula for disaster. Especially in a recession that is long in the tooth and shows no signs of recovery!" Even more agitated, he argued, "This could prove to be worse than the Great Depression and I'm, in large part, responsible! Please give me this time away?" he implored, lowering his voice considerably.

Indeed, he was not responsible for the current 2017 recession, but the guilt he felt for the part he played in causing the market collapse in 2008 continued to haunt him. It started all those years ago with a white paper he crafted describing the sub-prime mortgage market and its imminent collapse. It was designed with the intent to begin the downward spiraling crafted by Simon Hall as part of his strategy. And although Simon promised to contain the market crash once Abner Baari won the presidential election, he vanished and the collapse ensued. Chase blamed himself for the black swan event. As a consequence, he had spent the past eight years in and out of rehab centers for the treatment of depression.

His wife was just as afraid of a relapse. She had seen it come and go many times. But she had hoped, with the demise of Simon, that he could put it all behind him. Instead, Chase felt he had been stripped of a chance to set things straight. She had no choice but to give him the space he so desperately needed. She leaned over and wrapped her arms around him. "I've always trusted your judgment," she whispered.

Sensing that he was beginning to relax, she relented. "Take whatever time you need. But please rid yourself of this guilt once and for all." Then, turning to face at him directly, she said, "Do whatever it takes, but return home as the man I married."

Chase pulled her toward him and kissed her gently, while at the same time feeling enormous relief. After spending the last week brooding over his options—it was now settled.

5
AN OFFER THAT CAN'T BE REFUSED

The noon hour struck, but Noble planned to forgo lunch in preparation to placing a series of calls. One was to Florence, Italy. Granted, it was 6:10 in the morning for the Italians, but he couldn't put off the call any longer. So he readied himself for a conversation he hoped would meet with little resistance. After a deep and prolonged inhalalation, he dialed the number. Following several seconds of delay, he finally heard a sleepy voice on the other end of the line.

"*Pronto.*"

"Paolo."

"*Ciao fratello.* What a pleasant surprise. Even so early in the morning." He yawned.

"Sorry, you have my condolence on your uncle's passing, but you're needed back here in Washington A-S-A-P."

"*Mi dispiace.* I'm sorry, but I can't. After the funeral, I promised Natalie and Mario a family vacation while we're here."

"Paolo, trust me. This is the consulting assignment of a lifetime."

"What's it about?"

Noble detected he would acquiesce; Paolo could never resist a challenge. "It's at the request of the president."

"*Mama mia...*"

"Paolo," Noble was quick to interrupt. "You are not to breathe a word of this to anyone, including Natalie. Do you understand?"

Unlike the other members of La Fratellanza, Paolo Salvatore had survived the ordeal with the least amount of scarring. Except now, he feared the possibility of more incoming marital shrapnel. But he had no choice. "*Si, fratello*, but Natalie is not going to like this one bit," he warned.

"Is she with you now?"

"Of course—she's lying right here. If you could only see the expression on her face."

"Put her on." Noble had seen that look a multitude of times, but he always knew how to approach his sister. Most times, he was successful at winning her over.

"Noble, you're not going to ruin this vacation for us. We have very little family time together as it is."

"Nat, I'm just the messenger." He could hear her letting out a few yoga breaths and chose to proceed calmly or, as Paolo would say, *piano piano*. "There's a client who very much needs Paolo's services. I think this would be a real boost to his career. But it's his choice." Noble decided to play it cool. He knew if he pushed too hard, Natalie would become suspicious.

"Why now?" The answer didn't really matter. She assumed it was a done deal. She could fight one of them, but not both. At times, it seemed that she had two big brothers who would determine her fate. "Never mind. We'll all fly back together," she groaned.

"Hey sis, don't disappoint Mario. Tell him his uncle is setting up some great places for him to visit while you're in Italy. You'll be fine on your own. Give me a couple of hours to pull it together. And Nat thanks. Love you. Now let me talk to Paolo."

"Love you too." She handed the phone over, brandishing a look of defeat.

"It looks like you worked your charm again. I think I need remedial lessons," Paolo chuckled. "You win. We'll catch a flight tomorrow."

"No, just you. I have some friends in Florence and I'm sure they'll take good care of your family. Don't spoil it for Mario."

"I'm not the one spoiling anything, *fratello*."

"Let me set things up. I'll call you back in a few hours. *Ciao*."

"*Ciao*."

✑

Noble checked the time again; it was now 7:45 a.m. in Lyon, France. The next call could wait a while longer before his role as vacation planner kicked into play. He had decided that arranging some activities to keep Natalie and Mario in Italy for a few more days would make things easier for everyone in the long run. He continued to sip away at his second— or was it his third?—cup of coffee. He had lost track as he reflected on his close relationship to Natalie. As one would expect, there was a modicum of sibling rivalry, but Noble had always played the protector. Then, after losing their parents in a deadly car crash, while they were both at college, their bond strengthened. Without hesitation, Noble assumed the role of an overbearing guardian much to Natalie's dismay. Admittedly, his demeanor at times, interfered with the suitors vying for her affection. *How ironic that the one person I believed was perfect for her was a member of La Fratellanza,* he mused.

Noble had no way of knowing, in the beginning, that his brother-in-law was a member of the group. He was not even aware of the existence of La Fratellanza until months later. In fact, his first encounter with Paolo Salvatore was on the Harvard campus. It was not until many years later, when they reconnected in Washington, that their friendship quickly blossomed. Then, after a period of time, Noble decided to introduce Paolo to his sister. Soon after, Paolo and Natalie were married; the rest became history. Until, of course, it all started to fall apart.

Out of the blue, Noble shuddered as he brought to mind that frigid day in Franklin Park. The day he sat on the park bench and listened to an astonishing tale. Paolo had reached his breaking point and confessed the entire plot spun by La Fratellanza, first to Natalie, and then to Noble. It was heartwrenching for Paolo to divulge the details, for all the while he knew that the information would ultimately lead to the interrogation of all his fraternal brothers and the possibility of criminal charges loomed. In the end, the members of La Fratellanza did accept an immunity agreement in exchange for their testimony, wanting to bring it all to an end. But it fell short.

Suddenly, Noble heard some clattering outside his office, breaking up his thoughts. He dashed a glance at his watch. It was two o'clock and Doris had returned from lunch. Pleasantly surprised, she entered his office with a tray containing his favorite bill of fare: a turkey sandwich on whole wheat with lettuce and tomato, and another cup of coffee.

"Thank you Doris, but what makes you think I haven't eaten?" he inquired in a teasing manner.

Doris gave him the *look*. "And how long have I been working for you?" Not expecting a response, she then nosily inquired, "What put you into a trance?"

"Close the door on your way out, please," he ordered with a smile, ignoring her inquisitiveness. He then readied himself to place his next call. He was reminded of the last time he had spoken with Enzo Borgini. It was to alert the executive director of police services for Interpol that Simon might be heading his way. This call, however, would be a stark departure from the last. This time he had a personal request.

✑

"*Ciao, amico mio.* What a pleasant surprise."

"Enzo, I trust all is well with you and your family."

"All is well at home, but outside the doors the economic woes prevail. On a positive note, the weather in Lyon is absolutely spectacular this time of the year. You must come for a visit one day."

Noble quickly called to mind the last time he was in Lyon. It was at the request of Enzo, for assistance in tracking down the perpetrators behind the recent New Year's Eve bombings in Paris, Berlin, and London. Ironically, their investigation established a clear link between the bombings and several murders that had taken place in a desolate part of Utah, which Noble had dubbed the Dead Zone. All acts of violence pointed to Simon.

"I shall, my friend. But for now, we have our own challenges on the home front," Noble replied.

"I read about them every day. Europe is bracing itself against your country's economic decline. Anything coming out of the White House?"

Noble skirted the topic and maneuvered to the purpose of the call. "Any plans for visiting you parents?" he asked, hoping for a "yes."

"No. I was in Florence last week. What an odd question. What's the real purpose of your call, Noble?"

"My sister Natalie and her son are in Florence. They were with Paolo, but unexpectedly, he had to return home for a business assignment."

"And you thought I could show them around?" Enzo interrupted.

"You know the city far better than I do. Any suggestions?"

"Give me a minute; let me think. Ah, I'm scheduled to go to San Marino for some meetings next week. Why not have them take a train and meet me there? If they can get there by Monday, I'll be able to spend time with them and orient them to the city, but it's very easy to walk around."

"Great! I'll organize the train tickets."

"Then I'll go ahead and organize some activities for them. They'll have a wonderful time, and it will give them an entirely different experience outside of Florence."

"You're a prince, Enzo. I really appreciate you taking the time."

"*Piacere mio*, it will be my pleasure. Now, speaking of Florence, do you remember Alessandro, the owner of the restaurant Birreria Centrale?"

"Yes, of course; it was a favorite place of Hamilton's." At the mention of Hamilton, Noble had a quick flashback of his predecessor and mentor. It was his vision of Hamilton lying in his bed in his villa in Florence, minutes before he passed away.

"Have your sister and your nephew go there for lunch tomorrow. I'll give Alessandro a call now and see if his son Simone is available to give them a guided tour. Don't worry; they'll be in good hands."

"You're going to make me look like a real hero."

"But Director Bishop, you are a hero. Simon is dead and no longer a threat. On behalf of Interpol, we all thank you!"

"It didn't play out as expected. But that quest is over." Noble moved back on topic. "Let me check the train schedule and I'll email you their arrival time."

"*Bene.* Good; I'll plan to meet them at the station."

"You're too kind, my friend."

"No I'm not. I might need a favor one day."

Noble chuckled. "*Ciao*, Director Borgini."

"*Ciao.*"

"That was easy," Noble uttered. "Now for the pain and torture."

6
THE SABBATICAL

Max caught a glimpse of Noble as she passed by his office on her way to the conference room. Slowly, she backed up, noting his unusual posture. His feet were up on his desk, crossed at the ankles. His arms were stretched behind his head as he peered up at the ceiling, giving the impression that he was in deep thought. She snickered as she thought; *Deep thought for him is tapping furiously at the keyboard or frantically shuffling papers.* Not able to resist, she stuck her head in the door and inquired, "How did it go with the president?"

Noble continued to stare unaware of her presence. Flashes of breadlines, panic on Wall Street, and social unrest kept circling like sliders in his mind. Then the gyrating images paused. All he envisioned was an image of Atlas carrying the world on his shoulders.

"Noble, everything okay?" She hesitated, and then questioned him again. "Hey, anyone home?"

Startled, Noble shot a look at the door. "Yeah, sorry. I was thinking about something."

"Thinking or mesmerized? So how did it go with Post?"

"Fine, Max. Everything is fine," he said, knowing the opposite to be true. Worse yet, he couldn't even confide in Max, of all people.

"Seriously, are you okay?" she repeated. The gloomy sound of his voice gave her instant concern.

"I'm okay, Max! Stop asking," he grumbled, sounding gruffer than he had intended. He rotated his feet back to the floor and shifted to his usual posture in the chair. In a softer tone he asked, "What's up?"

She ignored his disposition for the moment and answered. "You'll never guess. The rogue hacker we've been tracking evidently became bored with the lack of attention he's been receiving in the press. So now that he's set up stakes in Russia, his new claim is to have proof that the CIA trained him as a spy."

Noble gaped at her. "You're not serious? Who does this guy think he is, Snowden?"

"Undoubtedly, he has a lot of hutzpah. Sadly, people are buying into his latest storyline."

"Haven't they figured out that if he did work for us, we wouldn't have him hanging out in the Kremlin, sipping tea with Putin?"

"He's managed to stretch this drama out over the last several years. We should have hauled Snowden and his ass back here when we had the chance," Max declared.

"It's mindboggling to think Snowden was able to convince millions of people that outing the government, with no regard to national security, was an honorable thing to have done. And now this guy has done it again, painting himself as the people's hero. But in my book, they both committed treason. Son of a bitch." Noble let out an exasperated breath and then shook his head. Then, in a more serious tone, he asked, "Don't tell me there is actual proof to support his claim?"

Max continued to relay what facts had been uncovered thus far.

Noble listened without interruption—but he was only half-hearing her words.

"I've begun the investigation to see whether or not there is any proof of the hacker's allegations. I doubt there are, but I'll make doubly sure."

He watched her lips signal she was about to conclude, then promptly jumped in to announce, "I need you to fill in for me for a few months."

She was dumbfounded.

He shot up his hand to silence the impending protest. "I'll be taking a temporary leave of absence. Since the Simon case is closed, it's a good time for me to take a break."

"Is this a *fait accompli*?" she asked with a hint of sarcasm.

"C'mon, you know that case became life-consuming for me. I simply need some time to figure out where I go from here."

"You'll never leave the agency. And the agency needs you."

"I have complete confidence in you, Max. You'll be able to handle things just fine."

"Thanks, Boss," she scoffed. "But this is a lousy time to leave; the country's a mess. And God forbid these periodic protests turn into nationwide civil unrest, as the media predicts *ad nauseam.*"

"Don't exaggerate. It's for only a few months. Just play director, Max."

She had learned the hard way; it was useless to argue. "When?"

"Not sure; possibly next week. I'm still making arrangements."

"So soon!" Max may have conceded, but she had no intention of backing off with the questioning. "So where are you and Amanda going?"

"I'm going solo. As I stated, I need time to sort out some life choices—decisions I've kept postponing thanks to Simon."

"Aren't you two supposed to be planning a wedding?"

"Trust me, Amanda can handle it on her own, and I suspect she would prefer to be extravagant without having to ask for my approval." He chuckled, trying to make light of his comment and to turn the conversation away from himself. Looking her squarely in the eye, he asked, "So how are things between you and Stanton?"

"Great, Noble! Don't change the subject. Is this what you truly want?"

"What, time off or the marriage?"

"Both."

He paused at the question and then answered in earnest, "I'm not sure—to both." Maneuvering away from the personal banter, he said, "Pull together your open case files and let's review them the first of next week. I'm sure there is nothing on the docket that you can't handle."

"Noble…"

"Max!"

She backed off, sensing it was not the time to inquire further. Then, cutting off the repartee, she refocused on her immediate concern. "Where can I reach you?"

"I'll have my cell, but most likely it will be out of range." He was aware that where he was going all frequencies would be frozen, and his personal time to get away would be limited. "I'll try to call in once a week for an update whenever I can."

"What do you mean out of range?"

"I'm playing it loose. Who knows, I may be trekking in Mongolia."

"You, Noble, playing it loose? Is that the best you can do?"

"Let's pick this up later. I have some calls to make."

She surrendered grudgingly and headed to the conference room.

7

LA DOLCE VITA

As Natalie and Mario traversed the streets of Florence looking for Piazza Cimitori, Mario spotted a *gelateria*.

"Mama, *un gelato per favore*?"

"Mario, we are on our way to a restaurant. Ice cream will spoil your lunch."

"Mama, I'll have my dessert first and then my pasta."

"You're impossible! Why do you have to look like your father and act like him too?"

Mario smiled. He was familiar with her expression and he knew she would concede.

Natalie rarely could win an argument with Paolo, mostly because she was overcome by his charm. And, as Mario developed into a young man, she found his charm equally hard to resist. As she looked at the joy on his face, her anger toward both Paolo and Noble, for leaving them alone in Italy, began to diminish. "It's not dessert; it's *dulce*."

"*Brava* Mama."

"*Prego*."

Natalie never had a facility for languages, but over the years she had picked up a few words from Paolo. Now little Mario was her teacher.

"Finish up. I think we're almost there."

Mario, trying to be efficient with the tiny spoon, scooped out the rest of his pistachio gelato and then licked his lips for one final taste. "Mmm, *buono*," he announced, thrilled at his conquest.

As they continued to wend their way through the streets, Natalie saw what appeared to be a church she recognized from the description she had read. She quickly retrieved her guidebook and flipped to the page she had marked earlier as one of her landmarks. "Yes, I thought so."

"Thought what, Mama?"

"This is the Church of Orsanmichele."

"What a strange name," he remarked, wrinkling his nose.

Reading from the guidebook, she explained, "It translates to the 'kitchen garden of Saint Michael.' This says the church was built on the same site where the kitchen garden for the monastery of Saint Michael was previously located. Mario, see how the exterior of the building is surrounded with statues? Each one was commissioned by a guild."

"What's a guild?"

"It's a union; or think of it like your clubs at school. But in Florence there were many guilds: one for wool, another for leather products, and banks, and even butchers. Each guild hired an artist to sculpt a statue of its patron saint to decorate the outside of the church. According to this book, it became a competition to show off their importance."

"Who is that one supposed to be?" Mario pointed out.

"Let me see." Natalie speedily scanned her guidebook. "Good choice, Mario. That's Saint John the Baptist. It was sculpted by the famous Lorenzo Ghiberti, best known for his bronze doors on the Baptistery. Michelangelo referred to them as the *Gates of Paradise*."

"Gates of Paradise?"

"Yes, we will have time to see them tomorrow with Simone when he takes us to the Duomo. It's one of the largest cathedrals in the whole world. Now let's go; it's getting late."

Mario spotted one other statue and hollered out, "One more, Mama! That one!"

"That sculpture is by Donatello. It's the statue of Saint George."

"Saint George. He's the one that slays dragons. You used to read that book to me all the time."

"Bravo, Mario. Now let's move along."

Finally, they stumbled upon via Tavolini, a small, charming street in the historic center of Florence. Like most of the streets, it was lined with various leather shops, a bakery café, and another *gelateria*. At the end of the street, toward the back of the piazza, Natalie spotted a welcoming sign above the door; it read "Birreria Centrale." Standing in front was a young woman with a pleasant face, clad in black with a matching long apron. She appeared to be greeting the hungry clientele, as she warmly gestured them to be seated.

Natalie and Mario stood by and waited their turn.

"*Buongiorno, tavolo per due.*"

"*Si, ma dov'è* Alessandro?" Mario asked.

"*Siete amici di* Alessandro?"

"*No, ma il mio zio è il Direttore* Noble Bishop," Mario replied.

"*Ah, devi essere il giovane* Mario *e tu la* Natalie. *Mi chiamo* Elena. *È piacere mio.*"

"Excuse me!" Natalie rang out, and then with slight embarrassment, she apologized, "I'm sorry, but I'm afraid my Italian is not as good as my son's."

The lovely women offered her a smile and then, in her best English, she said, "My name is Elena. *Mi ricordo bene il tuo fratello. Visitò Firenze appena prima è mancato il direttore.*"

"I'm sorry; I don't understand. Mario, please translate."

"Yes, Mama. Elena said that she remembers Uncle Noble. It was when he visited Hamilton before he died."

Natalie encouraged Mario and Elena to continue in Italian. She would patiently wait for the translation. As she listened to her young son, she noticed Elena pointing to another restaurant next door where a tall bear of a man was standing. Then she heard Mario and Elena exchange the word *grazie*, with Elena ending with "*Prego.*" Natalie knew enough Italian to know that once there was an exchange of "thank you" and "you're welcome," followed by "*buongiorno*," the conversation had concluded.

"Mama, that man is Alessandro." He pointed. "And that is Osteria da Ganino. He also owns that restaurant."

Natalie braved the language and offered a *buongiorno* to Elena, and then she and Mario walked toward the man whom Noble had described as a "gentle giant." From the expression on the face of Alessandro, Natalie understood why.

"Mario, please introduce us."

Even conversing in his childlike Italian, Mario suddenly seemed older than his years.

"It's my pleasure to meet Noble's family. Please come in," Alessandro greeted, in his best-limited English.

Seconds after being seated at their table, Natalie was presented with a glass of Prosecco and Mario with a Fanta. Then a parade of delicacies appeared one by one at their table. Natalie was familiar with *crostini*, the appetizer portions of bread topped with various ingredients. But with Mario's translation, she learned that one was topped with *fegato*, a delightful chicken liver pâté. Another slice of toasted bread was smothered with diced tomatoes and basil, more commonly called *bruschetta*. Then her little master explained a simple treat enjoyed by all Italians. First, he rubbed a fresh clove of garlic on a slice of toasted bread. Then he poured olive oil on top.

Mario didn't hesitate to bite into to his treat. And before scarcely finishing the first bite full, he announced, "*Delizioso*."

Natalie followed Mario's instructions, ending with a generous bite. "Yum, I agree; it's delicious."

No sooner did the words leave her mouth before another wooden platter appeared with generous slices of prosciutto, salami, and various pecorino cheeses, also to be enjoyed with more slices of Tuscan bread. As Natalie and Mario continued to enjoy the lavish meal, Alessandro stayed close by conversing with Mario and freely answering questions. Natalie was especially inquisitive as to why the bread contained no salt, tasting different from the bread at home.

Alessandro delighted in telling the various tales but the one he seemed most to enjoy involved blaming the port city of Pisa, Florence's warring rival. With Mario's assistance, he explained that in the 1500s, Pisa had a monopoly on the salt imports. During one of the fractious wars with Florence, Pisa decided to impose a salt embargo on the proud Florentines to make their daily lives difficult and thwart their means of food preservation. Florence's immediate response was "We do not need your salt!" and they devised other methods to preserve their food. To this day, they no longer add salt to the bread recipes. But as a proud restaurateur and lover of food, Alessandro also clarified that the bread was the Italians' third utensil, and was used to sop up the sauces on the plate.

"*Sale nel pane rovinerebbe la ricetta*," he declared.

Mario stepped in, anticipating the need for translation, and said, "Mama, salt in the bread would ruin the recipe."

Natalie beamed at both of them. Enjoying Alessandro's melodic Italian and watching her little man translate provided a double treat.

While it appeared Natalie had finished her questions, Alessandro still had a few of his own.

"*Lo conosceva il Direttore?*" he asked.

"Mama, he wants to know if you knew Hamilton," Mario translated.

Natalie spoke slowly as she replied, "Hamilton was a very dear friend and one of the few who attended my wedding. We were sad when he decided to retire and move to Florence, but I understand he was very happy here."

Alessandro appeared to understand and responded, "*Era anche amico mio. Lo considerava Noble molto. Penso che lo considerava come un figlio.*"

"Mario," Natalie beseeched and then quickly offered a "*Mi dispiace*" to Alessandro. The one phrase she had mastered—"I'm sorry."

"Hamilton cared very much for Uncle Noble and considered him a son."

With the grateful help of Mario, Natalie hung in and was reassured to discover that Hamilton had made a life for himself among friends before his sudden death.

During their pleasant exchange among the three of them, the wait staff had removed their empty plates and the wooden platter without notice. Then, not wanting to monopolize Alessandro's time further, Natalie started to signal for the check.

"*Cosa volete per pranzo?*" Alessandro asked, quickly stepping back into restaurateur mode.

Natalie was floored. She was positive that he had just asked them what they would like for lunch.

"Pasta *per favore*," Mario responded immediately.

"Mario, we have had more than enough food," she politely scolded, as she clutched her stomach.

"Madam, a little pasta for *Signore* Mario?" Alessandro suggested.

His English had be perfect at that moment, she thought, knowing she'd have no other choice but to surrender.

"Okay, but what is the word—*poco*?"

"*Si*, Madam, a little." Alessandro smiled with his gentle grin and then asked, "*Che pasta vuoi, Signore* Mario?"

"*Vorrei spaghetti e polpette*," he said with poise.

At Mario's response, Natalie could not help overhear the couple at the next table chuckle.

At the same time, Alessandro let out a little laugh. "I will return in one moment," he replied. Then, with a slight bow, he left to go to the kitchen.

"What did you order?" Natalie asked, curious at the reactions.

"Spaghetti and meatballs, Mama. My favorite!"

Natalie could not help but giggle herself, once clued in to the surrounding expressions.

"What?" Mario asked, wanting in on the joke.

"Your father told me once that spaghetti and meatballs is not an Italian dish. It was invented by Italians who moved to America."

"I don't understand. Alessandro must have meatballs," he stated with a confused expression.

"In Italy, meatballs are typically served as a main course or sometimes in soup."

Mario, still finding it terribly confusing, was pleased to see Alessandro walk out of the kitchen and head their way. Then, adding to his muddle, Alessandro placed a plate with a generous portion of spaghetti *al ragù* in front of Mario. To the side, he placed another plate heaped with small meatballs.

Mario, still not understanding the difference between the Italian and the American versions, promptly picked up the plate of meatballs and scooped them on top of the pasta. "*Vedi, spaghetti e polpette*," he announced with great pride, having solved the dilemma.

Laughter broke out throughout the restaurant; the patrons had just witnessed the humorous scene.

Hungry Mario paid no attention as he twirled his fork with agility.

Natalie sat back and sipped on the glass of red wine Alessandro had generously poured, while Mario enjoyed his lunch. During that time, she watched as customers continued to stream into the restaurant, asking either for a table inside or out in the piazza. She happened to notice one man greeting Alessandro with the typical Italian cheek-to-cheek hug, a charming habit Paolo could never break. Then, oddly, they turned and headed toward her table.

"*Questo è Eugenio. Egli e stato un amico di Hamilton è lui ha conosciuto il tuo fratello quando l'ha visitato a Firenze*," Alessandro introduced.

"Excuse me?" Natalie asked, still lost in the lingo.

"My name is Eugenio," the stranger quickly responded, noticing the fact that she didn't speak Italian. "I was a friend of Hamilton's. Also, I met your brother when he visited Florence."

"My name is Natalie and this is my son, Mario."

"*Piacere mio*," Mario acknowledged and then returned to tackling his meal.

Natalie was thrilled that Eugenio spoke flawless English and was able to engage in an actual conversation. While Mario was engrossed in an obvious activity and Alessandro scooted off to other customers, Eugenio explained that he was a curator at the Uffizi Gallery. It was there that he had met Hamilton.

"So you gave the tour to Professor Ducale's students?" Natalie asked.

"You know the story about the *professoressa*?" Eugenio asked, quite surprised.

"She was my husband's aunt."

"*Mama mia!*" Eugenio stated, finding the happenstance quite intriguing.

"Paolo hasn't seen her for years. She divorced his uncle soon after Hamilton moved to Florence. I never had the occasion to meet her."

"Yes, it was an odd set of circumstances," Eugenio replied, not sure how much Natalie knew about the story. *She most certainly wouldn't have known that the professor was accused of leaving a satchel of money at the entrance to the Vasari Corridor*, he mused. He knew it had been rumored that the professor was seen leaving a bank with money that Hamilton had prearranged as part of his sting operation to lure a notorious terrorist named Simon. That led Hamilton and Enzo Borgini to follow the professor through the halls of the Vasari Corridor, while on a tour with her students. Upon discovering they had been outmaneuvered, Hamilton interrogated both Eugenio and the professor. The professor told all she knew, including her involvement with Simon. Later Hamilton befriended Eugenio, and since that time, the story had taken on as many twists and turns as the Vasari Corridor itself. None of the rumors had ever been confirmed.

"Would you and Mario like to see the Vasari Corridor?" Eugenio invited.

"Mario?"

"*Si*, Mama!"

"Splendid. It would be my pleasure to give you a private tour if you are available tomorrow afternoon."

"We'd love to. Thank you."

"*Bene*, good, I'll pick you up here at four o'clock."

"We'll look forward to seeing you tomorrow. And thank you again."

Eugenio bid his goodbye and headed to the bar in the back of the restaurant wherein Alessandro had already prepared an espresso. In Italian fashion, Eugenio took the afternoon caffeine fix with two precision gulps and then left the restaurant with a friendly *ciao*.

When Alessandro rejoined them at the table, he had already discovered from Eugenio about the private tour and quickly reconfirmed the arrangement with his son Simone. It was settled. He would take them on a quick tour of some of the sights in the morning beforehand.

"Smile," Alessandro requested, as he snapped a photo of Natalie and Mario on his smartphone and then promptly sent it to Simone. He then gave Mario instructions for them to meet the next morning at ten in front of the Café Scudieri in the Piazza San Giovani. He told them they would find it near the Baptistery.

Natalie was thrilled. Noble's promise to make all the arrangements while they were in Italy had thus far exceeded her expectations.

"*Avete piacere di vedere il menu di dolci?*"

"Mama, Alessandro wants to know if we would like to see the dessert menu," he informed with an impish grin.

"No, Mario," she chided softly. And then, with the help of her son, she thanked Alessandro for a fantastic lunch and his generosity. At last, she asked for the check.

"No, *Signora*, it was my pleasure."

Natalie attempted to make the request a few more times and then graciously accepted. After heartwarming goodbyes and agreeing to return the following day, they headed out once again to venture through the streets of the magnificent Renaissance city, a veritable walking museum.

"Are you enjoying Florence, my darling?"

"Yes, Mama. It makes me feel closer to *Babbo*."

"Yes, it makes me feel closer to your father, too."

Natalie had learned that the endearing term *babbo* was the only Italian term for "papa." Paolo was especially proud that it came from the original Florentine language.

"Let's try to call *Babbo* tonight."

Mario's face glowed.

8
A MYSTERY TOUR

Seymour Lynx sat in a booth at Café Americano on Melrose Avenue in Beverly Hills, consuming his cappuccino with effortlessly timed sips. Moments later, he eyed the stretch limo pulling up outside the café. He reacted by drawing a deep breath, while bringing to mind a quotation from the renowned inspirational speaker, Tony Robbins: *"It is in your moments of decision that your destiny is shaped."*

He still had time to renege on the deal, but either way, he knew it would change his life forever. At that point, he was riding high in the film industry, with more awards and accolades heading his way. His personal life was in perfect order. *I don't have to do this*, he had repeated to himself boundless times ever since he received the call. After one last deep breath, he paid the check and headed for the car.

"Sir, would you like me to take your bag?"

"Thank you," he uttered, and then, with a tad of apprehension, he handed his carry-on luggage to the driver, save the briefcase.

The ride to LAX would take about thirty-eight minutes if the traffic flowed. He estimated that he had plenty of time to catch the flight and meet his connection on the other end.

Over the years, Seymour had made many attempts to flush the memories of his previous life from his memory bank. However, during the ride he could no longer repress his thoughts. Most specifically, he mused upon his role as the communications director, and then the documentarian, for the former president, Abner Baari. He openly admitted that it was an amazing gig, but he also acknowledged that it had ended badly. Rumors had surfaced regarding his creative, negative campaign ads and the fabrications of his original campaign sound bites. It sealed his fate in and around the Capitol. When he returned to L.A. he was all the worse for the wear, but without missing a beat, he began to revive his film-production career. After fighting the blowback, he was finally welcomed into the inner circle when his film *The Framework* was nominated by the Academy for an Oscar.

"What am I doing?" he questioned aloud.

The driver looked into the rearview mirror. "Sir, did you say something?"

"No!" he answered, in a dismissive manner to thwart off further intrusions.

By chance it was not long before the car pulled up to the curb. Seymour hurriedly retrieved his belongings and headed to the departure gate.

∽

The flight arrived at his destination as scheduled. Within minutes, Seymour made his way to the arrival lounge. Soon after, he spotted a group of men standing next to each other, all holding up tablets of various sizes. The name "Lynx" was scrawled on one of them.

So far, so good, he assumed, still unable to shake off his uneasiness. He shot his hand up into the air to signal the driver. As the driver approached, Seymour noted something different about his appearance. Granted, his mannerisms seemed appropriate, but strangely, the driver was dressed in a manner similar to the Secret Service agents Seymour had seen many times roaming the White House. But as expected, the driver offered to carry his luggage and then ushered him to the stretch limo waiting outside.

On impulse, Seymour checked his wristwatch as he entered the limo and noted the time. But it was not until he had shifted comfortably into his seat that he took the opportunity to peruse his surroundings. "Hey, what's going on?" he called out to the driver.

"This is for your protection, sir," came the voice over the intercom. "Please let me know if there is anything you need."

Seymour's eyes darted around, but there was nothing of interest except the wet bar stationed in front of him—all the windows had been blacked out. "Where are we going?" he asked, suddenly feeling uncomfortable.

"Sir, please relax. We'll be there before long."

"Where?" he demanded.

"Sir, you'll be given further instructions when we arrive. Please, it won't be much longer."

"It's obvious I have no choice," he grunted.

There were no more responses from the intercom.

Seymour sat back and waited to arrive at their destination—wherever it was to be. No less relaxed, he spent the time focusing on a prior conversation, one that had led him to this juncture. Then he began to second-guess his decision. He must have been deep in thought, because it was not until the limo's engine came to an abrupt halt before he was jolted back to the moment. He took note. Again, he cast a quick glance at his watch; they had been driving for less than an hour. Right away he realized the engine was silent, but, strangely, the car was still in motion. It was not moving forward or backward, but he sensed the car was descending at a slow speed—then he felt another jolt. The car came to a complete stop.

Seconds later, the right passenger door flung open as the driver reached inside and handed him a cloth object. "Sir, please put this on. In a few minutes we will enter the facility."

"Is this necessary?"

"Sir."

Seymour let out an audible breath. *I've come this far. I might as well play along—on this mystery tour,* he thought. Relenting, he placed the blindfold across his eyes and tightened the cord behind his head. Then, sharpening all his senses, he began to pay particular attention to his surroundings. First, he could feel himself being led down several narrow hallways, each one ending as he passed through a metal doorway. At last count, he had entered four different passageways. Throughout he detected a metallic smell circulating in the air. The echo from his footsteps as they hit the cement flooring resonated. The lack of sight only increased his anxiety. Most odd was the sense that there was not another soul around. *What the hell is going on?* he questioned himself as fear began to take hold.

"Sir, you may remove your blindfold."

Seymour ripped off the mask and took several deep breaths as though he had also been gagged. His eyes slowly adjusted to the lighting, until he found himself facing two large steel doors. The driver was standing to his left. There was no one else in sight. Without warning, the doors opened. In front of them was another hallway, just as Seymour had envisioned. Up to that point, he had been somewhat tractable, but then his doubts rose to the surface. He was urged to enter.

"Where am I?" he demanded.

"Sir, you are in a secure underground installation. Please follow me."

"You didn't answer my question," Seymour countered, losing his patience. This was not what he had signed up for, but then again the real purpose was not entirely clear to him from the start. All he recalled was hearing the two most dreaded words—*trust me*. He knew they always came with a price.

"All your questions will be answered soon. Please follow me."

Another steel door opened.

Seymour's jaw dropped.

9
MAXIMUM RESTRAINT

Noble sauntered into the conference room, not realizing he had naively walked into the lioness den.

"If we have to do this, let's get it over with," she scowled.

Noble sat down next to her and reassured, "As I said before, Max, you'll be fine. You're a real pro." The gentle pat on her shoulder was for extra measure.

The scowl softened somewhat.

"Okay, where do you want to start?" he asked, mindful of her level of angst.

Max, showing signs of relenting, obliged for the moment and proceeded to open one of the case file folders on her xPhad. While scrolling through the pages, she described in brief terms the latest case. "Remember a few years ago when the Chinese attempted to hack into the Office of Personnel Management database? When they tried to retrieve information on people who had applied for security clearances?"

"Yes, and it's fortunate that when the case was brought to our attention, we were able to quickly thwart the incursion."

"Well, no surprise, they tried again. There's been another series of hack attacks—this time to infiltrate the CIA. Again, they were disrupted. But each time they managed to break through more layers of security. They're inching along, and it's getting a little too close for comfort."

"Agreed. Who was it this time—the People's Liberation Army Unit 61398?" Noble asked.

"You've got it. They keep hacking; we keep changing the security. But it's an endless loop and a tiresome game."

"I've had to dodge their attempts to infiltrate many times over the years, but nothing appears to deter them from their cyber-attacks. What I find frustrating," Noble admitted, "is these attacks occur daily, but for some strange reason our government agencies are required to report an incident only in cases of personal identification being obtained. What were they sniffing around for at the CIA?"

"Same thing—personnel records. I surmise it's to locate agents operating in the field. I have a new team working on increasing the security levels." As Max spent the good part of the hour to describe some of the implemented programs, she appeared to have gotten back in her groove. Her disgruntled mood seemed to have almost disappeared.

It did not go unnoticed. "Has Max returned?" Noble jested, hoping she had finally come around.

She flashed the smile of old but offered no retort.

Noble moved the conversation forward and speculated, "Snowden didn't help the situation when he divulged that our government made similar attempts. The Chinese and the Russians think it's fair game. Even the Koreans joined the fray. It's in their DNA."

"Thus far, it's been a game. Stealing state secrets is part of the massive intelligence gathering that plagues the world, but the number of destructive hack attacks is accelerating at an alarming rate. We've had over four hundred critical attacks this year alone on our core infrastructure. We can't relax for a moment," Max cautioned.

"That gives me the creeps, especially after knowing how Simon attempted to bring down the national power grid. I shudder to think what the consequences would have been if he had succeeded."

"Yes, but the threats are also happening in our transportation and banking sectors."

"It may merely be a matter of time before some catastrophic event occurs dwarfing 9/11."

Max reacted as she looked up from her xPhad and made eye contact with Noble. "Now that's a chilling thought." Then with a half-grin she warned, "But it better not happen on my watch."

"Let's just pray we'll be prepared if it does. But one major problem that exacerbates the situation is the Internet infrastructure. It rests in the hands of the private sector and there is no uniformity in controlling the malware that allows these predators to access our most vulnerable databases. Hackers are aware of this lapse in security and treat it as an open invitation to wreak havoc."

"You're not suggesting it should be left in the hands of the government, are you?"

"Not totally, but there needs to be better coordination between the two entities."

"There are various congressional subcommittees working with the private-sector vendors." Max stated, and then lamented, "In the meantime, all we can do is to try to curtail the hackers."

"What else is on the docket?"

"You're aware that the number of transnational crimes has tripled over the past two years?" she asked, in an attempt to elicit his confirmation.

"Yes, it's been on an upward trend since the squabbling on immigration reform heightened during 2014."

"Well, the alliances between the South American and Mexican cartels have expedited the level of illicit activities, including arms smuggling, human trafficking and of course, their specialty, the drug trade."

"I know. But what is even more astonishing is that even with the increased border security and Coast Guard surveillance, over sixty percent of the two thousand metric tons of illegal drugs the cartels claim to produce a year, still makes its way into the U.S. That damn border has to be closed." Noble, no sooner than having lodged his complaint, felt his xPhad vibrate. "Hold on. I have to take this." He noticed the name on the display. It was Stanton.

"Yes?"

"Director, all the packages have been delivered."

"Thank you. That's all for now. I'll let you know if I need anything further."

"Yes, sir."

"What was that all about?" she questioned.

"Not to worry. Proceed," he urged, avoiding her probing.

Max got the message and continued. "We're also following up on an intelligence report from the U.S. Border Patrol of the possibility that Muhammad Nabi and Khirullah Said Wali Khairkhwa have entered the U.S."

Noble shook his head in disgust. "It still blows my mind that we traded five Guantanamo detainees—who were high-ranking Taliban officials—for Army Sergeant Bergdahl, an obvious deserter. A fact the government was well aware of at the time. Wasn't Nabi considered a high-risk threat and Khairkhwa a major narcotics trafficker?"

"Yes, and both are still heavily embedded in the al-Qaeda regime leadership. Don't forget—the deal was predicated on the Qataris monitoring their activities for just one year—the same government that supports Hamas. I never bet the ranch on that one."

"What a joke. Baari even admitted that there was a possibility that some prisoners released from Guantanamo would return to activities that could threaten us. But he continued to release other detainees, even though it was obvious the earlier attempts to put these bad guys out of business failed miserably. I can't imagine what the six detainees sent to Uruguay are planning."

"So I guess he was determined from the *Gitmo*—so to speak." Max managed a faint smile and then reverted to form as she fumed, "What burns my toast is he also opened the door for them by not closing the border sooner...What?" she asked, catching Noble's snicker.

"The expression is *fries my bacon*."

'Whatever," she huffed. "He pissed me off. His delays were contrary to the clear public sentiment, but Baari wasn't known for his open mind. In fact, he was more myopic and just focused on the event of the day."

"So now we manage the result of indecision and miscalculation. I suspect Khairkhwa is working with the South American cartels in drug trafficking?"

"It's probable, but more likely it was a ruse—a way to enter the U.S. illegally," Max speculated.

"Our vulnerability, both at the border and in our Internet structure, is also a gift to ISIS."

"There's evidence that ISIS is purposely stirring up trouble between the police and the local Islamic communities across the country. The Islamic State remembered the debacle that took place in Ferguson, Missouri and how a simple shooting between a white police officer and a black teenager turned into a national crisis. The tension was further inflamed by the *Chokehold Case* and the assassination of two police officers in New York City. They're playing on the fears of the minority communities and creating similar crises."

"It's clear they never got Baari's *degrade and defeat* memo. Worse yet, the victim's sympathizers fell into the trap and moved into the fracas."

"When is Sharpton going away?" Max snarled.

"I suspect with the White House no longer providing him cover, he'll become ineffective on his own accord very soon. In point of fact, he should be behind bars."

"He's the least of our problems. Trying to track the ever-increasing number of homegrown terrorists surfacing within our borders and attempting to identify those entering the country, many with British passports, is bordering on the impossible."

As much as Noble enjoyed the ideological conversations with Max, he needed to move it along. "Keep me posted. Anything else?" He knew that no matter the answer, all terrorist threats would become secondary concerns if President Post's analysis is correct.

"Noble, we don't need anything else. We're having a difficult time as it is keeping up with our current caseload. The national security challenges alone keep our inboxes full."

He nodded in agreement and then asked, "Max, would you mind closing the door for a moment? I need to speak with you in complete confidence."

Max was all of a sudden overcome with an unpleasant feeling that she wasn't going to like what Noble had to say, but she played along. When she returned to the table, she asked with uneasiness, "Okay Boss, what's up?"

"I've finished formalizing my travel arrangement, so I'll be leaving this evening," he announced in a calm manner. She sat in silence and listened while he relayed his fabricated plan in loose terms.

"So you really are just going to up and leave?"

"Max, we've gone over this. It's obvious that you have control of the cases and I know you have complete cooperation from the entire team. I don't see any challenges you can't handle."

"Thank you for the vote of confidence. But I'll state again, this is a vulnerable time. The country's in crisis mode and there are continuous outbreaks of civil unrest spreading from coast to coast."

"Those issues don't fall in our bailiwick, aside from playing a supporting role with the other agencies. The team is intact. But if anything arises on an urgent basis and you need to contact me, leave me a voice message on my cell or send me a text. I'll get back to you as soon as possible. In either case, use the secure line or encode the text."

"I don't understand why all the cloak and dagger?" Max grilled.

"I assume if it's an emergency, then it's agency business and should be conducted on a secure line. Simple as that."

Max was sparring for further repartee.

Noble evaded the opportunity. "I wouldn't leave you in charge if I didn't have full confidence in your ability. How many times do I have to assure you? You've proven yourself time and time again."

"By the way, what does POTUS think about you leaving?"

"He's on board and has complete confidence in your ability as well."

"Buttering me up doesn't help." She was, by design, trying to make it difficult for him to leave, although she knew she'd already lost the fight.

Noble stood up from his chair, startling Max before she had an opportunity to grill him further. It was a clear signal to end the inquisition. "Don't make this any harder on me," he implored, deciding to use pity as a weapon.

Max stood up to face him head-on. "You win," she conceded, and then worked up a disingenuous smile.

Noble disregarded her unwilling surrender and reached over to give her a gentle hug. "Thanks Max," he whispered. Then, in an atypical manner, he maintained the embrace for a moment longer.

Surprised by herself, she returned the hug willingly. But at that same moment, her mind swirled with fleeting thoughts. *This is more serious than he's letting on* was the most prevalent. The uneasiness persisted; she knew something was horribly wrong.

Just then, Noble pulled back and clasped his hands around her shoulders.

Their eyes met.

"Everything will be okay, Max," he said as though he had read her mind. Again he tried to reassure her. "Everything will work out. You're the boss now."

Not knowing how to react in that split second of intimacy, she turned away and walked out of the conference room, before saying something she might regret.

Noble watched her leave. He knew he had handled it badly. *She doesn't believe me for a minute.*

✍

Max returned to her office and closed the door behind her. Leaning back against it, as though she were bracing for an intruder, she played the scene of their embrace over and over in her mind, still surprised at herself for not resisting. One thing she could not deny was that something odd and inexplicable had just happened. Though unsure of her personal feelings, she couldn't help but ponder, *The one thing I am sure of—is that you're not leveling with me.* "I'm worried about you Noble," she muttered to herself.

10
BAD TIMING

The bartender spotted Max out of the corner of his eye and signaled her in the direction of the booth in the corner. As she approached the table she was stunned. "What's going on?" She couldn't help but notice the bouquet of flowers off to one side and the candle in the center.

"I wanted to do something extra nice for you, sweetheart." Stanton stood up and embraced her, and then followed up with a sensual kiss. All the while, he thought, *Tonight's the night.*

All the while Max thought, *Oh, please don't let this happen. The flowers smell like a proposal.* She pulled back gently and assumed her position in the booth across from him. Working up a smile, she remarked, "They're beautiful. Thank you," and then she thought *There's no way in hell I'll ask what the special occasion is.*

Stanton, still with an inviting look in his eyes, reached across the table and held her hand.

Max kept her cool as she tried to turn off his afterburners and looked for a diversion. "Noble just left me at the helm," she blurted out. "He's decided to take some time off to contemplate his navel, so he left me in charge."

Stanton, not pleased with the subject matter nor her timing, played along as though he had no clue as to what she was talking about. "Where's he going?"

"He's taking a temporary leave of absence. And I don't need this headache right now."

"Hon, you could do the job blindfolded while standing on your head. You're as tough as Noble—maybe even tougher. You'll step up to the plate."

"Thanks for the vote of confidence, but Noble already tried that approach. And with all the problems out there, his timing sucks. Besides, we've always worked together. He's the one I count on to bounce off my hunches and wild speculations—as he does with me. We keep each other grounded. You know me; I'm not the administrative type!" Max continued to lay out her concerns with her being elevated to the new position of director, despite its being temporary.

Stanton listened as she groused on, but could not help thinking, *What's going on with her?*

Abruptly, she stopped short.

"Max, what's wrong?" His annoyance turned to concern.

"See that guy sitting at the table over there? The one in the blue suit?"

"Yeah, so what?"

"His profile is identical to the guy in the hoodie that keeps coming into the Blackfinn."

"How do you know? You couldn't even see the face of your suspicious stalker—you don't even know if the person in the hoodie is a guy." Stanton let out a frustrating breath. "You want me to go talk to him?"

"And say what?"

"I'll tell him that I'm in love with a crazy lady who thinks he's a stalker, but is usually dressed in a hoodie with dark glasses. Then I'll compliment him on his elegant taste in clothing for this evening."

Max recognized how ridiculous the ploy sounded. She remained silent and gazed back at Stanton as she mused, *He's intelligent, handsome, witty, and the sex is great. Why can't I commit to him? Without a doubt he's drool-worthy.* Her mouth curled upward at the thought.

Stanton took note. "Sweetie, I'm really worried about you."

"Can we change the subject, please?" Max regretted that she had ruined the evening, but she was unnerved. She was being stalked; Noble had deserted her; and now she feared that Stanton was going to propose. She did love him, but for the time being she couldn't succumb to his wishes. She was sure of one thing: If he had popped the question, she would have said "no" and risked losing him in the process. That she'd try to avoid at all costs. Their relationship was far beyond platonic, but she was not ready to waltz down the aisle just yet.

Stanton picked up on the vibes and had already determined that tonight was not in the cards. So he tried to switch the tenor of the evening around and enjoy what remained. He reached over to refill her wine glass and tried to change the conversation. "Have you been watching season five of *House of Cards*?"

"You know I haven't had the time."

"Well, their depiction of the Secret Service is overly glamorized. I should be so lucky for such a job. Instead we've all been tainted by the 'Pierson' Syndrome."

Max knew that, for the past several years, all the agents were being second-guessed as to their effectiveness. It all began when Julia Pierson, the head of the Secret Service, stepped down under duress for flagrant incompetence.

"You're one of the good guys and everyone knows you would lay down your life for the president." She eased up and her smile of old appeared. "No more shop talk," she commanded, as she too attempted to salvage the evening. The repartee took an abrupt change and moved to small talk, with an occasional affectionate gesture.

As it became apparent that Max had returned to some vestige of herself, Stanton managed to restore some romance in the air—minus the planned proposal. After he paid the check, they left the restaurant and walked in the direction of her apartment. Strolling arm-in-arm, they'd stop along the way for a penetrating kiss. Once they arrived, Stanton was pleasantly surprised by her invitation for him to stay the night.

11
PLAYING BIG BROTHER

Noble had a final call to make before going out of cell range. It would also reduce the chances that Natalie would try to contact him, at least for the next few weeks. It was ten o'clock a.m.—a good time to catch her.

"Noble, *mama mia*, what a pleasant surprise," replied the energetic voice from four thousand miles away.

"Practicing your Italian, Nat?" Noble chuckled.

"Slow going, even with Mario's help," she groaned.

"I'm sure you two are having a grand time running around the streets of Florence, but I thought I'd check in and see how you're doing."

"We're having a marvelous time thanks to you." She sputtered on, "The other day we had lunch at Osteria da Ganino, Alessandro's new restaurant. He sends his best. He was wonderful and arranged for his son Simone to take us on a tour—and, oh, we met Eugenio…"

"Nat, slow down. You may be having a problem with the Italian language, but not with the rapid-fire pace."

"Sorry; it has just been so exciting." In a calmer manner, Natalie described how Simone had met them the following day in front of the Duomo. "First, we took a tour through the Baptistry of Saint John and then walked around the outside to admire the Gates of Paradise. Earlier, I had read to Mario about Ghiberti and his bronze doors, so it was wonderful to see them up close." She knew she was still jabbering away and expected some rebuff from Noble. "Are you listening?" she challenged.

"Rattle on. I find this all fascinating."

"Don't humor me. Anyway, thanks to Simone, who had already arranged for the tickets earlier, we were able to breeze past the lines and walk right into the Duomo. Noble, when we looked up into the dome, its enormity took our breath away."

"Did Simone tell you the story of the dome?"

"Oh yes, and Mario couldn't believe that the church had been without a roof for over a hundred years. You should have seen his face when Simone explained in great detail how Brunelleschi constructed the dome. Just imagine a building requiring a 150-foot-wide structure to be assembled 180 feet in the air. Mario found it fascinating to learn that Brunelleschi, who was a goldsmith by trade, had lost the commission to create the bronze doors for the Baptistery to his rival Ghiberti, but won the contest to build the roof. Even today, no architect or engineer can say for sure how the dome was built. But of course, Mario wanted to try to figure it out. I think we may have a little architect in the making, Uncle Noble."

"Wonderful. Anything but the spy business," he joked. All kidding aside, he was pleased that Natalie and Mario were enjoying themselves, and by the same token, pleased that she no longer seemed to be annoyed with him. He indulged her a while longer, urging her to continue. "Did you see the David?"

"Of course Simone took us to see Michelangelo's brilliant sculpture. You know the original is at the Accademia di Belle Arti? Florence's Academy of Fine Arts."

"Yes, they restored the statue several years ago. When I was there it had just been made available for public viewing."

"Then you must have experienced the overwhelming feeling when you stare up at the David. It makes you feel insignificant and small. Nothing in any of the guidebooks, or in any of the photos I have seen, prepared me for a sculpture to come alive. Am I boring you, dear brother?"

"No. But as I listen to you, it's reviving the fondness I feel for Florence."

"And the special memories of Hamilton?"

"Of course. Where did you venture next?"

"We walked back through the glorious Piazza Signoria, with Simone describing all of the statues. He had a bit of difficulty answering Mario's incessant questions about the Rape of Sabine."

"That's my nephew," Noble chuckled. "I hope he explained that rape meant abduction and it was the way men found wives in ancient Roman times."

"Yes, Simone handled it quite appropriately. Then he dropped us off at Birreria Centrale for lunch. Alessandro wasn't working at Ganino, but Elena was as wonderful and we had another delightful Tuscan lunch."

"You mentioned Eugenio was taking you on a tour of the Vasari Corridor."

"Yes, he picked us up at the restaurant." Natalie continued to wax on and describe how they weaved through the hallways of the famous corridor, considered to be one of the most astounding architectural masterpieces of the Renaissance.

While Noble half-listened, he wondered why he was feeling slightly homesick for a place where he had spent so little time. Whatever the reason, he began to reminisce about his time with Hamilton.

Noting his silence, Natalie asked, "Did you know it was built in 1565, in just six months, for the Medici family?"

He caught her question, and droned, "Yes, I remember that little fact."

Ignoring his apparent inattentiveness, she continued. "Cosimo I of the Medici family commissioned Giorgio Vasari, the brilliant architect of the time, to construct a covered passageway. It leads from the Uffizi, which is his place of work, across the Lungarno degli Archbusieri and continues along the north bank of the Arno River. Then the corridor crosses over the top of the famous Ponte Vecchio Bridge, meanders across the peaks of houses, and through their private church the Chiesa di Santa Felicita. Finally, it ends at the Palazzo Pitti, the final home of the Medici family."

"Nat, are you reading from the guidebook?" Noble teased.

"Sort of," she admitted.

Noble continued to egg her on. "Did you know that Cosimo I did not want to have to fight his way through the crowds nor tolerate the smells emanating from the butcher's establishments located on the bridge? That's why they removed the butcher shops and replaced them with goldsmith shops, which remain there to this day."

"And what are you reading from?" Natalie inquired.

Noble chuckled. "I just remember some of stories that Hamilton told me when I visited."

"Be serious, Noble. It was amazing to walk through the corridor and to be able to see hundreds of portraits and paintings dating back to the seventeenth and eighteenth centuries. It was an incredible experience. You should have seen Mario. He was so curious and it seemed as though he had asked zillions of questions. Eugenio was so patient with him."

"That's wonderful. It's a great experience for a young boy, especially Mario, who is so inquisitive."

"You know, Noble, at times I felt like we were tracing Hamilton's footsteps, while he was in hot pursuit of Simon. It was delicious fun!"

Noble listened as though the attempted capture of Simon had happened yesterday; bringing to mind the day Hamilton had called him from Florence to describe how the sting operation had failed. He could still remember hearing the heartbreak in Hamilton's voice when he admitted that Simon had escaped the trap. Lost in thought, it took him a moment to realize that Natalie was still rattling on.

"Both Simone and Eugenio were princes. They gave of their time and we felt privileged to have had an inside peek at their amazing city. They both send their best."

"Send them mine as well. Well, it sounds like you've had a great time," he said, ready to sign off. "Natalie…" *Damn delay in these international calls*, he thought, as it just robbed him from the opportunity to end the travelogue.

Natalie, oblivious, continued, "The next day, we walked through the city and found the other places Hamilton described to you. We went to the Perini Gastronomia in the Central Market. The entire team of Andrea, Moreno, Flavio, and Simone were amazing. Oops, I can't forget Sania and Yvonne. What a real treat." For the next few minutes, Natalie went on to describe in infinite detail the panino they made for Mario. "You should have seen his eyes light up when Andrea handed it to him. By the way, isn't that where Hamilton went for lunch while he was stalking Simon?"

"Yes, it was another one of the haunts," he grumbled.

"What's wrong?"

"Nat, you know I love Paolo like a brother, but I still hold some residual resentment that he involved you. Whatever possessed him?"

"The fact that I am his wife!" Natalie never understood why Noble had difficulty grasping the concept. But she chose not to belabor the point and instead offered some sisterly advice. "We've managed to work through the bad times and put it behind us in the family history books. It's now time for you to let it go. Besides, you're the one that told me Hamilton's story," she complained.

Natalie was the only outsider that was aware of the convergence of events that brought down Abner Baari. When it happened, Noble believed it was important for both Paolo and Natalie to know Simon had escaped and why they needed to be vigilant. Had Paolo not confided in his wife before confessing to Noble, it would not have been necessary to alert her. Part of Paolo's immunity agreement then had to include Natalie's silence.

"By the way, have you spoken to Paolo? I haven't been able to reach him and he is not returning my calls," Natalie asked, somewhat concerned.

"Not recently, but I'll try to track him down and have him give you a call." Noble decided that it was time to get off the subject. "When do you leave for San Marino?"

"Tomorrow afternoon. We're taking the 1:40 train to Rimini. Enzo will be picking us up at the station. I'll call you when we arrive."

"That's okay. I'll check in with Enzo. For now, you two have a great time. Give my love to Mario, along with a hug."

"I will Noble. And thank you again for making it such a special time for us. I love you. And if you can find him, give my husband an extra big hug from me and Mario."

"Love you too Nat. Talk to you later."

12
THE ASSIGNMENT

Noble had entered the underground facility on several occasions, but he was still in awe at the enormity of the complex and all of its technological treasures. Now, after passing through several security checkpoints, he had one last step before reaching his final destination, to pass the retina scan. He leaned in toward the metal grid, making contact with the camera lens, and then pulled back as he watched the metal doors part.

When he walked into the vast reception hall, he was pleased to see that all invited had been accounted for as they chatted away in the alcove off to the side of the main room. He remained standing in place for a moment, as he listened to the sound of backslapping and friendly banter, as old friends reconnected. All the while, his expression remained serious.

Seymour, the first to spot the new arrival, stood up. As he walked toward him, he demanded, "Where the hell are we?" still smarting over the blindfold.

The others followed behind.

Noble ignored Seymour's complaining and walked over to offer him a handshake, which he accepted—willing to let the question slide for the moment. Noble then moved along to greet Chase, and then Paolo, thanking them both for accepting his invitation. He saved Hank Kramer for last.

Noble was more than delighted that Hank had become a more compliant adversary since the death of Simon, and that he had been cooperative thus far. He had not forgotten, however, that Hank was a key figure among the members of La Fratellanza. Hank was not only the person aligned with Simon, but as the chief of staff of the former president, he was also the direct link between Simon and Baari. He was in the center of activity. On several occasions, he knowingly broke his immunity agreement and continued to communicate surreptitiously with Simon. His shenanigans seemed endless, following the *Chicago Manual of Politics*. As a result, his Chestnut Foundation continued to be slammed with lawsuits accusing him of misappropriation of federal funds and voter intimidation. Hank, not one to learn from his mistakes, found himself once again fraught with similar charges during the 2016 presidential election. And although the claims were unsubstantiated, they took their toll. In the end, Hank folded under the pressure, fearing Simon more than the long line of lawsuits.

Once the pleasantries were out of the way, Noble invited each of them to be seated at the table in the center of the room. However, he remained standing and watched as each of them pulled up a chair. He could not help but muse, *Habits are hard to break.* Ironically, they each chose the same seating arrangement they had occupied during their study group at Harvard. Hank sat to Chase's left, followed by an empty chair. Situated next to the empty chair sat Seymour, and then Paolo completed the circle.

Still, in an apparent huff, Seymour fingered the initials **LF** etched in the center of the table. "Nice touch, Noble," he allowed with a grin.

The table was the same one that La Fratellanza had sat around those many years ago. It was where they discussed their individual theses, and also, where they had joined forces and engaged in the intellectual game: to devise a shadow thesis identifying the steps necessary to bring an illegal immigrant to the U.S.—and get him elected president.

But the table held even greater significance. On the day their plot was foiled, Hamilton had transferred that table from his conference room to the interrogation room at the CIA Headquarters in Langley, Virginia. This was the same table he had confiscated years earlier from an apartment in Cambridge, based on clues that led him to Simon Hall's apartment—the scene of the infamous study group. Through fingerprint analysis, Noble and the former director were able to determine the seating arrangement each of the members of La Fratellanza had assumed. All but one.

Without explanation, Simon's prints were nowhere to be found. He had removed any trace of himself but, curiously, he chose to leave those of his brethren. Even that early on in their relationships, Simon was scheming to set them up at some future date. That table had remained in Noble's office ever since, as a reminder that one day he would bring Simon to justice. On April third, in a dramatic closing of the curtain, Simon robbed him of that satisfaction with his leap off the Peach Bridge.

As planned, each member had arrived at the facility earlier that morning, giving them ample time to scout out their new surroundings. With little effort, they had discovered the three bedroom suites, the central kitchen, and the fully equipped fitness center. The living room alcove was where Noble had discovered them lounging on the two overstuffed sofas, watching a baseball game on the gigantic screen. He suspected that they also noted the two large steel panels in the rear of the reception hall, and had snooped around trying to access a series of the other locked doors.

Up to that point, the group had been restrained, other than for Seymour's outburst. But the angst on their faces did not go unnoticed. Noble presumed they were waiting to find out in greater detail why they had been summoned—an explanation he would ease into a step at a time.

"I trust each of you has found your accommodations satisfactory? I hope they meet your lofty standards."

"What's with the bunking assignments? It reminds me of summer camp." Hank asked. Being the first to arrive, he quickly found the instructions posted on each of the bedroom doors, indicating the sleeping arrangements and any requests for dietary restrictions.

"I was thinking that, based on your Harvard days, it might be best to put the *strange bedfellows* in one suite and the *ladies' men* in the other suite." Noble abandoned his serious demeanor for the first time and smiled. "So you'll be sharing quarters with Chase. Paolo and Seymour will be in the other suite."

"What's with the room over there? Are you saving that one for Simon?" Hank asked, returning the smile.

"You never did recover the body. Did he in fact jump, or do you have him holed up in witness protection or who knows where?" Seymour prodded, adding his two cents.

The others offered a nervous chuckle in a bow to Simon's elusiveness.

Noble ignored the probing and simply stated, "That's my suite."

"What about those rooms?" Chase asked. He pointed to the closed double doors to the left of the alcove and the adjacent single door— both were locked.

Noble once heard a rumor that behind one of the doors was a rigged stage that looked like the Oval Office. Should it become necessary, the president would use the set to speak to the nation or to her enemies, giving the appearance he was safe and ensconced in the White House. The other door was believed to be a presidential apartment to serve as temporary quarters. Obviously, they were locked for a reason.

"The tour's over. Those rooms are unimportant to your mission," Noble answered in haste. He was eager to move the discussion forward.

Seymour, assuming the others had entered the facility in a similarly circuitous route, thought that they had to be equally curious as to their location. He pressed on their behalf. "Okay, so where the hell are we?"

On impulse, Hank scanned the room with a more studious eye, having not given the specific location prior thought. Then, in utter astonishment, he announced, "The Crystal Palace!"

The others were dumbfounded, other than Noble, who was impressed with Hank's conclusion. Of course, he would have had firsthand knowledge, as the former president's chief of staff.

"We're at Mount Weather?" Chase's voice dripped with concern, struggling to stave off the onset of claustrophobia.

They were all privy to the fact that Mount Weather was located about forty-eight miles outside of Washington, D.C. near the rural town of Bluemont, Virginia. It was a self-contained facility used for a variety of activities, most notably, the training ground for FEMA, the Federal Emergency Management Agency. It was the national-security stronghold utilized as a command center for over a hundred federal relocation centers in the event of a national emergency. Beyond that, what went on underground was less well known. The underground city was rumored to provide a safe haven for the president if the country were ever under attack. The code name for the presidential emergency facility was referred to as "The Crystal Palace." But its location was classified, known only to a small cadre of those at the highest level.

If Hank had figured out where we are, chances are Simon had also known of its existence. Noble took a deep breath at the thought and then stated, "As I told you when I first solicited you for this mission, you would be staying in a secure location and all your needs would be met."

Hank smiled. "It's obvious we're trapped inside the Crystal Palace, which is why we haven't been able to get any cell reception," he concluded.

Noble shrugged, as though to say, *Indeed.*

"Now we understand where we are, but we need to know the details as to why we're here!" Paolo insisted.

Noble looked at the wall clock. It was time to put the plan in motion.

He remained standing and began his elaboration. "I'm sure it hasn't escaped any of you that the reeling economy and the current number of people not participating in the workforce could push the economy deeper into a recession—even edge the country toward a depression." He hesitated. "If that should happen, the economic effects will not trickle—but will flood the world—causing global economic devastation beyond any adversity we've experienced in our history."

It did not take much for them to conjure up images. Not from old photos of the breadlines from the Great Depression, but from the latest series of apocalyptic films and television episodes that permeated the airwaves. The rebirth of shantytowns and wandering hobos had become Hollywood themes with firm messages against corporate greed and the plight of the poor.

"What does all of that have to do with us?" Chase asked, characteristically afraid of the answer.

"The president is well aware that a group of highly intellectual men were responsible for placing Baari in the Oval Office, which resulted in a market crash brought on by his policies, with all the attendant consequences. Furthermore, he's mindful of your actions that aided and abetted Simon's infiltration of the government."

Paolo interrupted forcefully. "We didn't know Simon's motives or the true measure of his master plan."

"None of us did!" Hank insisted.

"We've rehashed that narrative many times before," Noble reminded them and then emphasized, "Simon is dead, but the country still remains in a precarious situation. Gentlemen, in five minutes, the president will conference in and make his request to you directly."

All the members of La Fratellanza were speechless.

That presented Noble the opportunity to walk over to the table and sit down in the empty chair. At the same time, he pulled out a small remote-control device from his pocket and pointed it toward the wall behind him. Then the large painting of a seascape that hung on the wall suddenly began to lift up toward the ceiling, revealing a large flat-screen monitor.

The others continued to be mesmerized.

✑

"Good evening, gentlemen," came the voice from a speaker system. The view on the monitor was the President of the United States, seated behind his desk in the Oval Office.

The group around the round table immediately sat upright as if to stand at attention.

"Good evening, Mr. President," the chorus replied.

"I'm encouraged to see that all of you are present. And I'm confident that each of you understands that our country's sinking economy and sovereignty are in peril," he began. "There is a blatant cry for jobs, but the prior administration turned a deaf ear, caught up in their own diversions. They offered nothing tangible to counteract the stress."

The members of La Fratellanza shifted in their chairs, each feeling as though the president's piercing eyes were directed at them personally.

"Nothing tangible," he continued, "except to create hopelessness, which appears to be the impetus for people to drop out of the workforce in such large numbers, and opt to rely heavily on government subsidies to hold their families together. We're caught in a vicious spiral that could lead us deeper into a recession, or worse. We must climb out of this vortex. My primary concern is to put people back to work. It's our major building block to get our economy out of the doldrums. Without some positive steps we are on the road to unsustainability!"

Hearing the president use the word "unsustainability" had a frightening connotation.

Then he began to quote a recent analysis by the Congressional Budget Office. "As the cost of government subsidies continues to increase, it places a heavier burden on our debt. Absent drastic policy changes the federal debt is expected to rise to over 106 percent of the GDP by 2039."

He paused briefly before delivering the CBO's dire conclusion.

"If the federal debt continues to grow faster than the GDP, it will become unsustainable for the economy. Investor confidence in the government's ability to pay its debt obligations will inevitably cause another market collapse." The president leaned his elbows on his desk as he moved closer toward the camera, and stated, "Gentlemen, on the fifth of July, after the Independence Day weekend comes to a close, I will deliver a speech to the nation outlining a strategy to restore the economy, to alleviate the fears of the American families, and to reclaim their faith in their government. I ask all of you now to use your well-honed skills to devise that strategy. You have sixty-five days to do so."

He remained silent for the moment, giving them time to absorb his request.

"I recognize I'm asking you to make an enormous personal sacrifice for your country. Please take the evening to discuss it among yourselves. I must have your commitment by the morning. Noble will be on hand all evening to elaborate on the strategy. Thank you and God bless America."

The president signed off.

Everyone remained silent as they stared at the blank screen.

13
RULES OF ENGAGEMENT

"What? This is an impossible task!" Chase exclaimed, being the first to come out of their self-induced coma.

"I agree with Chase! What's he smoking anyway? Any changes in policy would require Congress's approval." Hank, not hesitating to chime in, pressed the point. "It takes years to wheel and deal to get any bill passed. Has anyone heard of Washington gridlock?"

"Hey guys, chill," Paolo interjected, attempting to slow the conversation down. "The wheels operate sluggishly in government, but let's make the operative word 'deal,' not 'wheel.' We'll need to make deals here. There's no other way!" Then, appealing to the egos of his brethren, he added, "We're at our best when thinking outside the box. Although, this may require us to meander farther from the box than anticipated."

Noble was pleased that Paolo appeared to be on board, savoring the challenge. Whatever the reason, he needed them all to pick up the cudgel. It was time to add more clarity. "The president sees the number-one problem affecting the economy is the paucity of jobs. After all these years, the feeble attempts at recovery defy historical norms. The snail-like pace of job creation is a key factor, along with the anemic employment participation rate. Our job is to decipher the underlying issues and prescribe a fix. The first step toward energizing an ailing economy. Our findings and conclusions must be based on facts, free of political biases. The entire exercise is classified and will be made an inseparable part of your current immunity agreements."

"I don't get!" Hank questioned, "The president has lots of brainiacs at his disposal. Why us?"

"The president has a Plan B that his so-called brainiacs devised. It would force him to squander more stimulus money to stop the bleeding and to stem further social unrest. But it doesn't solve the long-term problems. It's just another Band-Aid and won't stop the hemorrhaging!" Noble exclaimed. Then he elaborated, placing his words with care. "The public is distrustful about another president with an executive pen and a printing press. FDR tactics would be a desperate choice. It comes down to a question of trust. The country is polarized at this moment and we all know that past attempts to resolve these problems have failed miserably. The blame can be laid on the personal interests, biases, and political chicanery. The president needs you to devise Plan A—one that will face up to the real issues and attack them openly, honestly, and transparently."

"So what's in it for us?" Seymour asked with skepticism.

"An unequalled opportunity to preserve the country's future." Noble then reminded them of the "Truth or Dare" game they played at Harvard and how Simon used it to test their loyalty. "Consider this the supreme test of your loyalty. This time to your country, sacrificing your own ideology and personal circumstances aside. More on point: consider it an opportunity for your own *redemption*, not a usual gift for those who have gone astray."

The members of La Fratellanza shifted uneasily in their chairs, contemplating Noble's last statement. Apprehensive about where he was going with the issue, they began to mull over their options. Caught in a moment of deep concentration, they paid no particular attention to the fact that Noble had sat down in the chair Simon would have occupied.

Hank, quick to revive, was the first to notice. "Are you assuming the role of self-appointed leader this time around?"

"I'll function as the moderator, but we'll all work together. Now listen up; here are the ground rules," he stated with more seriousness. "You will have no communication with the outside world, other than at designated times. The calls will be placed on the secure phone over there." He pointed toward the set of steel doors they had entered earlier. "It requires an access code, which only I possess. Once a week, you'll be allowed to chat with your loved ones or business partners, although your conversations will be somewhat restrained by the circumstances. You are never to reveal your whereabouts or your assignment. I trust that you've already conditioned your families and associates for your absences. As Hank discovered, your smartphones will not work inside these walls." He paused to ensure that they were following, and then continued. "Each day your meals will be delivered at seven, one, and eight o'clock sharp. Not knowing your dietary preferences beforehand, I took the liberty of selecting palatable choices for your meals this evening; I trust they will suffice. The kitchen will be stocked daily with beverages and snacks at your disposal. I recognize the difficulty that comes with being isolated for long periods of time, so I urge you to use the workout room to keep you physically, as well as, mentally fit. All laundry will be collected every Friday and returned on the following Monday. You'll find individual laundry bags in your rooms marked with your first initials, for obvious security reasons. Should you need anything else to make your stay comfortable, please don't hesitate to ask." With a bow of the head, Noble bragged, "Our service is second to none." Scanning each of their faces, he noted their acquiescence, at least on the surface. Somewhat relieved, he thought, *So far, so good.*

"How about a few attractive young ladies to help us lap dance into the night?" Hank wisecracked.

As usual, Chase found his humor distasteful and was already beginning to dread his roommate. *These are not the days of old*, he reflected. "Seriously, what the hell is this—a conclave? You're going to lock us in here until we arrive at a decision!" Chase's own use of the word *lock* caused a momentary relapse, as he felt the tightening in his chest.

Noble responded. "Your task mirrors the process of electing a new pope. As I stated, all your personal needs will be accommodated." He stood up and walked over to a keypad on the wall near the secure phone. Blocking their view, he tapped in a series of numbers.

The others heard a distinct noise from the opposite end of the room. As their heads spun around they watched as the two large, unidentified, steel panels parted open in opposite directions.

"Far out," Seymour broadcasted, as a fairly sizeable room appeared.

Contained in the mysterious room were a series of monitors plastered along the walls and hordes of computer equipment. Positioned in a semi-circle were five tables that appeared to be set up as makeshift workstations. Each table provided ample workspace, in addition to housing an oversized all-in-one touch-screen tablet resting in its docking station, with a printer attached. Nearby was a large industrial-sized shredder.

"Looks like we have our own little communications center." Hank joked.

"Consider it more of a Situation Room. And what happens in the Situation Room stays in the Situation Room." Noble teased, recognizing they would not be allowed any outside communication.

"Perhaps we should call this place 'Sitcom,'" Seymour kidded.

"There is nothing funny about the miracles we are being asked to accomplish in that room," Chase admonished, in a professorial manner.

Noble sat back and let the banter continue for a few minutes longer, hoping to set them more at ease. Then he continued. "Work among yourselves to divide the responsibilities and determine what documentation you'll need. I've been authorized by the president to provide you with classified materials as they become necessary to the task. I will assist in performing any research analysis you require. Consider me your analyst-in-residence."

Paolo, with a puzzled look, pointed toward the Situation Room. "We can retrieve everything we would need from the Internet ourselves, right?"

"You'll have full access to the Internet, with certain restrictions. All email and social networking connections have been disabled for fear of messages being traced back to the facility. You'll only need to use a propriety search engine we refer to as the *DataSmasher*. Think of it in terms of the atom smasher and its ability to produce infinite results. The clever master indexer optimizes the search over all engines, scanning the results before downloading them into the highly classified DataSmasher."

"Sounds simple enough," Seymour boasted.

"The tablets on each of the workstations have been loaded with all the possible software you would need. Once your mission is complete, all hard drives will be scrubbed and all documents will be shredded."

"You mean the old 'Lois Lerner' Maneuver?" Seymour joked.

"Noble, I'm getting the feeling you don't trust us. Not a good start to a beautiful relationship," Hank challenged, adding to the levity.

Noble let them have their fun and then reminded them, "Our mutual trust is well established, harking back to the days of the immunity agreements each of you signed admitting to felony crimes; need I say more? We must all keep our eye on the ball."

Chase asked, this time in earnest, "Why all the secrecy?"

"If the country were to become aware of the existence of La Fratellanza and your immunity agreements, it could place you and your families at risk." *Act Three has yet to begin—watch out,* rang in Noble's ears, as he recalled Simon's last statement.

The group seemed to have caught the hesitant look on Noble's face, but he ignored them and continued.

"There's also the potential for immense political fallout. It could signal a weakness in the new president before he has a chance to carry out the plan. We can't resort to the usual Washington shuffle with endless hearings, free-flowing words, and no results. There needs to be some element of a workable solution to capture the imagination and support of the people. But it can't be accomplished in small increments—we must seize the bull by the horns and flip it over. If we succeed, the economy will turn around and confidence will be restored. That of course, will be up to our plan."

"So POTUS wants us to make him look good?" Seymour asked, with a hint of sarcasm.

"No, he wants solutions—let the facts fall where they may. You'd be surprised. President Post is a new breed of political leadership. But forget the president. Your job is to devise a plan for your country to stave off an economic disaster that could have global repercussions." Noble sensed they were beginning to understand the enormity of their task, but he was not convinced they had committed fully.

He pushed a little harder.

"If we can't stave off a disaster, the consequences will be unbearable. Life as we know it will change forever." He remained silent for a moment to let his words sink in, and then chose the personal appeal. "I've given a lot of thought to how my life and the lives of loved ones would be affected. There's no choice. We must change the course!"

"Noble, we've never seen you so pensive," Chase reacted, offering a sympathetic ear.

I had hoped to cause them to think about their own lives, not mine, he thought, but appreciated Chase's concern. "Let's move on—the clock is ticking."

Noble had held off with one final challenge. Now it was time to play out his hand.

Paolo was his ace in the hole.

He didn't like using his brother-in-law to promote their cause, but knowing where Paolo's sentiments lay, he needed him to convince the others. Facing Paolo directly, he said, "You, my friend, will be tasked with writing the speech—the one the president will deliver to the nation on July Fifth. It will be the opening salvo!"

"I'm humbled. I would consider it a privilege."

His brethren appeared surprised at Paolo's obvious acceptance and that it came so fast.

"Don't worry brother," Hank quipped, "you've defended both sides before. You're the spinmeister, capable of pivoting sentiments on a moment's notice."

Noble looked askance at Hank, but spoke to all of them. "I'll say this one more time. The president wants the facts. Political ideology has no place in the final solutions. We must first face the raw truth to fashion those solutions. The president will have it no other way."

"I'm not convinced we can do this. Maybe I should reconsider," Chase balked.

Seymour waved his arms in the air, displaying the seeming hopelessness of it all. "Chase is right. This is impractical. Why should we give up a couple months of our lives and lie to our families. For what? To fail the president of the United States. Tell him it's impossible!"

"He can't keep us here against our own will," Hank interjected, solely to provide solace to Chase and Seymour. He had no family responsibilities and no one to lie to, except perhaps to himself. Hank was ready for a new adventure, but he was not completely sold on the fact that this was the trip he wanted to take.

Over the next two hours, Noble continued to answer their questions and fend off their concerns. Finally, his effort to persuade was over. It was now up to Paolo to step up to the plate and convince his brothers. But Noble sensed some hesitancy in the room. It was difficult to read the expressions on their faces to determine whether they were all on the team. Conjecture told him Paolo, yes. Hank, most likely. Chase and Seymour, doubtful. Now he had to pass the baton to Paolo to state the case and influence the outcome.

To the others, Noble's plea was reminiscent of the year 2000. It was the time when Simon summoned all of them to Chicago and then devoted hours trying to convince them to bring their master thesis to life. Simon also laid out the ground rules, as Noble had just done. In silence, they each wondered whether they were heading down another wrong road with painful consequences.

"Forgive the pace of our deliberations, but time is of the essence," Noble apologized, and then pounded his fist on the table. It worked— he had their full attention. "This time it's not a game. It's reality all the way."

It was as if he had read their minds.

∽

Right on cue, a red light above the steel entrance doors began to flash.

"Dinner's arrived," Noble announced.

With the word "dinner" came a series of stomach pangs among the group. The source being either anxiety or hunger. In either case, they were pleased to see a large metal cart being pushed through the door, but confused by the force behind the cart. Suddenly, a tall, slim, muscular man dressed in khakis and a black sweater appeared.

"Good evening fellas. Anyone hungry?"

"This is Jax," Noble noted. "He will bring in our meals each day—and cater to other requests." He looked over at Jax. It was hard to miss the smile on his face. He surmised an outstanding debt was about to be paid.

"That's me, Jax, a jack of all trades," he quipped and then, making light of the situation, he said, "Welcome to our humble cave-like abode. It's as homey as we can make it." Hurriedly, he opened the doors to the metal cart. "Okay, fellas, we have grilled chicken with mashed potatoes, ravioli filled with spinach, and steak with fries. All expertly prepared by our version of an executive chef. Now, what say you mister with the bowtie?"

"The chicken will be fine," Chase replied.

Jax continued to pass out the rest of the meals according to their requests, while attempting to invoke some humor along the way. He finished off by placing a set of wine glasses on the table, followed by the welcome bottle of red wine.

"Will that be all guys?"

With mouthfuls of food, they all managed to mumble, "*Thanks Jax*," and then proceeded to devour their meal. There was no doubt their hunger had taken priority, as they ignored the polite table manners for the evening.

"Hey Jax, here is a list of their food preferences. See what you can do to accommodate," Noble requested.

Jax scanned the list. "Hmm, you must be Mr. C. You look like a gluten-free sort of guy. And you with the ravioli must be Mr. P. Bet your name ends in a vowel. Okay, which one of you two doesn't like fish?

"That would be me, Jax. I guess I'm Mr. S," Seymour responded, noting the obvious naming conventions.

"Then that would make you Mr. H?" Jax asked, looking over toward Hank's meal.

Hank offered a smile as he continued to gobble up his steak and fries.

"Low-fat, low-carb, good choice," Jax snickered.

"I thought it would be a great time to shed a few pounds—starting tomorrow," Hank retorted.

"All right, gentlemen, you enjoy yourselves," Jax hailed, as he executed a military salute. Then, with an about-face, he wheeled the cart out the entrance doors. Once again, he heard them utter, "Thanks Jax," as he departed.

∽

After several more bites and sips of wine, their hunger slowly abated.

Nodding toward the door, Seymour asked Noble, "What's his story?"

"Jax. He's ex-CIA. We used to work together. And from time to time, he does me favors. This is just one of those times."

"What was he, one of those undercover spies—a man who came in from the cold?" Hank prodded.

Chase interrupted. "I thought this was supposed to be a big secret."

"All anyone at the facility knows is that a group of men are working on a special project that is classified—and Jax doesn't talk. He can be trusted; you have my word. He also conducts training sessions in the facility and he knows his way around, so it doesn't raise any red flags. Now, eat up; it's getting late," Noble instructed.

It was obvious that no other information about their surprise guest would be forthcoming. They were willing to wait for the rest to unfold. Content for the moment, they calmly finished off the last of their wine.

It was an opportune time for Noble to leave the others alone to share their thoughts on more complex issues. He stood up and made his final plea. "The president will not force you to accept, but he appeals to your sense of duty to your country. Talk among yourselves and give me your decision in the morning. This will be your last chance to opt out. Remember, while you're deliberating, your country needs you— but it has to be all of you or none. Good night, gentlemen." He left and walked to his room.

The group watched without a sound.

14
THE NIGHT OWLS

The members of the now-defunct La Fratellanza remained immobile and silent for a few passive moments longer, while waiting for Noble to retire to his suite. Each spent the time contemplating his next move.

When safely out of earshot, Seymour, true to form, was the first to voice his opinion. "Need I remind any of you that the last time we sat around this table it didn't turn out so well?"

"Except when Baari won the presidency," Hank harked back, chuckling.

Finding no humor in his remark, Seymour griped further, "You can't paint a happy face on that fiasco! It was a colossal lapse in judgment on our part."

"Hey guys," Paolo interrupted. "We all have to admit that when we sat around this table at Harvard—and planned the impossible, albeit thinking it was just a game —it was one of the most exhilarating times in our lives. That's what turned us on and kept us going."

"That was then, before we had to spend years rebuilding our lives because of it," Seymour retorted. "Noble has no idea what he is asking from us, the sacrifices we'd have to make. He can't possibly comprehend the impact our misdeeds had on our families. Do we want to go through this again?" he queried, that time with more emphasis.

"Let's not forget; Noble also suffered immeasurably because of Simon," Paolo chimed in. "But putting all that aside, this is a chance for all of us to find some redemption for the damage we inflicted. We all bear the emotional scars of our actions. Why not seize this opportunity?"

Seymour attempted one more passionate plea. "What if we get it wrong? What if the president stands at the podium, delivers a plan to the nation, and it ends up creating more panic and devastation? We will not only fail the president, but the country once again. Can we live with the consequences? How much scar tissue can we carry?"

Chase and Hank had remained silent while listening to the discourse, and pondering their own stances. Then, to the surprise of the others, Chase entered the dialogue and was the first to take a softer line.

"It would be our job to make sure it doesn't happen by providing unbiased, logical solutions. We aren't charged with producing a miracle, but only a course that will right the ship."

All eyes shifted in his direction, each wondering if they had incorrectly concluded that he would have been the hard sell.

"Hey my friend, are you sure? We're all aware of how you've suffered. If this takes a bad turn, you could have the most to lose," Hank cautioned, in a surprisingly avuncular tone.

"I listened to Noble. And Paolo is correct. It's a chance to redeem ourselves. For me—it may be my last opportunity. I never dreamed I'd ever have a chance to clear my name fully!"

The others listened with admiration as Chase continued to make his pitch.

"If we were to do this, then we'd have to work together to come up with concrete solutions to present to the president. We know each other's strengths and weaknesses and have played off them successfully in the past. I'm confident we have the collective right stuff."

Paolo grinned, delighted with Chase's demeanor. "I've never seen you in such an effusive role. May I add it's to your credit? I like the new, new, all-new Chase."

Appreciating the comment, he softened his expression, and asked, "If we decide to move forward then we must first define the priorities and then fashion a strategy that will serve as a road map for POTUS, with both short-term and long-term strategies."

"Wait a minute—before we commit," Seymour said, somewhat softened by Chase's stance. "I suggest we first lay out a tentative plan to see if it's even possible given the timeframe. We'll need to challenge our premises before drafting a blueprint."

After a brief pause, they all agreed to prepare the agenda outlining their mission. But first they would review the interrelated issues they believed might be responsible for the failing job market and then determine the threat level of an impending market collapse. They would also take into account other areas that perhaps would require further scrutiny.

Chase continued to elaborate, "There are statistics cited by various sources that show that the healthcare bill, in particular, has had a deleterious effect on the economy, especially on jobs. But we'll need to dissect the numbers to determine their impact on the economy."

Hank stepped into the breach. "The verdict is still out on the healthcare bill!" he disputed. "It has just been a few years and more people enroll each day. There are no statistics that condemn the plan outright or lead to the conclusion it should be scrapped."

"Calm down. I agree we can't accurately pinpoint at this juncture exactly what is causing our economic pains, but for certain the healthcare bill deserves our attention," Chase underscored.

"We do know for a fact," Paolo said, "that out of all the people who enrolled for healthcare insurance, over seventy percent enrolled in Medicaid versus private insurance. So it's clear the Medicaid expansion aspect of the bill has created huge deficits in many states." Not being able to resist a good jab, he continued, "Hank, what about your beloved state? The city of Chicago alone was left with a sixty-two-million-dollar deficit. Thirty other states rejected the federal funds to expand Medicaid for their cities, not wanting to be forced under the federal guidelines."

"Paolo's right, and I'm sure once we research further, we'll uncover other policy issues that have had a direct effect on the job market," Chase concluded. "Besides, being the last man standing in the former administration, you, Hank, more than anyone, knew where the problems lay. Your knowledge will be most helpful."

Hank remained silent. He knew that Chase was correct, for he personally was against much of what was included in the bill. But Baari was unrelenting on making the Universal Healthcare Act his legacy and refused much of Hank's advice, pouring salt in the still-festering wounds. Hank was not alone.

"The immigration and energy policies can't be ignored either," Seymour stated.

"They're all areas of concern," Chase allowed. "But first we have to dive deep into the real job numbers to understand the magnitude of the problem we are setting out to resolve. We can't be led by the headline analyses that are often figments of political imaginations."

Seymour, with more vigor, insisted, "Whatever solution is proposed to the president, it must also have a corresponding marketing plan to ensure successful execution."

Chase and Paolo were happy to ease back into their chairs, wanting to hear more from the marketeer.

Hank coaxed him to continue.

"Most people have tuned out and distrust anything coming out of Washington for good reason. Despair blankets the country. If the president is going to deliver a speech to jumpstart the country out of its malaise with plans to reenergize the economy, it needs to be understood by all and repeated often. Primarily by the younger generation, who are the most skeptical. Otherwise, what's the point?" Seymour sensed that his brethren were buying his argument. He continued. "It would need a huge media blitz, including a website to be operational moments after the president gives his speech. Social networking must be used to the fullest capacity. It's imperative that the message ring true founded on factual transparency, an element that's not existed in Washington in the past. In the end, it will be all about the message."

"Seymour, it sounds like you've signed on to lead the charge!" Paolo cajoled.

"I didn't say that. I'm only pointing out that without a marketing campaign, a plan of that magnitude, meant to reach out and enlist the support of the populace—would fail. That's how we succeeded to get Baari elected, not once, but twice."

"There's another point that mustn't be overlooked," Hank posed. "Seymour's correct about conducting a full-fledged marketing campaign, but it would have to continue long after the president gives his speech. We'd have to commit to more than sixty-five days."

Hank's comment caused them all to slouch back into their chairs for a moment of scrutiny.

However, Paolo, not willing to let up, pushed the point. "There's one person I know who could put together a believable and inspiring media campaign—and he's in this room."

Chase had been watching their expressions and had sensed they would all sign on. He chose to take the offensive. In a serious tone, he asserted, "We should hold our first session two days from now, when we can more accurately pinpoint the problems. Before then we should use the time to research various dimensions of the major issues and to agree on priorities. Then as each day proceeds, we can determine how to allocate our time, whether or not we spend our mornings to further research or move right into debating the current topic. Remember our purpose is to weed out specific ineffective policies and to formulate changes the president can adopt."

"Excuse me, Chase, am I missing something? When did we agree to accept this insane assignment?" Seymour asked.

"We'll let you tell Noble that he'll be building the website," Paolo teased, sensing that when it came to a vote, Seymour would make it unanimous.

Hank played along. "Okay, I'll formally ask the question. Are we going to sign up?"

Silence took hold. Then each offered a grin of varying degrees in tacit agreement. The nonverbal answers became evident.

Then without missing a beat, they began to divide up the assignments.

"Hank, can you run through the numbers on the recent unemployment report?"

"No problem."

15
THE BROTHERHOOD'S GAME PLAN

Noble looked over at the alarm clock. Through half-closed eyes he deciphered that it was 4:10 a.m. He also surmised he had been lying in bed wide-eyed for hours. In reality, he had spent the last few hours in a fitful sleep wrestling with his past demons. As he eased out of his haze, he evoked memories of sporadic dreams blurred in perspective. First, he recalled obsessing over the president's dire words, and then contemplating aspects of his own life. Strangely enough, there was even one with Chase pounding the gavel, calling a meeting to order. Most troubling were the flashes of faces that kept reappearing. Natalie, Amanda, Max, but in no particular order—although Max's face always seemed more in focus and calming.

He punched his pillow in frustration. He knew he would now have to wait a few more hours to discover whether or not he had failed on his pledge to the president. And if by some miracle, all the members of La Fratellanza were willing to take on this enormous undertaking— then the tension, without a doubt, would increase. There was only one acceptable outcome, a plan destined for success.

Noble tussled a few more times with his pillow, trying to induce sleep, until it became impossible. "Dammit," he called out. He was quick to empty his head of all thoughts and force himself out of bed. As he tossed on his robe, sudden visions of hot coffee replaced the unpleasantries. He quietly eased open his door, cognizant of the others sleeping nearby, and crossed the reception hall. As he headed toward the kitchen, he was suddenly startled by four shadowy figures seated at the round table.

⚮

"Pull up a chair," Hank invited.

Without offering any small talk, Chase plunged in with an outline of the discussion points from their overnight meeting and described how they had divided up the various responsibilities.

"Wait a minute," interrupted Noble. "Chase?" he questioned warily, looking for confirmation.

"I'm in," he acknowledged.

Noble scanned the faces of the others.

Hank threw up his right hand and pledged, "I'm in as well."

"I'm in," Seymour averred.

Paolo repeated the same two words in unison.

A few minutes of eerie silence filled the room, as those two little words brought back memories of an earlier time in the spring of 2007. Having followed their own rules, they took a vote whenever any doubt loomed as to whether they should continue to carry out their far-fetched plan. Basically, if one person opted out, the group would cast a vote—the majority decision would be honored—and, as agreed, it would be all or none. There was one desperate time when Simon handed each of them a piece of paper, saving one for himself. They were to cast a vote either to end the game or to continue to the finish line. At that point, they had already invested seven years in grooming Baari. With their orchestration, he had become a U.S. senator, and the time had come to enter him into the presidential race. Each member brought to mind a vivid memory of casting his own ballots and listening with apprehension as Paolo read them aloud. IN, IN, IN, IN, IN. The sound still resonated in their ears. Ultimately, even with all the doubts Paolo had at the time, he could not bring himself to part with his brothers. In fact, he had read his ballot first, not knowing how the others would vote.

Hearing how Paolo had voted this time brought it all back.

"The entire country will be indebted," Noble stated, with disciplined reserve, even as his heart was racing. He took a deep breath and then urged, "Chase, please continue."

"We have the distinct advantage of having members of the Baari administration present." He cast a glance in the direction of Hank and Paolo. "So we've reached total agreement as to which areas are most crucial in terms of potentially affecting the unemployment rate and the creation of jobs. As we debate each topic, we will clarify whether it presents a positive or adverse effect and then decide whether it requires further focus. In due course, we will attempt to identify ways to stimulate the economy, by spurring employment through monetary and fiscal policies." Chase paused for a brief moment to scan his notes. "At first pass, it appears the major areas are immigration, the Universal Healthcare Act, and various energy policies, including climate change and the vaunted cap-and-trade legislation—acknowledging they are inextricably entwined. We also recognize that other topics may surface and will address them accordingly." He then looked at Seymour, signaling him to chime in.

"There is another aspect we need to consider." Seymour explained, "A speech alone will not have much impact unless the ordinary citizens grasp the concepts. Therefore, the president will need a major marketing campaign to work in tandem, giving the public the opportunity to follow along with his solutions to turn the economy around, say, a scorecard if you will. A constant flow of messaging must reach the young and the old to convince them of the validity of the president's plan in real terms, allowing the private sector time to demonstrate actual results."

The group sat back, waiting for Noble's reaction.

"I like it!" Noble asserted, not requiring a second thought. "The only change I would make is that when we sell it to the president we refer to it as a 'communications campaign.' The president will want the public informed and not to feel as though they are being sold another bill of goods. The scars from the Universal Healthcare Act rollout are still healing. "

"Point taken, but the techniques will be basically the same," Seymour said.

"But this time around no astroturfing. There will be no mis-information; only honest messages will be conveyed," Noble warned, and then he softened his tone. "You realize, however, if the president buys into the concept of a full-blown campaign, he will expect you to remain here after he makes his speech to provide guidance in the early stages? It could be a matter of weeks."

"We surmised as much," Hank said, with a slight shrug.

"Great! Any ideas for a name?" Noble was thus far pleased with the outcome.

Seymour cocked his head and looked at the others. "I hadn't given it any thought until you posed the question. But considering we are here for our own redemption—how about the *Renaissance 2017 Project*?"

"Brilliant," Paolo commended, accompanied with a pat on the back. The others wholeheartedly agreed.

"Oh, Noble," Seymour grinned, "I forgot to mention, you get to program the website."

Noble glanced at them for a moment, and then retorted, "Silly me, I didn't see that set-up coming."

They all had a good chuckle and then Chase requested, "Can you get us copies of the Universal Healthcare Act? Unless, of course, you want to print us copies."

"I'd rather spare another forest from being cut down to provide the paper."

"Funny, Noble. Two quips in one day. I didn't know you had such a sense of humor," Hank teased.

Noble ignored Hank. "I'll inform the president of your decision and have copies of the healthcare plan delivered to you within the next few hours." Completely satisfied, and much more at ease, he solicited, "Anyone for a cup of coffee?"

Chase looked at his watch; it was 6:45 a.m. "Not for me, thanks. Mr. Sandman is beckoning. I'm going to hit the sack for a few hours of shut-eye. What do you say we reconvene at ten o'clock and then spend the day doing our homework? We can then begin the jobs discussion the day after tomorrow as agreed."

"Works for me," the others chimed in as they retreated to their respective suites.

❧

Noble remained alone at the table, while his stomach did a few somersaults. *They're all good to go,* he thought. *Amazing!* He couldn't have been more pleased. He was a bit surprised, though, that Chase had taken the lead and appeared more resolute. Aside from his emotional wobbles at times, Chase was the most honest and levelheaded individual in the group. Most important, he was a numbers guy and believed the numbers never lied.

"Yes! We are good to go!" he exclaimed aloud.

Given the time, Noble chose to wait another fifteen minutes before making the crucial call. First, he'd call Stanton to request that he deliver the monstrosity of a healthcare plan that had a pass-first-read-later instruction for the Congress, according to the then-Speaker of the House.

He glanced again at the wall clock—the decisive moment had arrived. He took one deep breath and placed another call—this time to the President of the United States.

16
BEAUTY ABOUNDS

After an exciting week in Florence, Natalie and Mario arrived safely in Rimini on schedule. It was 4:55 p.m. to the minute and Enzo was there to greet them. He spotted them getting off the train, a beautiful American woman with a young boy in tow.

"*Ciao bella*," Enzo welcomed, with the Italian cheek-to-cheek kiss. "Your brother forgot to mention how exquisite you are my dear."

"*Grazie*," Natalie replied, slightly flushed.

"And this must be *Signore* Mario." He offered the young master a firm handshake.

"*Piacere mio*," Mario replied.

"Ah, *si parla italiano*?"

"*Si, signore. Mio babbo mi ha insegnato.*"

"Your father is a very good teacher," Enzo replied, and then noted Natalie's confused expression. "Would you prefer I speak English, my dear?"

"Yes, and please call me Natalie."

"*Certamente*; I mean, certainly. And please call me Enzo." Enzo patted Mario on the shoulder and said, "You must be a little tired from you trip. Let's get you to the hotel so you can rest a while." He reached over for Natalie's luggage and directed them toward his car, which was waiting just outside at the curb.

The official-looking black car impressed both Natalie and Mario, especially when the driver stepped out to help them into the back seat. Enzo sat up front. Natalie knew all about Enzo and his relationship with Noble. How he first worked alongside Hamilton on the sting operation in Florence and then later he worked with Noble on the European New Year's Eve assassination attempts. However, she was still she curious to learn more about this interesting man, thinking Noble may have left out some interesting tidbits.

"The Republic of San Marino is the oldest independent city-state in the world," Enzo explained and then remarked, "Its first governing body dates back to 1243, although the city's first historical documents date back as far as 885." It was obvious that Enzo was proud of his knowledge as he continued to pontificate. "Geographically, San Marino is located in the country of Italy, but technically wedged in between two Italian regions, Emilia Romagna to the northeast and Montefeltro in the Marche to the southwest, but she still remains independent."

Although he sounded more like a travel guide, Natalie asked, "What brings you here from Lyon?"

"There are roughly thirty-thousand inhabitants here, but Interpol's role is vital in promoting cooperation between San Marino and other member countries. But I always delight in coming to this beautiful, charming medieval treasure. Even if it's for the usual business."

They had been on the road only a short time when Natalie spotted a sign that read "San Marino." Soon after, the car veered right and began the ascent up the twisting country road. As the car continued to corkscrew up the mountain, Natalie sensed they were about to reach the top. "Mario, look back. You can see how high up we are," she urged.

"In a moment, we will arrive at the top of Mount Titano, where you'll be able to have a three-hundred-and-sixty degree view. You'll even be able to spot the Adriatic Coast, near the train station where I met you," Enzo continued.

About ten minutes later, their car pulled in front of the Hotel Titano, named after the mountain. While the driver stayed in the car that blocked the narrow street, Enzo carried in the luggage. Natalie and Mario followed behind.

"I've taken the liberty of making reservations at one of the best restaurants in San Marino. It's the Ristorante Righi, just up that street. I'll meet you here in the lobby at ten to eight." He then quickly checked them in at the reception desk.

"Thank you Enzo, but you've been so kind to arrange this for us. We don't want to impose on you any further."

"Please, it's my pleasure. At dinner we can discuss some sights for you and Mario to take in tomorrow. Although you'll find San Marino very easy to maneuver."

"Thank you again." She relented. "We'll see you in a few hours."

Enzo dashed out to the waiting car, and the bellman directed the two American visitors to their room.

༥

Rested and feeling energetic, Natalie, Mario, and Enzo walked out of the hotel, turned left onto the narrow, stone street, and then walked up the steep hill less than a half-city block to an open plaza.

"This is the Piazza Libertà and that is the Public Palace," he said, pointing toward the end of the square. "Come with me."

They followed Enzo across the square, although they were both curious as to the direction. They had noted as they entered the plaza that they were heading away from the row of restaurants lined up on the opposite side. But within seconds, they had reached the edge of the square and lined up to lean against the waist-high, ancient stone wall. Then they peered to the right.

"Oh my!" Natalie exclaimed.

All the visitors in the plaza had turned their heads in the same direction. The sun had just begun to gently set down and dissolve into the sea.

"What a most glorious sunset. I feel like I'm on top of the world," Natalie said.

"Sanmarinese think they are." Enzo smiled and then gestured them in the direction of the restaurant.

Standing outside was a pleasant-looking man dressed in a business suit, seemingly expecting them, as he appeared suddenly to walk in their direction.

"*Ciao*, Enzo. And these must be your lovely American friends."

The man patted Mario on the head and offered a handshake to Natalie. "My name is Giovanni. Welcome to my restaurant." Effortlessly, Giovanni and Enzo immediately moved into the Italian embrace as they each greeted an old friend.

"Please follow me," Giovanni gestured.

Natalie and Mario followed behind and entered the small but charming restaurant. Then, quite by surprise, they continued to follow up a narrow staircase to the right of the bar and, suddenly, they entered an elegant dining room with gorgeous views out over the plaza and to the valley below.

"How lovely," Natalie remarked, as both Enzo and Giovanni

swooped in to offer her a chair at one of the large round tables.

From the moment they sat down, waiters appeared from various directions, pouring Prosecco and laying out platters of Italian delights. Then, interchanged with Giovanni's description of the different meats and cheeses, Enzo suggested an itinerary for their first day's adventure, until Giovanni stepped in.

"I agree, Giovanni, they must visit the towers, but first they must stop to see the Basilica of Saint Marinus. It's an exquisite church with altars embellished in precious stones. There are also many valuable paintings to view."

"They can see the church after, but first they must see the towers. Early in the morning, when the air is still crisp and the streets are quiet." Giovanni took a moment to kid Enzo, reminding him that he was the real Sanmarinese, and then continued with his preferred plan. "After they walk up Salita alla Rocca to Guaita, they should walk along the Passo delle Steghe to Cesta, and then continue on to Montale. Naturally, that will bring them right past the Kursaal Congress Centre and Interpol's office." They continued to jabber, agreeing and disagreeing, on the other churches or museums they should visit, and in which order they should be seen. Finally, it was settled.

"Brilliant suggestion, Giovanni."

It must have been the perplexed looks on both Natalie's and Mario's faces that prompted both Italian gentlemen to laugh, realizing that their rather animated conversation might have seemed odd.

"Excuse me, my dear," Giovanni said, while motioning one of the waiters to bring him a map. "Maybe this will help." He proceeded to explain what had transpired and then proudly began to describe the history surrounding the three towers perched high above the city and how they were an integral part of the city walls that protected the citizens of San Marino. From time to time, he would point to the map for clarification. "Here's the road that will take you to Gauita, the first tower you'll encounter and the first one built in San Marino." He explained that it dated back to the eleventh century and, in modern times, functioned as a prison until 1975. "I suggest you walk up Passo delle Steghe to Cesta, the second tower, for a magnificent view of the valley and the Adriatic Coast. Mario, do you know what Passo delle Steghe means?"

"Path of the witches," he replied hesitantly.

"*Bravo*. But I promise you won't run into any along the way." Giovanni winked. Then, pointing to the map, he followed along the path with his finger to the second tower. "This is Cesta and it was built over the remains of an ancient Roman fortress. It dates back to about the thirteenth century." Again using his finger to trace along the path to the third tower, he said, "This is Montale. It dates back to the fourteenth century and was erected for defensive uses, but also functioned as a prison. Look here; if you walk down this path you'll end up here at the Kursaal Congress Centre."

"That's where the National Central Bureau of Interpol is located," Enzo interjected. "If you'd like a tour, I can arrange it for the day after tomorrow."

"Cool," Mario replied.

"Be careful Enzo, Uncle Noble is deathly afraid that Mario will want to become a spy," Natalie warned in good humor.

"Perhaps he'd rather visit the Torture Museum, or maybe even the Reptile Museum," Giovanni quipped.

Mario let out a big grin at the same time Natalie winced before being saved by the waiter. Large platters of pasta suddenly appeared on the table.

Giovanni explained that one platter contained ravioli, filled with almonds surrounded by a saffron sauce. The other was called strozzapreti. "It's a penne pasta with cream and bacon sauce. Both are local dishes."

"They both smell divine," Natalie complimented as she inhaled the aroma.

Enzo took to serving Natalie and Giovanni served generous portions of each to Mario. Then, after the platters had been emptied, and Natalie feeling sated, more platters appeared.

"This is *coniglio*, or rabbit. It is stuffed with pork. And this *baccala*, a roasted cod with a chickpea cream and glazed onions. I hope you will enjoy both. Again, they are local recipes."

Over the course of the meal, interspersed with delightful conversation, the first day had been scoped out, ending with a funicular ride down the side of the mountain to Borgo Maggiore, the second largest town of San Marino, which lies as the foot of Mount Titano. Feeling slightly queasy at the prospect, Natalie was not sure that she was ready for what would come next.

"Mama, look."

Suddenly paraded in front of them were a variety of desserts, each looking somehow more decadent than the others.

17
BROTHER, CAN YOU SPARE A DIME?

Precisely at ten o'clock, a band of freshly showered and refreshed men strolled into the reception hall. Straightaway they noticed the hard-to-miss eight-inch stack of papers that had been placed in front of each of their workstations. They presumed it to be the highly disputed Universal Healthcare Act, a subject that had monopolized the attention of the U.S. population.

"Good morning gentlemen," Noble greeted them with gusto. "Jax already loaded up the kitchen with a breakfast buffet. I'm sure you'll find something to satisfy your craving. Sorry Paolo, no caffè *corretto.*" Noble winked.

"What the hell is that?" Hank asked.

"It's espresso with a shot of grappa," Paolo replied, adding, "If I even sniffed it, my day would end."

"Go help yourselves and then let's get started," Noble urged, recognizing that he had created the delay.

Without a word, they scurried in the direction of the food.

Noble carried on with his croissant and coffee in hand while he waited for the others to return. Not surprisingly, it required very little time before they returned with their favorite goodies. The unusually large portions of yogurt, fruits, and pastries stacked on their plates did not go unnoticed. It was obvious that they had worked up an appetite during their overnight session.

Earlier that morning, Noble had placed a smaller tablet, compared to their fully loaded desktop version, on the round table in front of each of their chairs.

Hank was the first to notice. "What's this for?" he asked curiously, holding up the device.

"Any data you enter on either your workstation tablet or this device will be synced with one another."

Setting their plates aside for the moment, they immediately started to power on the tablets.

"Since you're all anxious to get started, you'll notice an app in the upper right hand corner. Please tap it."

Instantly, a document displayed.

"Whoa, what's this about?" Chase asked, noting its formality.

"Let me start off by letting you know that I've spoken with the president and he extends his gratitude to all of you for accepting this assignment. But he requests that you first sign a confidentiality agreement. Please read the document carefully and then sign at the bottom." Noble offered no further instructions for the moment. He sat back and watched as they read the wording.

"Is this really necessary?" Hank questioned. "You already have immunity agreements you can use against us."

"I'm sure all of you understand what's at stake," Noble explained. "The president requests that all of what is discussed, any information retrieved, and final outcomes be classified."

"Are you going to sign the document as well?" Hank challenged.

"I already have."

Hank looked at others for confirmation. They all seemed satisfied. "Okay, where do we sign?"

"Have you all read the document thoroughly?"

With affirmative nods, Noble passed along the instructions. "Place the pad of your right thumb in the box at the bottom of the document. When the green light flashes, hit the *Submit* button. Your documents will then be sent to the president's private email address. He will have the only copies."

Noble watched as each complied.

"Cool," Seymour announced. "The document just crumpled into a ball and then poof! It disappeared.

"A little graphic touch I added," Noble admitted, with a modest smile. Then he used the remote-control device once again to move the painting up toward the ceiling and reveal the large monitor. "Now, if you swipe the left side of the screen on your tablet, your screen's image will project on the monitor as well. One at a time," he cautioned, "or you'll override the other tablets."

"I'll go first," Seymour volunteered. Unable to resist, he quickly tapped the OneNote App and drew in large lettering the initials *LF* and then swiped the left side of his screen. "Hey, pretty wild."

The others in the group chuckled, except for Noble. As usual, he ignored Seymour's wit and continued. "While you guys munch away, listen up while I reiterate our mission." He set down his own plate and laid out the strategy for the group.

"When I spoke with the president he requested that we be prepared to provide him with periodic status updates. He'll conference in at a prearranged time. I'll try to give you as much warning as possible, but it will be, of course, according to his schedule." Noble perused their faces. It was hard to measure whether they were pleased at the opportunity to convey their ideas straight to the president or it just added another stress point. He chose not to give them time to contemplate either and moved on.

"Now as I explained before, the president needs—for lack of a better description—an economic triage. Troubled times demand drastic measures, and these times exceed the mark when it comes to being troubled. Yesterday, you identified certain policies that could have a potentially negative impact on the job market, in terms of employment, capital investment, and job creation: what we know to be the primary engines of economic growth."

"So, the president is asking us to identify resolutions and assign priorities where the country can achieve measurable success in the shortest possible time," Paolo clarified.

"Exactly, or we'll just be floundering," Noble replied.

"Then let's cut to the chase—no pun intended," Hank interrupted, hoping to move along the conversation.

"Thanks for the intro, Hank," Chase said, "but it's reasonable to assume that as we drill down into the topics, we'll also arrive at other plausible approaches that will take a longer time to execute."

"I agree," Noble allowed. "We'll likely have long-term goals and short-term milestones. And you have my assurance that all credible solutions will be submitted to the president for timely consideration." After noting their expressions, he opted for an obsequious interval, and lauded them with "Only a group of your stature has the vision to create and execute these solutions."

Noble understood these intellectuals well enough to know how to appeal to their egos. Apparently it worked. They seemed pleased that any cogent ideas would make their way to the president's desk.

"But you must focus on deliberate changes he can invoke to launch the overall strategy without delay!" he emphasized.

Their serious demeanor remained in check. It was apparent that they had grasped the enormity of the task at hand. A sense of commitment pervaded the room.

"Finish up your breakfast and then let's get to work."

18
TRUTH IN JOB NUMBERS

The group had devoted the past two days pulling together all the necessary information to debate the elusive job numbers. Their first official session was about to begin. Everyone seemed enthusiastic to get the ball rolling.

"Take it away," Noble suggested, nodding in the direction of Chase, who seemed overly eager.

Already prepared with an opening statement, Chase didn't hesitate. "Our brief analysis of the situation suggests that we must first identify the causes behind the lack of jobs being created, sufficient to sustain the workforce. Slow job growth can only produce a moribund economy in our consumer-driven country. I believe that, in large measure, employers are being hampered by policies and regulations imposed on them by the prior administration. There's a clear cause-and-effect relationship that's evident." Then, after downing a quick sip of coffee, he threw a personal jab. "After all, they were policies all of you orchestrated." With a nod of exception to Noble, he added, "Your fingerprints are all over them."

Not wanting to give them an opportunity to lose focus, Noble said, "Despite the numbers that are pumped out monthly by the government, they are defective and confusing. Let's begin by ferreting out the real numbers relative to the workforce versus those murky numbers conveyed in the monthly job reports that we've dissected. Reports we know that have been contested for good reason."

Hank, noting the earlier inference, consumed the last of his muffin and then challenged, "As you so rightly pointed out, Chase, we were at the scene when it happened. That's why I would suggest that before we wander too far afield, we zero in on why people are dropping out of the workforce. This is a key element not reported for political motives and largely unreported by biased news sources. How can one ignore the fact that less than half the population is participating in the workforce. It's an abysmal statistic; even I would have to admit."

Great start! I was counting on you Chase, to stay in the neutral zone, Noble mused, but was glad he had done his homework as usual. He tapped away at his tablet and retrieved the most recent copy of the U.S. Census Bureau's report. He then flipped to the page he had previously bookmarked and chimed in. "Valid point Hank, but I'd like to go back and address Chase's point. As reported, the current unemployment rate is stagnant, holding at ten percent. The U.S. Bureau of Labor Statistics, or BLS, had projected that as of today the rate would be somewhere around five-point-eight percent, which is completely out of whack. And according to the latest census poll projections, the population is tipping over 331 million people." Noble paused and refocused his attention to the group. "Another national census will not be conducted until 2020, which doesn't include the twelve million illegal immigrants who recently became 'amnestitized' citizens, thanks to the former president…"

"Amnestitized?" Seymour interrupted.

"It seemed like an appropriate term for a person being pardoned for an illegal act, without ever losing consciousness of their ill-gotten gains." Noble noticed Seymour wince, but continued. "Also, consider that for the past three years, we still haven't processed all of the illegal immigrants. There's a real possibility that millions more could be added, as a result of the lack of enforcement of our immigration laws on the books. Sorry to digress, but it's one of my few hot buttons." He apologized and then directed a question back to Chase. "Given these numbers, how is it possible to determine how many people are actually out of work, and how can we calculate a real unemployment rate?"

"It's impossible to do a reliable calculation for a number of reasons, one of which you just stated. First of all, the labor force does not include the entire population, only eligible workers." Chase further elaborated, "According to a strict interpretation of the data, there are approximately a hundred million people who've already abandoned the workforce and are not seeking employment. In fact, the *Labor Force Participation Rate* is at its lowest level in forty years. Retiring baby boomers alone account for half of the drop in the labor force! Statistically, there are around one hundred and fifty million people still in the workforce, and roughly fifteen million unemployed. Using simple long division, dividing the unemployed by the number in the workforce gives us the ten percent unemployment rate. It's that simple."

As chief financial officer of a major bank, Chase was at home with the data. Picking up the pace, he stated, "As I mentioned, a large number of the baby boomers left the workforce, which was considered a natural progression toward retirement. But it doesn't speak to the remainder of the labor force. For the purposes of this discussion, let's focus on the fifteen million people who are unemployed, ten million of whom are collecting unemployment benefits."

"Pardon me, Chase, your number of fifteen million can be misleading," Hank challenged. "The unemployment rate only counts the jobless who are still in the workforce. As I addressed earlier, dropouts are not counted because *marginally attached* workers are not treated as unemployed." This was something Hank could relate to because many of the volunteers at the Chestnut Foundation fit neatly into that category.

"Excuse my ignorance, but can anyone tell me what is *marginally attached*?" Seymour asked.

Hank was pleased once again to be handed the opportunity to boast. Adequately armed with the data on his tablet, he swiped the screen from left to right and displayed a section of the BLS statistics on the monitor. The others read along as he paraphrased. "Marginally attached persons are not actively looking for a job even though they are available for work. They are the dropouts. BLS also has a subcategory for this group called *discouraged workers* because they are not seeking employment for a variety of reasons, but have not officially dropped out of the workforce. What's alarming is the total number of the marginally attached is over three million, no piddling number."

Everyone in the room, including Seymour, was aware that the BLS was a government agency under the Department of Labor. They were tasked with churning the data to support not only the reported unemployment rate, but also the Consumer Price Index, among other indices.

"It sounds like a euphemism for *voluntarily unemployed*," Seymour quipped.

Hank smiled in agreement, but continued to explain that BLS' unemployment rate is extrapolated from the Current Population Survey, or CPS. "Approximately sixty thousand eligible households that equate to one hundred twenty thousand people or two wage earners per household are surveyed each month. It's a representative cross section of our population."

"I recognize the survey is used to measure the extent of unemployment," Paolo stated, "but what I don't understand, is how the questions in the survey—based on the participants' recent activity rather than whether they are employed—can provide accurate numbers?"

"It's an attempt to obtain a more honest answer," Hank opined, and then expanded further. "A series of questions are split between demographics and labor-force items. They do ask the recipient if he or she worked for wages, performed any jobs for a family business or farm without pay, or were seeking other jobs. It's difficult to administer, as you can imagine, because the person being surveyed is counted once, ignoring the possibility he or she holds more than one job or is self-employed and not paying themselves."

"Hank's correct. And adding to the confusion," Chase explained, "it doesn't take into account that almost twenty percent of the total jobs reported are involuntary part-timers. That's over thirty million workers. Another huge number with which to reckon. A major reason is the recession, which caused many employers to reduce payroll costs by limiting workers to fewer than thirty-five hours of work per week, adversely limiting their healthcare benefits, another cost-saving measure. There are also various government disincentives to working full-time, affecting both employers and job seekers."

"To that point," Noble interjected, "the chairperson of the Federal Reserve Board recently noted—give me a second—here it is." Noble read from his tablet:

"'The existence of such a large pool of partly unemployed workers is a sign that labor conditions are worse than indicated by the unemployment rate…Research shows employers are less willing to hire the long-term unemployed and often prefer other job candidates with less or even no relevant experience.'"

Noble, adding his own two cents, concluded, "Conceivably, that number could grow to millions working part-time stemming from UHA, the Universal Healthcare Act, which was instrumental in redefining the work week. We'll save that for another discussion. But the real number of eligible workers without full-time jobs is reportedly seventy-five million."

Over the next several hours, they continued to debate the job numbers, sometimes heatedly, challenging the various methods used to calculate the unemployment rate. In the end, they found them impossible to reconcile.

"No wonder some numbers are open to question. It sounds as though *Common Core* math may be the real culprit and responsible for all the discrepancies," Seymour joked.

Noble moved to rein in the group. "So let's see. The real number of unemployed full-time workers is somewhere around seventy-five million people. Then factoring out those with part-time jobs, and factoring in the marginally attached, are we looking at approximately forty-two million eligible workers that are not working, using plain old arithmetic?"

"Given what we know, it's in the ballpark," Chase agreed. "What's most disturbing is that six million of that number includes young adults between the ages of sixteen and twenty-four who have dropped out altogether; they are neither working nor going to school. Imagine dropping out at that age! I know I'm going astray, but according to the BLS, almost ninety-one million people over the age of sixteen aren't working for a host of reasons." He glanced at the others to see if they grasped the significance. Then, to drive the point home, he stressed, "That's almost one-third of the population!"

The point was noted.

The group continued to question, debate, and recalculate the numbers into the early evening—until Seymour had reached his limit and began to flail his hands in the air. "Hey guys, my mind can only comprehend what my seat can endure. This is pretty heavy stuff and we've been at this all day."

"My seat says we pick it up in the morning," Paolo joined in and then suggested, "A libation and dinner will help to put us back in balance."

"I second that, especially the libation." Hank's enthusiasm was obvious.

Noble capitulated; pleased they had become so engrossed in the material. He also recognized they were driven by the desire to arrive at quick effective solutions. So it was not a surprise from day one that they opted to keep the sessions moving and waived the lunch break. They were satisfied to nosh on the snacks from the kitchen, so as not to miss a beat. Jax was quick to pick up on their daily routine and began to deliver salads and sandwiches along with the morning meal. It meant for less distraction throughout the day. Now dinner was prevalent on everyone's mind, naturally kicking off with the welcomed aperitif. So it didn't take much coaxing for them to adjourn to their respective suites and freshen up for the evening meals.

19
UNEMPLOYMENT ABYSS

By the first week, they had established a working rhythm and were firing on all cylinders. Each day began promptly at nine o'clock in the morning with the guys orchestrating their own limited free time. Seymour and Paolo managed an hour in the fitness center before breakfast, Hank managed breakfast, and the anal-retentive Chase spent his mornings pouring through the documents in preparation for the day's topic. Noble, after a quick breakfast, would spend time either working on the website-in-progress, or collecting any data he may have needed for their upcoming discussion. Thus far, it was working like a Swiss watch.

After days of data gathering, Paolo had done his fair share of pulling the numbers together. Even though he held to Hank's point about focusing more on the causes of the numbers generated, he continued to help slice and dice them in an attempt to quantify the stats. Consequently, he chose to begin the session.

"*Attenzione, amici!* The dissection of the numbers thus far has helped to describe the complexity of the unemployment situation. Through a maze of smoke and mirrors, various employment rates were produced. But it's become clear that any change in policy we propose must target the true causes of why people are not working in the first place. We must go behind the scenes to clarify the numbers we have bandied about in order to have a direct effect on the job market. Granted there are sundry reasons; identifying them is our starting point." Shooting the next question at Hank, he asked, "So in your view, why are people dropping out of the workforce at such an alarming rate?"

Hank, the supreme showman, was happy to accommodate Paolo and to pontificate on the question. "We've already discussed the influx of baby-boomer retirees. Also, people are living longer, many with chronic illnesses, and a vast number of them are being placed on disability, unable to work. Then there are a substantial number of people who can't find a job or believe there are no jobs in their occupation. Some of the older-set are being phased out by new technology and many of the young simply lack the necessary skills for the entry-level jobs. That also explains why an unusual number of people are returning to school, which is a positive. But I would suggest the majority of the unemployed find themselves in one of two categories: unskilled or unmotivated."

"Isn't that rather simplistic?" Paolo challenged. "Don't forget many have determined that the jobs available don't pay enough and opt to collect unemployment insurance until their benefits run out and the checks no longer flow. The House of Representatives choked again and extended unemployment insurance for another full year. For many, it extends unemployment benefits beyond two years. C'mon, sounds like an inducement to remain unemployed."

"When did you become so cynical?" Hank scolded.

"Don't shoot the messenger. There was a Harris poll taken recently, where forty-seven percent polled stated they had completely given up looking for a job. Out of that number, eighty-two percent said they would only start looking when their benefits ran out. Did you hear that?—*When their benefits ran out.* Also, the combination of government subsidies that help to bolster household income has become a disincentive to many prime-working-age adults, between the ages of twenty-five and sixty-four. Many of whom have given up full-time employment or have chosen not to work at all. It's a matter of simple logic. Why work when you can live reasonably well on the dole?"

Chase cut in. "I have to agree with Paolo. Given the slow-growth economy, Americans have lost confidence in the government to fix the problem. Their patience has expired because they feel the government has given up on them. We stressed that earlier when we discussed the young adults."

Paolo persisted. "Poll after poll shows that Americans believe they are financially worse off than they were a year ago and have real concerns about their future. Even recent polls show conclusively that American believe their children will be economically worse off than they."

"Okay, I agree," Hank acquiesced, raising his arms to surrender. "Admittedly, even the Congressional Budget Office has stated that the weak conditions in the labor market have caused people to leave the workforce permanently. And I'm smart enough to realize that the effect of reduced consumer buying power on Main Street will also diminish the outcomes on Wall Street."

Hank trusted the numbers coming from the CBO. Despite the fact that the Congressional Budget Office is a federal agency operating within the legislative branch of the government, it had an earned reputation for being objective and nonpartisan. He knew the job of the CBO was to report the economic and congressional budget numbers, for both spending and revenue, however the numbers tallied. "I broke down the figures and I saw no intended room for manipulation. The numbers tell the story."

"You're right on the money," Chase agreed. "Ignoring the double entendre, when the Federal Reserve was forced to raise interest rates, predictably the banks tightened further on credit lending. The negative effect on the financial markets added to a lack of business confidence, holding back capital expenditures. That's one of the major forces leading to people leaving the workforce and a reduction in consumer spending. The housing market is once again heading south." He shook his head, visibly dismayed. "It's the perfect storm that could push us deeper into a recession, teetering on a depression—the one the president fears."

"That's the exact reason why we're here!" Noble punctuated. "The president is well aware that fewer people in the workforce erodes the lives of income-producing families."

Paolo postured, "Fewer people employed equates to less revenue in the way of tax dollars, especially the payroll taxes necessary to fund Social Security and Medicare, which run dry without new participants."

"It also has a direct effect on our exports and bloats our national debt further, placing additional strain on the government and the taxpayers," Chase added. "But there is a catch-22 here."

That statement caught their full attention.

"As the economy continues to lag, more and more companies will downsize. In many cases, employees will be made redundant, mainly men and women edging toward retirement age. The prospect of finding another position is bleak and many will opt to retire early, placing an even heavier burden on pension plans, including Social Security and Medicare benefits. If the trend continues in the number of people claiming disability, as Hank cited earlier, the safety net of entitlements will, for sure, become threadbare. We've already seen evidence of the unraveling."

"You paint a pretty bleak picture," Seymour interjected. "But speaking to your point about companies downsizing, there was a prediction that more than half of the major retail outlets will close over the next five years, being no longer able to compete with online retailers. Reportedly, hundreds of thousands of people would be laid off. A devastating effect on the job market, with no alternative at hand. Imagine your favorite department store going kaput."

"Wasn't it Michael Burden, a principal with Excess Space Retail Services, who predicted the closings?" Noble asked. "He called it a *Retail Apocalypse.*"

"Yes, and you've already seen the early stages. Giants like Sears, Macy's, and J.C. Penney have closed many of their outlets and seem to be hanging by the fingernails. And the blockbuster of them all of course, was Blockbuster. Some ascribe it to ecommerce, but others point to the frightening aspect of the shrinking middle class, which brings us full-circle to the unemployed," Seymour observed.

"We've already seen the impact on jobs by technology. Two examples are in the use of 3D manufacturing printers and in the use of robotics." Noble cited, "In a *Time Magazine* article, written back in 2014, Rana Foroohar cited a study by the McKinsey Global Institute that estimated one-hundred-forty million service jobs were at risk over the next decade. Foroohar pointed to companies such as, 'Zillow, Uber, and Airbnb as fostering *creative destruction* in new sectors like real estate, transportation, and hotels.' A stark difference from the days of old. The article points to the fraction of jobs produced by the social networking sites compared to the dot-com companies in the late nineties."

Hank quickly inserted, "Innovative technology comes with a price, while I personally believe the positives outweigh the negatives. Granted, the impact on skilled labor needs to be factored into the equation."

All at the table were outwardly disturbed by the specter of the devastating effects of more people falling into the unemployment abyss and those making a Hobson's choice to drop out of the workforce entirely.

Seymour, reiterating Paolo's earlier statement, affirmed, "It's clear; either scenario is an encumbrance to an already snail-paced economy: fewer people producing, less income, less taxes being collected. It is a vicious cycle. They are inextricably bound together and move in tandem."

"All true, but I'm not sure this is getting us closer to a solution," Noble determined. "But there is one policy that has had a monumental effect on the job market. Anyone want to take a guess?" It was unfair of Noble, but he was more than aware that the topic was one of Paolo's sore spots. So he gave it a little nudge.

"I know where you're heading," Paolo presumed, and then took a deep breath. "We've all been reluctant to mention the dreaded 'I' word. While we briefly touched on the increase in population, we also need to discuss the total broad effect immigration has on the job market."

"Oh please, that horse has been beaten to death," Hank groaned. "This is a country founded on immigrants. By the way, aren't you first-generation?"

That question created a firestorm, so Noble and the others sat back and listened to the jousting between Paolo and Hank. Then, noting the time, Noble realized that he had introduced the wrong topic for such a late hour. "Hey, hey you two," Noble interrupted, "You've just touched on a new issue that could inversely affect jobs. So without a doubt, it places a burden to some degree on government resources. Just look at our rising expenditures over the years. It's evident we need to look at immigration a little more closely. Perhaps we'll uncover some areas that will be useful to the president straightaway. Let's pick up on it tomorrow."

Everyone happily agreed. They were indeed getting into the groove and wanted time to refresh their minds on the immigration policies and be armed with facts for the next day's discussion.

The meeting was adjourned.

20
AN INQUIRING MIND

"**H**as Noble called in?"
"Not yet, Max."

"Shit. He just doesn't get it!" Max blurted as she whisked into her office.

Doris flinched, although she was becoming accustomed to Max's outbursts and to calling her by her first name. After years of being Noble's secretary, always referring to him as director, and having rarely heard him swear—things started to change around the office as the language became more colorful. Doris had to admit: Max was growing on her.

Max plopped down at her desk and glanced around the room as she thought, *This is temporary. I shouldn't get used to it.*

It had been over a week since Noble took his leave of absence, placing Max in charge as Director of the SIA—a position to which she aspired. But for which she wasn't quite ready to seize the reins. So, as Noble set off for parts unknown, Max grudgingly agreed to assume the position. Stanton was right. She'd step up to the plate, but on one condition: Noble had to promise to call her weekly. His call was way past due.

As fate would have it, the phone buzzer sounded at that moment.

"Max, Natalie is on line one."

"Thanks Doris." She had hoped for a different caller.

℘

"Natalie, what a pleasant surprise. How was your family vacation in Europe?"

"Doris said you were filling in for Noble. Where is he?"

Max was surprised by the sound of panic in her voice and was a bit worried. "He's taking some time off. Didn't he tell you?" she asked with wonderment.

"I spoke with him from Florence about a week ago and he never mentioned going on a trip. Sorry to be abrupt, Max, but I need to speak with him now," she pleaded.

"His cell appears to be out of range, but he promised to check in. I'll tell him you're trying to reach him. Is there anything I can help you with?"

Natalie's voice began to crack. "We returned home last night. The house was completely ransacked. But all they stole was the art off the walls," she wailed and then continued to babble. "They're not worth much, but they were from my parents' collection and have sentimental value. Each painting represented a childhood memory for Noble and me. Max, the house is a mess! Who would do this?"

Max sensed that Natalie was waffling between hysterics and rage at that point and tried to help her to refocus. "Calm down. Did you call the police?"

Struggling to regain her self-control, she acknowledged in a more even tone, "Yes, they came over and dusted for prints. They also happened to mention that there was a slim-to-none chance they'd find the intruder. Particularly given the lack of value of the paintings. But they said they'd check with the local art fences whom they knew to be dealing in stolen art." She gulped a few times to hold back the tears, but failed. "Max, I'm scared! Mario and I are all alone in the house."

Max was flabbergasted. "Where's Paolo?"

"What! Noble didn't tell you that he set him up with a client who needed him for some urgent assignment?" she questioned with a hint of annoyance. Then, in a calmer tone, she explained, "He's supposed to be away for about a month. I'm waiting for his call now. It's all so strange. And now this has happened."

"I'll speak with the chief of police and advise him that I'll be sending over our own forensics team. They'll go over everything again. Don't worry; I'm sure they'll come up with something." Max was making every attempt to put Natalie at ease—it was the least she could do for Noble's family. But the level of defeat in Natalie's voice made her feel even more helpless. "Do you want to stay with me?" she offered, mindful that Noble was Natalie's only living blood relative and all of what remained of Paolo's family lived in Italy.

"No thanks. I'm just unnerved by the entire episode. We'll be fine— really."

"I'll get in touch as soon as I find out anything."

"Max, please call me as soon as you hear from Noble."

"Likewise."

⤬

"Odd that both Noble and Paolo should be away at the same time," she said aloud. "Even odder, Noble didn't tell his sister that he was going away."

From nowhere, Doris appeared at her door. "Did you need something?"

"No, just conversing with myself as usual." She paused. "On second thought, would you please get Hank Kramer on the phone?"

"Right away." Doris left to place the call.

Max always had a knack for raising her antennae whenever the dots didn't connect. This time she questioned herself as to why Kramer would pop into her head, but reasoned there had to be a link. She was well acquainted with the former president's chief of staff, who earlier had been the campaign manager for both Baari's senatorial and presidential campaigns. She was also aware that Kramer was a member of La Fratellanza—one secret Noble entrusted her with, which had been crucial to their investigation in the hunt for Simon.

While contemplating, she caught the intercom light flashing.

"Mr. Kramer's secretary is on line one."

"Thanks, Doris."

⤬

"Hello, this is Deputy Director Ford with the SIA. May I please speak with Mr. Kramer?"

"I'm sorry Deputy Director, but he's on an extended leave with an uncertain return date. May I give him a message when he calls in?"

"Yes—please have him call me." As she hung the phone she thought, *Curiouser and curiouser*, and then shouted, "Noble, what the hell is going on?"

21
CURIOUSER AND CURIOUSER

"Max, Amanda Kelley is on line one."

"Thanks, Doris." *What now?* she thought as she reached for the phone.

⚬᷾

"Hello Amanda."

"Have you heard from Noble?"

"Not in the past several days, but I'm expecting him to check in any time now. Haven't you spoken with him?" Max was beginning to tire from the repetitive dialogue.

"I left messages on his voicemail and I've texted him repeatedly, but he's not getting back to me."

"He told me he may be out of range from time to time. Try to be patient. I'm sure he'll contact you soon."

"Max, what's going on? He was acting so strange for about a week and then out of nowhere, he announced he had to go away on a mission for a while. I'm really worried."

Max was too, but didn't let on. "I'll let you know when I hear from him."

"I don't need this right now!" Amanda bellowed, in an extremely unusual manner.

Neither do I, Max thought, but she set her concern aside and asked, "Amanda, is everything okay?"

"Notwithstanding the fact that I'm trying to plan a wedding with the groom-to-be nowhere to be seen, I think someone is screwing around with my financial accounts."

"What makes you think so?" Without giving it a thought, Max had shifted into director mode.

"Since Noble's been gone, I've been flooded with medical bills that are not mine. A string of credit-card charges for things I never purchased. And the bank is sending me letters threatening legal action if I don't make the back payments on a line of equity I supposedly had taken out on my home to the tune of one-hundred-seventy-five thousand dollars. I don't have an equity loan!"

Max listened to her rant, but Amanda had it right; somebody was royally screwing around. "I'm sorry to say, it appears you've become a victim of identity theft. And it's unfortunate there's not much the authorities can do. This type of theft runs rampant and there's no way to keep ahead of it. Reportedly, there are over ten million people a year in the U.S. that become victims."

"That's comforting, coming from the States Intelligence Agency." It was clear that Amanda was not pleased with Max's advice.

"I'm sorry, Amanda, but it falls back on you to rectify. You'll first need to submit a report to the Federal Trade Commission. Hold on—here's the number: 877-IDTHEFT. Also, go to their website and complete the *Identity Theft Affidavit*, which you can then print out and give to your local police precinct. You'll need to report the crime there as well."

"Anything else?" she groaned.

"Don't forget to notify the three major credit agencies, Experian, Equifax, and TransUnion, to have a fraud alert placed on your file. And definitely, notify the IRS. Most likely, your Social Security number was used to obtain a medical insurance card and the equity loan. Also, I would suggest you change your bank accounts."

"That's it?" Amanda was exasperated that Max couldn't offer her any better guidance.

"Other than to watch your accounts. There may be more activity." She was certain they were not the words Amanda wanted to hear, but the sooner she responded, the more chance Amanda would have to restore her financial health.

"How could this happen?"

Max could hear the despondency in her voice and resisted overloading Amanda with any more unpleasant information. "Take the necessary steps to protect your identity at all costs and trust nothing to the Internet. I wish I could be more helpful, but it's virtually impossible to trace these crimes, unless we suspect someone, giving us some plausible lead. Is there anyone you can think of who would do this to you?" She gave it one last shot.

"No one! Please have Noble call me as soon as you hear from him."

"Good night Aman..." The call ended before Max could finish. *How rude*, she thought.

This is all so odd. First, Natalie and then Amanda, at a time when Paolo and Noble are out of contact. She continued to ruminate. *There has to be a connection.* "Kramer is missing too!" she murmured.

She never knew who the other members of La Fratellanza were and suspected she never would. But one thing she did conclude, aside from Paolo and Kramer, was that there were two other men who also worked on the same political campaigns for the former president.

Having yet to reel in her antennae, Max placed a few calls.

22
HUDDLED MASSES

They had been debating the issues for the past two weeks. For the past four days, they had been battling over immigration. Not surprisingly, Hank was on the receiving end of most of the brickbats. So with the morning rituals out of the way, the group convened around the table, raring to proceed with the next round.

Chase didn't hesitate to launch the discussion, but with an unusual moment of levity. "Paolo, would you like to start after yesterday's ten-rounder with Hank? Or has the final bell rung?" He grinned.

Paolo bowed to Chase from a seated position and gladly began. "Over the past eight years, the majority of jobs created went to immigrants, both legal and illegal, crowding out American workers from the workforce. We all know this to be true; we were the ones pushing the policies while we were in control."

"Are you starting in with that tired old theory again? Paolo, I'm disappointed in you," Hank rebuked. "Immigrants competed across the board from low- to high-skilled jobs, losing out most of the time to native-born Americans."

"Then how do you explain why the number of immigrant job holders increased as domestic job holders declined?"

"Excuse me?" Hank questioned.

The others listened, curious as to where this line of banter was taking them.

"It was the policies that we helped shape in the last administration that exacerbated all the problems!" Paolo stated categorically. "And don't tell me it was unexpected. A certain former president said as much in his book, *The Audacity of Hope.*"

"Please," Hank chastised. "That was when he was a junior senator."

"It doesn't make it any less true." Paolo reached for his tablet and said, "And I quote, directly from the man himself:

> 'Still, there's no denying that many blacks share the same anxieties as many whites about the wave of illegal immigration flooding our Southern border…Not all these fears are irrational…The number of immigrants added to the labor force every year is of a magnitude not seen in this country for over a century. If this huge influx of mostly low-skill workers provides some benefits to the economy as a whole—especially by keeping our workforce young, in contrast to an increasingly geriatric Europe and Japan—it also threatens to depress further the wages of blue-collar Americans and put strains on an already overburdened safety net.'"

Hank and Paolo continued to joust until Noble stepped in to keep them on point. He said, "The fact remains that in 2014, even before the Immigration Reform Act made it to Congress, ninety-nine-point-five percent of the applications applying for legal status were approved. Two hundred and fifty thousand formerly illegal immigrants waltzed into the workforce, ahead of those waiting for years to enter legally."

"And what's wrong with that?" Hank posed, equally willing to take on Noble.

"I'll throw the question back to you. Is it fair to those who played by the rules? How well screened do you think the applicants were, considering they were required to have a high-school diploma or equivalent degree, with no criminal record—ninety-nine-point-five percent is quite an amazing hit rate, wouldn't you say? Are we living in Brigadoon?" Noble asked in frustration.

"I still fail to see your point," Hank challenged.

Paolo rejoined the fray, eager to make a point. "After the act stalled in Congress and Baari signed the executive order granting Amnesty, allowing over six million plus illegals to avoid deportation, the flow of illegal immigrants steadily increased. Aside from the potential criminal element, the existing job market has been invaded by workers who have monopolized lower-paying jobs, at a time when jobs are not being created to accommodate the unemployed."

"Paolo, you know as well as I do; we need immigrants to fill the vacant jobs created by an aging population. We've already discussed why people are dropping out. Don't forget the baby boomers. Immigrants only help to create a younger workforce," Hank reminded.

"Even if that is true," Chase interjected, "current federal regulations will continue to hinder job growth, no matter the makeup of the workforce. A time will come very soon when even the immigrants are unable to get jobs given the current trends. Then they'll join millions of unemployed Americans looking for relief, placing an even greater drain on government resources—meaning a growing demand for assistance will be funded by a smaller base of taxpayers."

"When it comes right down to it," Paolo insisted, "citizenship is not the prime goal for many immigrants crossing the border. They're not just here for jobs, but also for healthcare for their families. Reportedly, over three million illegal immigrants signed up for the Universal Healthcare system—and the system has never been reconciled. Hank, you can't negate the fact that seventy percent of legal immigrants take some form of government subsidies. That's much higher than the suffering general population who pay their bills."

Noble eyed Hank as he geared up, ready to pounce, but Noble didn't hand him the opportunity to belabor the point further. "You're all making effective points, but we'll get nowhere if we allow our ideology to cloud our thinking. We are a country of immigrants. There will always be a segment of immigrant workers willing to take lesser-paying jobs than those of traditional American workers. The economy depends on it. But this debate is not getting us any closer to finding a surefire solution to solve the widening gap between available jobs versus the unemployed."

"Other than freezing immigration." Paolo persevered. "We blew billions of dollars while trying to deport over a hundred thousand children. Open your eyes; the government is disinclined to stop the influx of illegals. Sealing the borders is the only answer."

"It's never going to happen, nor should it. These immigrants are future generations who will add to the GDP as they have throughout modern history," Hank retorted. "There is no empirical evidence that immigration is going to have a negative effect on the job market. That's the mantra of the 'Party of No' fodder."

Paolo pushed back. "Hank, take off your blinders. Don't lose sight of the fact that hordes of immigrants, who crossed our borders illegally, created a humanitarian crisis. We spent over three billion taxpayer dollars, including yours, to process the children and families from Central America in 2014, most of whom slipped through the net. Our border patrol have become caretakers and are stuck with duties that have taken them away from their first responsibility to protect our borders. That left the floodgates open for more to enter illegally, including those with criminal intent. Today, three years later, many of those children are still in this country, feasting on government aid."

Chase came to Paolo's rescue. "And as long as the administration's policies continue to encourage illegal immigration, it will continue to be an impediment to an unsullied competitive job market. The constant incursion is destined to become unsustainable. It's been reported that during the great influx of 2014, over seventy percent of the illegals caught at the border failed to report back to the authorities as ordered when they were released to other family members already in the U.S. Not surprising, but not returning the children to their country sent a bigger message. Because of our open borders they are still coming in. As far as they're concerned the border is a huge welcome mat."

"Hank, we're speaking about *illegal* immigration, not those waiting in the queue." Paolo reiterated. "The immigration law today sets the cap at seven percent to any one country, thus controlling the total number of people allowed to enter the United States in a single year. For refugees the cap is a total of seventy thousand people from any corner of the world. The last administration—our administration— gummed the bullet and allowed illegals to enter this country unabated. You can't deny the facts," Paolo underscored, as if to rest his case, but he carried on. "Baari's amnesty ignored the long-held quotas and flooded the labor market, which in turn added to an economic imbalance, not to overlook our national security. And if you wonder why this is happening, think about the fact that over fifty percent of the illegal immigrants consistently support the Democratic Party."

"What the…" Hank attempted to blurt out.

Noble cut him off. "Back on point!" he admonished, attempting to stop any further digressive debate.

Hank dug in his heels. "Excuse me, Noble, and the rest of you who conveniently keep quoting the non-partisan CBO. You might find it interesting that they recently released a report claiming that granting amnesty to illegals would naturally increase the size of the labor force, but as a result, we would see an increase in both capital investments and productivity. As a direct consequence, your statement omits a key part of that report."

"The CBO also reported it would produce a glut in cheap labor producing higher unemployment. Hey bro, it's already happened," Paolo countered.

Seymour, having been silent up to that point, felt that one issue had been overlooked. "Aren't we forgetting the employer? The influx of immigrants in the past several years has created a disincentive to increase wages, making it impossible for American workers to earn a living wage. To that end, there is a greater divide between Americans and immigrants competing for jobs. More and more protests are breaking out in the streets, many of them violent. The American workers feel they're fighting for jobs, at the same time they are competing for government subsidies that are also handed out to illegals. Household income is the overriding issue."

"Right on point!" Paolo agreed. "And even when the job picture improves, millions of people who might have re-entered the workforce may be less willing to sacrifice subsidies, if they're only able to compete for low-wage paying jobs that lower household incomes." With a wink and a nod at Hank, he added, "Kind of takes the audacity out of hope."

Noble gave another attempt to redirect the conversation, this time more forcefully. "Clearly, there are a multitude of reasons why people are dropping out of the workforce or are not able to compete. Your statements only support the urgency for a laser-like focus on the goal of job creation. We need to move on!"

"But still keep in mind that job-killing government policies do fit into the mix and must be addressed," Paolo advised.

"At the top of the list should be the issue of minimum wages," Seymour added.

"I agree. I've made note of the immigration issues, along with the concerns from both sides." Noble looked at the wall clock and noted the hour. "So I guess the battle on tomorrow's docket is now minimum wage, a debate that has undoubtedly gripped not only Seymour, but the nation?"

From the reluctant nods of their heads, the next day's topic had been decided.

"Good," Noble asserted, but as he was about to adjourn he noticed Seymour signaling for their attention.

"If you guys can hang in for a few more minutes, I have an idea I want to bounce around."

The others at the table sat back to listen, even though their appetites protested.

"I've been working on the Renaissance 2017 Project and I've put together a mock-up of the website's *Home* page for you to ponder tonight. I'd like your input. Compliments are gladly accepted." Seymour pulled up the site on his tablet and then swiped the screen from the left and displayed an image on the monitor.

The others perused the tabs on the menu bar that included **JOBS, MINUMUM WAGE, IIMMIGRATION,** and **ENERGY.** They all took note that the 'minimum wage' had been included.

"Aren't we confident?" Paolo teased.

"I considered it a valid issue and was confident in your wisdom that you would as well," Seymour grinned. "You'll note by the tabs that other pages can be added easily if necessary. Each page will be set up to display a simple slideshow explaining the topic and the direct correlation to jobs, with real numbers and proposed solutions, as we arrive at a conclusion. There will also be links directing the user to various resources available for assistance. Of course, all topics will coincide with the president's speech."

"Whatever the message—it must be uplifting," Noble urged. "Aside from solutions, one of our main goals is to instill confidence in the government. The people have to believe their plight will improve and the cloud over the country will lift."

"Of course, that will be the main thrust."

"You mentioned a media blitz?" Hank asked placidly, having exhausted his ire for the day.

"I'm also working on several thirty-second commercials to tackle each of the topics we cover in a massive YouTube video strategy. From the moment the president completes his speech, one of the videos will be blasted over all the outlets on the Internet and repeated throughout the day. Each day a different video will be transmitted. While each of the infomercials will focus on a different topic, they will all feature job creation and the economy."

"How long will the campaign run?" Chase asked, looking more for an end date.

"The videos will be programmed to run consecutively for one month and will direct the listener to the website. After that we'll have to reassess its effectiveness," Seymour answered, and then he took a few more minutes to give a brief outline of each of the infomercials. He then sat back, looking for a reaction.

Noble was the first to respond. "It looks like it has potential to work. I like it!"

The others concurred and waved high-fives in the air to Seymour.

"Hey guys, we've got some homework tonight, so let's limit the conversation over dinner and then get to work," Noble suggested. "Keeping our shoulder to the wheel is the fastest way to get back to home-cooking."

All but Noble stood and departed to their suites to freshen up before Jax arrived with their evening meal. He hung behind, running the issues of the day through his mind. He knew that everyone was working hard to come up with solutions, but as of yet, it looked like they were lagging. Everyone had been to bat but there were no runs on the scoreboard. The pressure was beginning to mount. Tomorrow they were heading into day fifteen. He knew he was not the only one sensing the burden that had been placed upon them.

23

WAGING THE WAGE DEBATE

O kay, who's brave enough to tackle the minimum-wage hike?"
Noble asked, suspecting that Seymour would take up the cudgel.

"I will," Paolo said, "because it fits exactly in with the immigration argument. The imposed increase in the minimum wage in 2015 did not close the floodgates. More immigrants flocked into this country, creating more competition for American workers, vying for the same jobs."

Hank didn't hesitate to take issue. "As I said before, there is no evidence that immigrants are taking jobs away from anyone. They're filling the void where Americans won't take the jobs. How many times do I have to make this point? Is anyone listening?"

"Obviously, you weren't listening to the former president, the then senator's own words. Tsk tsk," Seymour scolded. "Hank, you can't deny that over a half million jobs have already been lost since the hike went into effect. The higher wages cost small-to-medium businesses billions of dollars. Granted, a gradual increase would have little to no effect on unemployment, but not a forty percent increase. And let's not forget the imposed wage hike on government jobs is estimated to increase the deficit over a billion dollars in the next several years."

"It flies in the face of economic common reality," Chase added and then elaborated. "Employers will hire less or cut basic benefits. That's their answer to higher overhead expenses. We've already seen how the wage hike forced many small businesses to hire fewer workers at entry-level positions—jobs that are a starting point for young people to enter the workforce and to begin earning an income. And for other employers who also couldn't absorb the increase, it was passed on to the consumer in the price of products. There's already a disconnect in the job market between the highly skilled and the McDonald's cashier before the rise in wages, by way of example. The fact is there are fewer employees working for minimum wages."

"According to the BLS," Noble pointed out, "there are three-point-six million workers at or below the minimum wage. Forty-four percent of those workers are in the food-service industry."

Hank jumped back in. "You guys are in outer space! You're missing an important point. I know firsthand, from the volunteers at the Chestnut Foundation, that many of the people in low-paying jobs are also receiving benefits from social programs to make ends meet. It's likely that with increased income the need for government subsidies will be reduced. While, at the same time, families earning more money will generate more revenue for the government by way of payroll taxes to bolster our threatened Social Security system. It will certainly help to lift the poor out of poverty."

"That's a false premise," Paolo countered. "Many in the welfare ranks have stipulated over and over again that they would only search for work if forced, if wages do not equal the government subsidies they receive, which is understandable. It's a matter of simple arithmetic."

"You're making my case. If wages were higher, families could afford to go off welfare," Hank postured.

"In this instance, Paolo's correct. Your premise is inaccurate," Chase noted, "but for another reason. You mentioned a positive effect of increased social security taxes. However, Social Security is not limited to retirees as originally designed. There are twenty million recipients under the age of sixty-five collecting benefits from our Social Security system under the Supplemental Security Income (SSI) or the Disability Insurance (SSDI) programs. Strangely enough, since the Great Recession, twice as many people have signed up for one or both of these benefits compared to the number of jobs being added to the system over the same period. So, even with an increase in minimum wage, the Social Security fund would not benefit and the threat remains. Fact is, we're dishing out money faster than what we're taking in."

"Adding to that," Seymour argued, "many of the low-paying jobs currently go to teenagers or to the elderly who are not considered poor, but are supplementing other sources of income. Some are second or third earners in their family's household income, which defeats the argument that those low-wage earners are uniformly poor and struggling."

Chase reaffirmed, "Hank, the people to whom you refer would not be able to boost their wages to a level to offset the government subsidies they are receiving, unless the minimum wage increased to fifteen or twenty dollars per hour, depending on where they live. And over sixty percent of the low-wage earners work less than a thirty-hour week."

Seymour followed up. "Studies have also shown that two-thirds of minimum-wage employees end up earning more within the first year of employment through their company's merit system. The myth that minimum-wage workers are doomed to remain at that level continues to be believed."

"What are you all saying?" Hank asked, directing the question to the group. "That raising the minimum wage was just an attempt to preserve class warfare?"

"We weren't in the administration at the time, but you were," Chase shot back and then quickly apologized. "Sorry, we're not here to question past motives. We are here to tackle the anemic job market. But a minimum-wage hike traditionally worsens the problem. Especially for small business employers and large companies managing low-wage jobs. I say, let the marketplace work it out."

"He has a point," Paolo concurred. "Companies like Walmart did just that by paying above-average minimum wages, a smart business decision for the largest U.S. employer, providing them huge returns, wouldn't you say? After all, Walmart employees are also Walmart shoppers."

"That wasn't your stance when we worked together," Hank resisted.

"At the time, I served at the pleasure of the president," Paolo counterpunched with a grin.

Chase cut in. "To further the point, the wage hike also provided an incentive for employers to escalate their move into automation, replacing human resources with technology and machinery. McDonald's is a prime example. Pressured by the union to raise the minimum wage backfired when McDonald's began installing self-ordering kiosks to reduce employee payroll costs, thus reducing the number of jobs. The food-service industry experienced the same apocalyptic effect that the retail market felt when supplanted by ecommerce. That's why the workforce needs to be retooled with updated skills."

"Without question, to be competitive, workers will need the right skills for the available jobs. Perhaps, the money that was allocated for wage hikes should have been used for education and job training to help boost people out of minimum wage jobs," Seymour proposed.

"You're not proposing the government get involved? Granted, it's another problem to add to the heap," Paolo volunteered, "but let's not forget that many graduates with a secondary education or college degree are unable to enter the workforce because they acquired skills for which there is no demand. Government training for the sake of training is a road to nowhere."

"Good point," Chase seconded, "but there's another impediment—and I apologize—it inevitably brings us back to immigration. And that's the professional worker with no job."

"Oh, please," Hank grumbled.

"Maybe this is a good place to call it a night," Noble suggested, noting the time. "Let's pick it up tomorrow for perhaps a less spirited debate."

No further encouragement was necessary. None of them wasted time retrieving their tablets and other paraphernalia before scattering off to their suites.

Noble remained behind to review his notes. Then he stopped short. Shaking his head in dismay, he thought about how Baari had lit the torch on the minimum-wage debate that started a firestorm across the country—even with all the warnings. He also thought about how odd it was that throughout their discussions, no one had thus far invoked Simon's name. *"Clearly, he must have been part of the strategy, but they've manage to avoid his involvement,* was a thought he could not put to rest. He would continue to take note.

Eighteen days had passed since they first embarked on their mission, and while, at times, the debates were testy, they continued to march on in good spirits. That morning was no different.

Now, after a quick break to grab some sandwiches from the kitchen, they once again settled back in their seats.

Noble picked up on the discussion. "We've been rehashing the minimum-wage debate all morning, but Chase, go back to the point you made a few days ago about the professional worker without a job. Will you elaborate?"

"I'd be happy to with Hank's tolerant indulgence."

"You have the floor," he allowed with a cocky grin.

"Everyone in this room is aware that the prior administration adopted policies to encourage high-skilled foreign workers with STEM degrees, those possessing skills in science, technology, engineering, and math, to enter the country on the premise of attracting the best and the brightest. Looking south of the border is not the only issue."

"What's wrong with attracting talent? We're just filling a recognized need." Hank was genuinely curious as to his point. Then he admitted, "I was the one encouraging Baari to push that policy."

"I think you've missed the point. There's nothing wrong with attracting the best, as long as we first try to acquire talent within our borders." Chase tapped on his tablet to retrieve a study that was conducted by the Economic Policy Institute. He then swiped the tablet to display the information on the monitor. "According to the EPI,

> 'Immigration bills proposed in Congress included various provisions to increase the supply of guestworkers for STEM employers. Proposals included expanding the current temporary visa programs by increasing the H-1B visa cap and providing permanent residency to nonresident foreign students who graduate from a U.S. college in a STEM field.'"

"What's the justification?" Noble inquired

"Basically, there aren't enough STEM workers in the domestic workforce. Hold on." He paged up on his tablet as the others in the group watched the motion on the monitor. Chase continued, "Here it is. This analysis is by the Center for Immigration Studies, another non-profit research organization. They indicated that the country has two-point-five times more STEM workers than STEM jobs. In this case, Americans are subtly being forced out of high-skilled jobs as well. All because employers prefer to hire immigrant workers for lower wages. There's a fundamental unfairness here. CIS reports that one-third of Americans graduating with STEM degrees take STEM jobs. This practice will continue to hold down wages for these high-skilled professional positions and at the same time, crowd out American graduates."

"So it's easier to hire foreign workers than to increase salaries to attract American citizens residing in the U.S.?" Paolo asked.

"Yes." Chase swiped the left side of his screen again. "As you can see, the EPI concluded from their study,

> 'that current U.S. immigration policies that facilitate large flows of guestworkers appear to provide firms with access to labor that will be in plentiful supply at wages that are too low

to induce a significantly increased supply from the domestic workforce.'"

"All of this is quite scintillating," Hank postured, feigning a yawn, "but you've made the case that those holding STEM degrees don't want the STEM jobs, so we have no recourse but to import foreign workers. And let's not forget that there are many other occupations available for American workers. In fact, the strongest current job growth areas are in the healthcare and construction industries."

Paolo ignored Hank for the moment and pointed back to Chase's earlier comment. "You mentioned that the men and women made redundant, the ones too young to retire, but too old to hire, were edged out of the workforce. Reportedly, twenty percent of them had degrees but still couldn't find jobs. Somewhere there is a disconnect, between domestic talent and available jobs."

"Quite correct," Chase replied, "but according to the BLS they project that the labor force will only increase point-zero-five percent over the next decade, slightly below previous forecasts. Here's the crux. They also project that more than half of the new jobs created will require a high-school diploma or less. That's a clear dumbing down of the workforce."

"Be careful, Chase; you're cheerleading to make my case." Hank chuckled.

Noble sat back and continued to observe the debate, chiming in when necessary to keep them on track or to follow the agenda. But he couldn't help marvel at how each member still ran true to form. Hank was still the staunch liberal of old. Chase was still the mossback, although his conservative values tended to outweigh his political stripe. Paolo continued to enjoy the devil's advocate role and to goad Hank. A complete surprise was Paolo's shift from apolitical to center-right. Noble surmised it might have been Natalie's influence. Most shocking was Seymour's swing from political agnostic to center left. His newly adopted liberal mentality most likely came from the Hollywood set with whom he hobnobbed. Suddenly, Noble noted that the din in the room had quieted. On instinct, he glanced at the wall clock; they had worked right up to the dinner hour once again.

"This has been a particularly fun debate," Noble quipped. "I've enjoyed it, especially the dueling between Hank and company. But while listening, it became clear that the answers to the job-creation problem will more likely be addressed as we examine the other subject areas we've identified. Thus far, nothing quite fits into our quick-fix scenario."

All agreed that it was time to move forward.

Hank was most pleased that they had finally finished beating his horse.

Everyone was pleased to see the flashing red light above the door.

∽

"Good evening fellas," Jax announced as he pushed the large metal cart through the door.

The guys, without giving it a second thought, pushed their tablets and papers aside and made room for their dinner trays. Then, before Jax had the opportunity to set the last tray down, the others had already begun to feast.

"Hey, where did you get a name like Jax?" Seymour asked, in between bites.

"Funny you should ask. My poker buddies gave me that name. It rather stuck."

The others gave their forks a momentary rest, curious as well.

"You see, I was known for holding on to the jacks. Much to their chagrin, I've pulled out a lot of flushes and quite a few straight flushes in my day."

"Kind of hard to have a poker face with a name like that," Hank suggested.

"Sure is, that's why I tell any newcomer that Jax is short for Jackson." He winked. "Now you all keep my secret, you hear?"

They all had a good chuckle but then quickly put their forks back to work.

"You fellas enjoy your meal now. And don't forget, tomorrow's laundry day." Jax turned and offered a backhanded wave as he exited with the metal cart in tow.

∽

The usual chitchat, aside from the day's topic, continued around the table, mostly involving teasing one another about anything innocuous. Then, as the hour ticked by, the food was devoured, except for a few sips of wine they had savored.

While they polished off what remained in their glasses, Noble reminded them, "Tomorrow morning the president will be calling in for an update, so don't forget to change your socks."

"Other than recapping our discussions over the past few weeks, is there anything you think we should add?" Chase asked.

"Not for now. At this point, we'll just tell it like it is. But Chase, as agreed, you should take the lead and fill him in; we'll stand by for questions. And Seymour, please be prepared to describe your media blitz."

"I'm good to go."

"Me too."

"Then, gentlemen, let's call it a night."

24
THE PRESIDENTIAL UPDATE

"Get settled; we've got five minutes."

While this illustrious group organized itself and finished off the last sips of their eye-opening coffee, Noble reached over for the remote and turned on the large monitor.

"Are we ready?"

No sooner was the question posed than a voice came through the speaker system. "Good morning, gentlemen." Up on the monitor sat the president at his desk in the Oval Office.

"Good morning sir," came a round of voices.

"Let me reiterate once more," the president spoke, in a solemn but earnest voice, "you have my greatest appreciation and my full confidence that you will deliver the solutions necessary to pull our country from the edge and restore the people's faith in their government."

It was clear from the expressions on their faces that they each felt the gravity of the situation.

Then, knowing the president's time would be limited, Noble said, "Sir, Chase is prepared to give you a brief outline. Then we'll be happy to answer any questions."

Chase picked up on his cue and began to provide the update. "Mr. President, we are making progress," he affirmed. "It's abundantly clear the current unemployment situation has the potential for further volatility. With the lagging economy and a predominantly low-wage workforce there are not enough jobs to lift the American workers out of their current doldrums. And with the current government restraints on small businesses and corporations, we can expect to see further downsizing. Without some relief, companies will be forced to reinvent themselves. While we touched on retooling the workforce, it's something that must be seriously addressed. There is no doubt that the American worker must get back to work. Tomorrow will be our first real opportunity to dissect one of the major forces we have identified as part of the conundrum, the Universal Healthcare Act." He paused, awaiting a response from the president.

"Is there anything I can do to further your progress?"

"Sir, we have a good handle on the job market and the impact of immigration, along with the implications of the increase in the minimum wage. But we feel there are other areas still up for debate that will hold some answers."

The president sat upright and began to fire off a series of questions, mostly related to the job numbers and whether they could be relied upon.

Chase, along with the others, provided the answers, as best they could, until no more questions were forthcoming.

"Anything else to report?"

"Sir," Noble responded, "Seymour has begun to design a communications campaign to coincide with any strategy you will implement. He is prepared to give you a rough outline if you have the time."

"Talk to me, Mr. Lynx."

Seymour stiffened in his chair. "Sir, on the Monday before your speech, I'd like to suggest that your press secretary leak to the media that you will be speaking to the nation to appeal to the American people for their support. We can provide the specific wording once we formulate the plan." Over the course of the next five minutes, Seymour detailed his Renaissance 2017 Project, including the infomercials and the website.

The president listened, appearing pleased at the conceptual design. Though neither endorsing nor renouncing Seymour's strategy, the president allowed, "I'll look forward to your final proposal. Is that all gentlemen?"

"Yes, sir," Noble replied, speaking for all in the room.

"Good luck. I'll speak with you soon." The monitor went blank.

The group remained in their chairs, mesmerized, for the moment. However, the sense of doubt on their faces remained.

"C'mon, what's going on?" Noble asked, trying to pull them out of their fog.

Chase was the first to respond. "We've been here for three weeks. That's all we had to offer?"

"There are no easy answers. It's a building process."

"Chase is right. We are supposed to be the smart ones. What are we missing?" Paolo asked.

"The pressure is on guys; let's move it along."

"That's not helping, fratello; excuse me, Director." Paolo flashed the *I'm sorry* look. He knew not to make it personal.

"I was mistaken," Seymour admitted. "Perhaps we need to go back and look more closely at the specific parts of the immigration and minimum-wage policies. We need to find the direct link that is impeding the job market. There are many related but indivisible factors that must be taken into account."

"I agree. It's worth the investment," Noble allowed, and then he divvied up the assignments. "Why don't you and Paolo take immigration? Hank work with me on minimum wage. And Chase, you run over the jobs numbers again, and make absolutely sure that we're making the correct assessments."

Everyone agreed with the approach, and that they were moving in the right direction.

"Refills anyone?" Hank asked, with coffee cup in hand, as he headed toward the kitchen.

"Hey everyone," Noble called out. "Don't forget, first thing in the morning we will begin to tackle the eight-hundred pound gorilla, the Universal Healthcare Act. And for anyone who is tempted, there's no escape from here." His humor did not go unappreciated.

While everyone was busy getting his caffeine fix, Noble excused himself. "I'll be back in a few minutes."

They had learned not to question his sudden disappearing acts, knowing he was the only one with the luxury to step out of captivity.

Once outside the Crystal Palace, he reached into his pocket and pulled out the secure sleeve and inserted his xPhad. Now his smartphone could break through the security and function within the facility on a secure line. He tapped at the options and retrieved his messages. Several were from Max. He quickly decoded her last message; it read, "call immediately."

25
A CALL FROM NOWHERE

"Noble, where the hell have you been? I've been waiting for your call for days."

"Calm down, Max; I just received your messages."

"Are you calling from a secure line?"

"Yes, boss, as agreed," Noble teased. "Now, what's so urgent that you think you couldn't handle it on your own?"

"Have you heard that Natalie's been robbed? Are you aware Amanda's a victim of identity theft?" she blurted out in rapid succession.

"Hit the brakes and tell me what happened." Noble insisted, attempting to steady his voice.

Max proceeded to fill him in on her conversations with both Natalie and Amanda.

"The entire art collection?"

"I'm sorry. I know they were prized possessions you and Natalie retained from your parent's estate. I sent our forensic team over, but you know how these cases go. Maybe we'll get lucky."

Noble was disheartened, but remained controlled. "And Amanda?"

"You know better than anyone that identity theft always falls back to the victim, leaving it up to them to sort out their financial affairs. I gave her the usual list of things she needs to do and asked her to call me if she needed any more help."

Max gave him a moment to digest the events at hand, before she unleashed more information that wasn't going to make him any happier. "Noble, I find it peculiar that both you and Paolo happen to be away at the same time."

"Max, your imagination is running wild again. I simply needed time away and Paolo got an assignment with a major client."

She took a deep breath but wasn't backing down. "Kramer also happens to be away for an extended period of time."

"Kramer. What are you suggesting?" Noble tried to sound impassive.

"That all of your disappearing acts are connected."

"Leave it alone, Max." *Damn, she was good. She must have bloodhound genes*, he mused, and then tried to divert the interrogation. "Don't you believe in coincidences?" he asked in a more jocular manner.

"No, Noble—I don't—and neither do you. So don't play me."

"Max! I'm shocked you would suggest such a thing."

She knew that was his way of saying "*back off.*" Naturally, Max persisted. "You yourself told me that Kramer was a member of La Fratellanza. Are Paolo Salvatore, Chase Worthington, and Seymour Lynx also members?"

Noble was not surprised that she would sniff out the connections, but stunned that she made it in record time. Thankfully, she was not able to view his expression. Without confirming or denying, he asked, "What led you to such an outlandish conclusion?"

"First, two people you are close to were vandalized. Second, Paolo and Kramer departed to places unknown, as you did. Both of them were members of Baari's election campaigns and members of his administration. As you would expect, I was curious as to what the other president's men were up to, so I called their homes."

"And?" Noble asked with trepidation.

"According to his wife, Worthington went back into rehab. She was quite open and willing to share personal information. I guess being the sitting director of the SIA has some cachet." Max pressed on. "Lynx's wife explained that he was out of the country working on a documentary and was not expected back for some time."

"So, what's the problem? They're plausible explanations." Noble held back from seeming overly curious, but he was certainly interested as to where she was heading.

"I also discovered that Worthington's wife had reported to the local police that someone was siphoning money out of their bank account. Lynx's wife was also worried because she has been receiving obscene phone calls day and night, many of which her children have answered." Max theorized, "Somebody's messing around with these families, all of whom have a connection that leads back to you." She waited for his response. None came. "I'll ask you again—are these members of La Fratellanza?"

Noble diverted the question a second time. He surmised that she already had the answer. "Max, focus on the crimes. Work with the local police to see what they've uncovered. Then use whatever resources you need to track down the perpetrators."

"Maybe there's only one," she remarked brazenly. "Simon's body was never recovered."

"Max, don't let your imagination run wild again. You'll find that it's a mere coincidence these crimes have been perpetrated against these families."

"I don't believe it, nor do you," she said without hesitation.

"Are you suggesting Simon is getting back at them from the grave?" He shuddered at the thought.

"Noble…"

He interrupted, hating that he posed the question. "Max, focus on the crimes. I must go. I'll call you later."

"Noble!"

The line went dead.

She sat at her desk and fumed for a few minutes more until she got her ire out of her system. Then she began to wonder what Noble was really up to and wished he were there. She was able to manage on her own, but she just wanted to know he was not in danger. All of a sudden, Stanton flashed into her mind. She quickly looked up at the wall clock.

"Dammit, I'm late again." She grabbed her coat and rushed out of the office.

26
HOODIE BEWARE

Max walked into the Blackfinn and noticed Stanton sitting on his usual barstool. As she approached, she began immediately with an apology. "I'm sorry about the other night." Then furthering her request for forgiveness she leaned in for an affectionate hug and a discreet kiss.

It was willingly accepted.

"Feeling better?" Stanton asked as he reluctantly pulled away.

She half-smiled and admitted, "No."

"What's going on now?"

Max was unable to reveal her suspicions about La Fratellanza, but she was able to clue him in on the suspicious crimes occurring to the families of Baari's political campaign staff, and of course, to Amanda. She sketched out the details.

"Simon? This new responsibility is obviously taking a toll on you. That's insane."

"Hear me out. All logic points to him being dead, but he could have directed someone, in the case of his death, to carry out these revenge acts. It's all within the realm of possibility." She seemed to have gotten his attention.

"Okay, lay it on me."

"I know it's no longer part of your official duties, but I could use your help. If I hand over copies of the interrogation reports you conducted at Dugway, would you determine if anyone fits the profile?"

"Off the top of my head, the only one I recall who had a direct connection with Simon was the mole and he's behind bars. I'll run through them again. But it will take a little time to sift through the data."

"Great! You'd have a better fix on the detainees than anyone. I appreciate it."

Max knew he was privy to firsthand information, having been the one to interrogate the prisoners captured from the underground encampment during Operation NOMIS. The prisoners were followers of Simon who had been recruited and trained to serve as a militia, as part of his plan to shut down the national power grid and darken the nation. Regrettably, one prisoner escaped. Simon craftily walked out of the maximum-security prison in Draper, Utah where he had been detained.

Stanton was relieved they seemed to be back on track. Both personally and professionally.

Max, satisfied that she had enlisted his help, switched the conversation. "So what have you and the prez been up to these days?"

"Ah, today was education day—his education. We visited a traditional elementary school and a charter school where he spoke with several of the children at the sixth-grade level. Then he visited two families who homeschooled the children."

"That sounds exciting," she droned.

"Surprisingly, the conversation was quite enlightening."

"I assumed he discussed the Basic Core standards?" They were both aware that its predecessor, Common Core, crashed and burned within the first year of implementation. Basic Core was a somewhat improved version. However, the verdict was still out as it limped along.

"Naturally, it was the topic of discussion."

As Stanton rattled off several areas of controversy in great detail, Max sat back sipping her beer as she listened with interest. She was always impressed with his acumen on a wide variety of subjects. But as she was about to reengage on a different topic her eyes trailed toward the end of the bar.

"Max, am I boring you?"

"There's Mr. Hoodie again."

Stanton glanced over and saw a tall person with a hoodie and dark glasses. As he was about to stand up from the barstool, the mystery figure turned and walked out the back door. Stanton headed in the same direction.

Max followed closely behind.

The door led out to a deserted alley behind the Blackfinn. There was no one in sight.

"Let's go back inside. I'm assigning an agent to keep an eye on you. It's time for some counter-surveillance."

"Absolut…"

Stanton cut her off. "Max, I insist."

She refrained from taking issue in the hallway and abruptly turned to head back to her bar stool. Then she lifted her beer mug as if she were about to make a toast and announced, "I insist you leave this alone. After all, how would it look if the deputy director of the SIA couldn't insure her own protection? It would also hinder the cases I'm working on. Agent, you do what you do and leave me to handle my job." She reached over and clinked his beer bottle, as if to say, "subject closed."

Stanton knew when Max got her back up there was nothing he could do to convince her otherwise. *She's right; she can take care of herself. Maybe it's the black belt that gives her such confidence,* he thought, hoping his words would not come back to haunt him.

"Deal?" she asked, lightening her tone.

"Deal." And he sealed it with a kiss.

27

IS THERE A DOCTOR IN THE HOUSE?

Tensions were running at full speed as the clandestine group rolled into day twenty-four. They continued to press hard on a variety of peripheral issues hitting the job market. Then, days after laboriously dissecting the Universal Healthcare Act, they came up empty.

All were exasperated.

"C' mon guys, settle down." Noble sensed the pressure mounting, but they needed to push forward.

Chase appeared the most frustrated. "We've been tearing into this for a week and we've arrived with no concrete proposals other than to repeal the mandates *per se*, which we granted would take time."

"One thing we did agree on." Noble highlighted, "is that the CBO was correct when they stated that the two-point-six-trillion dollar UHA was neither universal nor affordable. Two erroneous selling points."

Hank looked up from his tablet. "That's just not true," he protested. "Look at the numbers. Forty million people have health insurance coverage who couldn't afford it before. An additional thirty million people have been given tax breaks to help them afford the coverage. Medicaid benefits have been expanded to include those at one-hundred-thirty-three percent of the defined poverty level, basically those earning thirty thousand dollars per year for a family of four. And it reduced the overall cost of healthcare by controlling the insurance-company premiums. How can that be a bad thing?" he fulminated.

Noble pulled back on his claim a tad to reel in Hank. "I don't believe any of us here are saying it's not important that everyone have healthcare coverage. What we're saying is that the Act isn't self-supporting—and there are unintended consequences facing the workforce."

"Taxing the wealthy an additional three-point-eight percent on their investment income, and charging fines and imposing business taxes on employers, are not motivating forces to impel economic growth." Chase qualified, "We've all agreed that business is the engine necessary to spur the economy and jobs. To me, it looks like we are killing the golden goose with taxes of a thousand deaths."

"You're forgetting that small businesses with less than twenty-five employees have been given tax credits to offset the cost of covering their employees," Hank stressed, as he became more intransigent. "So actually, both the middle class and small business are enjoying the benefits."

Paolo entered the discourse. Staring down Hank, he asked, "What about firms with over fifty employees? The ones that will either be forced to insure full-time workers or pay a fine."

"We're talking about..."

Cutting Hank off, Paolo pressed his point further. "In many cases, jobs will never be created because of UHA. More and more, small business owners are shying away altogether from expansion, afraid of hitting the threshold for the newly defined full-time workers."

Noble stopped the tit-for-tat before it went any further. "We have already determined that it would be too costly to repeal the entire act. Moreover, it would adversely affect millions of people unable to afford the benefits of healthcare. However, recasting selected aspects of the employer mandate provision might be a place to start. Let's focus on the direct negative effect on the employer in terms of job growth."

"Well, since we have been relying heavily on the CBO's 2017 predictions," Chase noted, "don't overlook their estimate that due to UHA, employees would work two percent fewer hours, equivalent to two million jobs. They were correct in principal, but underestimated the number by one million. We're actually looking at three million."

Chase was confident with his new calculation and continued to explain that, included in that number, five hundred thousand workers were fired as a direct result. The remainder was a disproportionate number made up of low-wage workers whose hours had been reduced, or who left the workforce for many of the reasons they had cited before.

Paolo, with confidence, suggested, "The employer mandate appears to be the Achilles heel of the plan."

Hank took immediate objection. "That's a sophist argument. It's the crux of the plan and it was well thought out."

"What? You mean to say nineteen hundred and ninety pages were carefully crafted in a matter of months? Among the American people, it's an article of faith that Congress did not read, nor do they understand it to this day. Even the simplest explanation of the plan was confusing." Paolo rebuffed. "Ask Nancy Pelosi. Or perhaps, Jonathan Gruber. His unmasking proved the entire plan was a ruse."

"Get it right! It was intended to force employers to cover full-time employees by offering up the government-approved healthcare insurance."

Clearly, Paolo had managed to get under Hank's skin, but he wouldn't back down.

"I don't understand your point. UHA incorporated various provisions depending on the number of employees, whether or not they offer insurance, whether one, or some of the employees are receiving insurance subsidies, and the list goes on. And sure, in every instance there is a tax or fine attached. That was to ensure widespread coverage for the uninsured and, of course, to cover the cost of the coverage."

"Sorry, that one passed by me," Seymour admitted, looking for some rationality.

Hank, becoming inimical by the moment, explained, "If an employee receives insurance from a federally subsidized insurance exchange, in lieu of the employer's plan, then the employer is taxed two thousand dollars for each subsidized employee."

"How do you rationalize the argument when the worker can't afford the employer's plan without the subsidies, which applies to a majority of people in the low-income brackets?" Seymour questioned.

Paolo sat back, happy to have Hank's ire redirected.

"That's the point—to provide coverage for those who can't afford healthcare."

"It all seems rather topsy-turvy. Especially for the employer," Seymour insisted. "The imposed fines equate to roughly a fourteen percent increase in wages, which has the same effect to their bottom line as a higher minimum wage."

"Sounds like a double whammy to the employer, especially since the increased national minimum wage was imposed," Chase was quick to point out.

Retrieving his notes from his tablet, Noble elaborated. "During the minimum-wage debate the point was made that the employer passed off some of the cost to the consumer. Well, I discovered the same thing happened with UHA. According to a past study by the Federal Reserve Bank of New York and supported by a similar study by the Federal Reserve Bank of Philadelphia, they predicted the healthcare act would have an adverse effect on the economy. Their predictions appear to be quite accurate and are a clear indication of how companies coped with the effects of UHA. Clearly, anyone can see how it can negatively affect the job market." Noble swiped his tablet from the left and placed his major findings on the monitor. He cited each of the bullet points at a swift pace.

HIDDEN COSTS TO THE CONSUMER

- 10% of the manufacturing and service sectors firms increased healthcare costs
- 55% of the firms made modifications to their healthcare plans
- 70% of the firms increased employee deductibles or co-pays
- 20% of the firms increased their proportion of part-time workers
- 20-30% of the firms raised the prices they charged to the consumer

Chase took the opportunity to jump in with more numbers to cogitate. "Don't forget about the Health Insurance Tax that was levied annually against the insurer. As predicted, the insurers increased their premiums between two-point-five to three percent to offset their cost. That additional cost fell to the businesses that paid the insurance for their employees, placing a further burden."

Hank offered no rebuttal and stepped back into his shell for the moment.

With no retort in sight, Chase continued. "Jobs have taken a hit in the medical device industry as well. The Medical Device Tax, imposed on the producers of these vital medical aids, saw a reduction in their gross revenues by two-point-three percent."

"That was a poorly conceived tax," Paolo punctuated. "According to a report from the Advanced Medical Technology Association, an industry trade group, over thirty-three thousand jobs have been lost, with the expectation that one-hundred-thirty-two thousand jobs will be lost in total due to this tax. In the first year of implementation, the IRS couldn't even figure out which companies to tax!" Paolo, still reeling from the Supreme Court's shocking decision, offered a parting shot. "I guess Chief Justice Roberts was correct when he called UHA a tax. Although, it was the one opportunity to stop the Act in its tracks. Now we are faced with the unpalatable consequences."

Chase nodded in tacit agreement and then pointed out, "It was never presented as a tax, which was a theory wholly unbeknown to employers. Hank, wasn't it factored into the equation all along that the government would reap around ten billion dollars in annual revenues? From whence would it come other than the taxpayers?"

"That's my understanding. It was one of the necessary evils to insure the uninsured," he admitted.

"And thanks to Gruber it's now everyone's understanding that the government covered up the fact that it was a tax—all to make it more palatable to the public," Paolo reiterated. "Clearly, when businesses began to discover the hidden costs, they delayed business-expansion plans in a defensive move to avoid negative effects to the bottom line."

Seymour pushed the point. "It's evident from the number of small firms with fifty or fewer employees—even with the tax credits— found that growing their business beyond fifty employees added unacceptable new costs. Companies that wanted to expand resorted to outsourcing whenever possible to evade the added prohibitive costs. It's what any smart businessperson would do if they wanted to stay in business."

Noble had been listening to the conversation, although his mind kept wandering back to his phone call to Max. Most unsettling was the prospect that Simon's fine hand may have somehow perpetuated the crimes. And why to the families of the group before him? He knew he had to tell them but feared it may take precedent over their crucial task. *I have no choice*, he thought.

"Noble, are you with us?" Seymour asked, noting his apparent distraction.

"I'm following. The costs are becoming prohibitive." He quickly refocused. "A clear example was when Walmart cut healthcare insurance for thirty thousand part-time employees, forcing them into state or federal insurance exchanges. At the same time, they increased their healthcare premiums for other employees."

"I recall Walmart's healthcare costs in the first year alone rose over five-hundred-million dollars more than expected," Paolo noted, and then added, "Trader Joe's, Target, and Home Depot, to name a few, took similar steps to reduce cost to their bottom line. It's a good bet that many of these part-timers forced into the exchanges also became eligible for other government subsidies."

"Sounds like, thus far, UHA has backfired miserably, in particular for those whom the plan was meant to help," Seymour declared.

Hank put the gloves back on and reproached them. "Don't act as though you were an innocent bystander."

"I just produced the infomercials to sell the plan. I wasn't the architect. I could have as easily been selling lemons. It was just a product."

"Sounds like you did sell a lemon," Paolo chuckled. "Now it's time to make lemonade with the lemons we've uncovered."

Chase stepped in to recap. "The fact remains that the government lost tax revenue from a shortcoming in anticipated enrollments and from the continuous delays." He went on to describe how the bungling of the enrollments on the website added to the pain. How they had to resort to a handout of waivers to select groups in an attempt to keep the healthcare plan on life support. And how government incentives and tax breaks induced some workers to reduce their hours voluntarily, to qualify for the tax breaks and other financial benefits, including Medicaid. "But in the end, the workers were affected the greatest with their loss in labor hours," he said to bring the argument home.

"Adding to Chase's point," Paolo said, "we've already discussed how the massive expansion of Medicaid has had an adverse affect on the deficit. Enrollment continues to increase, due to loosening the eligibility requirements by lowering the federal poverty line to one-hundred-thirty-three percent to qualify."

"You're not attributing that entirely to the Universal Healthcare Act?" Hank asked in earnest.

"No, but according to the CBO the biggest decrease in full-time work hours was among persons earning less than forty-six thousand dollars per year. Clearly, the lower income groups."

Seymour pulled back, and challenged, "To Hank's question, for some individuals it made economic sense to choose the option that gave them the best result. You're not suggesting that UHA directly and intentionally penalized low-income households, those who automatically qualify for subsidized insurance?"

"That's how it appears on the surface, even though it may be an unintended consequence," Chase stated. "Naturally, employers that are fined for employees receiving subsidies are discouraged from hiring from low-income areas. There are already nineteen million people receiving exchange subsidies at the cost of fifty-seven billion dollars."

Seymour again plunged ahead. "So you're suggesting UHA is encouraging discrimination, forcing those who need full-time work the most—to part-time jobs—or accept unemployment?"

"Precisely. The Fair Labor Standards Act defined the workweek as forty hours per week." Chase clarified, "But by giving employers an incentive to cut hours below the thirty-hour threshold, to avoid the employee mandate to provide healthcare, counts for the rapid and continuing increase in part-time jobs."

"So, the redefinition of the work week, in essence, flies in the face of traditional definitions," Seymour responded.

"You said it."

Paolo, showing his concern, interjected, "The ugly reality is that many part-time workers are desperate for full-time jobs, but the jobs are far and few between. When it comes right down to it—the very people that UHA was supposed to help are being punished."

Seymour, equally disheartened, muttered, "It all seems rather inhumane." Then, as though a lightbulb went on, he bolted upright in his chair and gathered their attention. "But it has given me an idea for an infomercial."

The others listened while he explained his new vision.

"Remember *The Life of Julia*? It was an effective strategy to paint conservatives as anti-women. It was a foolish cartoon depiction that forced voters to look away from the facts. I admit that's what it took at the time to appeal to the targeted audience. But I'm willing to dumb it down again." He offered a mischievous grin, taunting them.

From their body language, the others were eager to see what bunny Seymour was going to pull out of his hat this time.

"Okay, you have our attention," Noble urged.

"Here goes. It would be a similar takeoff of the cradle-to-grave infographic, but this time it would focus on Julia's healthcare and how she was forced from full-time to part-time, lost her doctor, and then was forced into an exchange, all costing her more money in the end. It will provide a realistic picture of what's in store."

"That's a pretty cynical view that sounds rather dire," Hank remarked.

"Isn't that the argument that's been made?" Seymour challenged. "Even I recall the original intent for UHA was a means to provide healthcare coverage for thirty million uninsured citizens. But after debating the facts over this past week, it's become evident the intent was to force all citizens into a universal national healthcare system."

"Something you may want to take into account," Paolo suggested, "is Julia's economic status because the biggest losers are the least educated, least skilled, and those with the fewest options. It's the low-wage earners that are definitely being squeezed. UHA in its current state will only increase the surplus of low-wage earners, which obviously will increase the dependence on government subsidies."

Hank sat back and listened to the exchange, while noting the others' expressions.

They, in turn, took note of Hank's demeanor and his level of withdrawal, but chose to keep the discussion moving forward.

"To add to Paolo's point, when people work fewer hours, they produce less income," Chase noted. "That reduces their spending power. Consequently, businesses will have less demand for goods and services, which directly affects the gross domestic product."

"It's a vicious cycle that can't be good for the country, especially when coupled with a slow economy and a high unemployment rate," Noble interjected.

"That about sums it up," Paolo agreed. "If I were cynical," he smiled, "I'd say that the entire effort to bring every citizen into a government-run healthcare system has been a monumental failure. I plead guilty; I kept writing the speeches back in the Baari days to sell it. But it seems clear to me now that the Act managed to escalate the insurance premiums, instead of reducing them as promised. After all, it was the only means by which it could pay for itself. So, I think we're all in agreement—the plan clearly is not universal or affordable."

"I reluctantly agree—with reservations," Hank capitulated, forcing a hint of a smile.

All heads shot up in his direction, each with a shocked expression.

"What? You made the case, not one hundred percent, but enough to sway me." Hank threw his arms in the air and then made a final confession. "I'd be foolish to ignore the multitude of polls that consistently show over fifty percent of small- and medium-sized businesses have found UHA to have a negative effect on their companies." Hank, suddenly, in a less defensive tone, stated, "Even Chuck Schumer said the healthcare act was undermining the larger political project, calling the law a distraction from the middle-class-oriented program."

The others couldn't have agreed more with the ranking Democratic senator from New York. But winning Hank over in the final stretch was the coup d'état. Notwithstanding, the hour had arrived when the group collectively became antsy and hungry.

Noble was aware of the time, but he could not stall any longer. It was time to fill them in on his call with Max. "Hey guys, good discussion today. But before we break for dinner, I need to speak with each of you separately and in private—not to worry—it's nothing earth shaking. I'll try not to keep you too long." He thought it best to begin with Chase. "Please stay seated and the rest of you go relax in the living room until I call you."

Each of them shot Noble a variety of curious looks but were willing to wait their turn. Hank, Seymour, and Paolo each stood up, gathered their belongings, and headed for the sofas.

Chase complied.

28
THE TRUTH BE TOLD

I could refrain from telling them. Noble gave it one last thought, and then immediately reconsidered. *They have the right to know, but I have to keep them focused on the mission at hand.* He remained quiet for a few minutes more, until he could see the others seated in the other room and out of earshot.

Chase remained silent as well, nervously waiting for Noble to unleash some unknown announcement.

"Chase, my deputy director Max Ford spoke with your wife recently. Your bank reported that strange activity had been occurring with your account."

"What?" Chase exclaimed, while at the same time trying to keep his voice low.

"Some unknown person or persons has been siphoning funds. The bank has put a hold on the account pending further investigation."

The concern on Chase's face was evident. "Simon?"

Noble ignored the direct question, but filled him in loosely on the details of the crime. As he relayed the conversation that took place between Max and Chase's wife, Chase appeared more relaxed. Then he asked a few follow-up questions.

Noble answered as best he could and then assured him, "Trust me, Max has it under control, and your wife has been put at ease. I'll let you know if there are any new developments." But then he cautioned, "You are not to let on that you are aware of these events when you speak with your wife. Obviously, she'll wonder how you became privy to this information, forcing you to contrive an answer. I trust you will act as though you're shocked."

Chase understood, but there was a more pressing question on his mind. "Do you have a similar message for the others? Has something happened to their families as well?"

"Would you ask Seymour to come in and then wait in the lounge?"

"You didn't answer my question."

"I believe given the personal nature of the situation that everyone deserves the courtesy of learning about this in private. If you choose to discuss it among the others that is your choice, but please refrain from doing so until I've spoken with everyone."

Without hesitation, Chase relented and headed to the lounge to summon Seymour.

Noble proceeded to conduct similar conversations offering varying degrees of details, specific to the situation. Again, he cautioned them when speaking with their wives. Seymour was naturally pissed off and Paolo reacted with classic Italian melodrama.

"Noble, I'm sorry about the art collection," Paolo whispered, as he agonized over the home invasion and the thought of Natalie and Mario home alone.

"Natalie's fine and Max is there for her. You don't need to worry," Noble insisted, trying to alleviate the helplessness he knew his brother-in-law was feeling.

"You want me to send in Hank?" Paolo asked forlornly.

"It won't be necessary." Noble stood and headed for the lounge.

Paolo was surprised by the answer, but took his cue and followed.

When Noble entered the alcove, Hank took no time to launch in. "Who the hell is screwing around with us?" he asked, as though his hair was on fire.

With great calm, Noble replied, "Evidently, you have been discussing the situation freely among yourselves. Hank, nothing has been reported where you are concerned..."

Paolo cut him off. "If it's happening to us all—former members of La Fratellanza—then I sense the fine hand of Simon."

Everyone in the room shot a look at Paolo as if he were holding the pin from a grenade.

Hank had a sudden flashback of recent news events and stated, "Does anybody find it interesting that Baari had a heart attack around the same time Simon took his grand leap?" *I wonder what he has in store for me*, was his afterthought.

They're becoming suspicious, Noble thought, and quickly moved in to squelch their concerns. "Simon is dead, guys. Someone's just messing with us. More than likely it's a coincidence that these crimes are happening to each of you." *The truth be told,* he thought, *Max and I have not completely dismissed the fact that Simon may not be dead.*

"*Us*—that means you too?" Chase asked, missing Noble's direct connection with the group.

Seymour and Paolo threw out similar questions, talking over one another.

"Listen to me!" Noble demanded. "Your families are safe. The investigation of these petty crimes is being conducted by experts in the field. Max is heading up the individual cases and you have my word she'll get to the bottom of it." Noble passed over the personal reference and stated, "I share your concern but I have full confidence in how the situation is being handled. Now, the pressure is on and we must stay focused. The nation is counting on us."

"That doesn't help," Hank asserted.

Blowing off the comment, Noble asked, "I trust you'd like to speak with your wives. Who wants to place the first call?"

Chase, looking rather sheepish, replied, "I'd like to."

"Remember the rule," Noble advised. "Choose your words carefully."

Chase nodded in agreement, even though he was disappointed in the *lack of trust* factor.

"Follow me." Noble stood up and left the lounge, with Chase once again in tow.

The rest of them remained behind. As they waited their turns, they continued to talk among themselves. Simon was the topic of discussion, which didn't help to stave off the concern they shared.

In the end, each managed to deal with their personal at-home situations, having found a modicum of comfort after speaking with their wives. Although the question of whether or not the crimes were a coincidence still circled in their minds. Noble certainly felt more at ease after Paolo revealed his conversation with Natalie. However, chancing a conversation with Amanda negated the effect. Noble could never recall a time when she appeared so frazzled. He was unsure as to whether it was due to the identity theft or to having to plan their wedding.

Quickly, the topic of dinner replaced the earlier conversations.

29
THE GREEN DEVIL

The first obstacle of a personal distraction had been abated for the moment. And after rehashing some of the finer, often complicated points of the healthcare mandates, and witnessing the astonishing acquiescence by Hank, the group was prepared to take on an equally heated subject. The challenge on the docket for the week was to determine the overall effect the climate-change policies had on the job market and the economy in particular. Those in the room suspected Hank had not finished sparring and were prepared for him to unleash his weapons.

Seymour threw the first jab. "We can't refute the negative impact of the global warming initiatives to the economy. We must bear in mind, as we address the initiatives undertaken, their effects on the economy and their rationale."

"Excuse me—it's climate change," Hank interrupted, somewhat indignant. "Seymour, you know it was your idea for Baari to adopt a new term—a term no one could deny. It's a simple matter of scientific fact. Climate change has been with us since the birth of Earth."

Paolo couldn't resist entering the fray. "Wasn't it Jay Leno who once referred to the White House's slogan as 'Hope and change the subject?'"

"Funny," Seymour chuckled. "But whatever you call it, the initiatives Baari put in place were over the top. And taking into account the lackluster economy at the time—the country needed policies that were more evolutionary in nature. Furthermore, there is no scientific evidence to support revolutionary action now."

"I thought all of you guys in Hollywood were latte-sucking tree-huggers," Hank chided.

"You've forgotten I once was a political agnostic. My conversion didn't take me all the way to the far left. I still have a brain, which gratefully intervened."

Tiring of the repartee, Chase interrupted. "Go back to the starting gate. This debate has been heating up ever since the 1992 Earth Summit that resulted in the United Nations' Agenda 21, the infamous plan to develop the world into a sustainable environment, including global warming as an intricate and indivisible part of the so-called *agenda*." He paused for the moment, and then asserted, "If my recollection is accurate, it started with a casual, unfounded statement by Edmund de Rothschild. It was at a wilderness summit a few years before. His statement became wildly accepted as fact without discussion."

"I remember. The gist of his statement was that an increased CO_2 level was the cause of man-made global warming. Not surprisingly, it resulted in founding a burgeoning cottage industry." Seymour alleged. "Might I add, where many have profited. Al Gore leads the pact. And as one of the beneficiaries he's had a monetary motive, as well as other profiteers, to keep the issue alive."

"There is nothing to keep alive!" Hank argued. "It's a real and present danger that must be addressed."

"Baari at least thought so," Paolo acknowledged. "He wanted all the guns blazing on this issue, even though the science wasn't there."

"Excuse me?" Hank challenged.

"Then, why did we change the terminology away from global warming and establish a new mantra repeating *ad nauseam* that ninety-seven percent of the scientists in the world agree on climate change? They are not synonymous. Remember Aristotle said, 'To say of what is that it is not, or of what is not that it is, is false, while to say of what is that it is, and of what is not that it is not, is true.'"

"That was a mouthful!" Hank was taken aback, losing his train of thought.

Paolo grinned. "It's one of my favorite quotes. After all, they're the words a spin-meister lives by."

"Which is another way of explaining a false premise," Chase added. "Every scientist in the world—in fact, most thinking people—would agree that the world has warmed a little since the turn of the nineteenth century. But the climate-change supporters never cite the number of scientists who still remain skeptical that the carbon dioxide levels are at dangerous levels."

"Be careful, Chase. Remember Senator Robert Kennedy Jr. said, 'All climate deniers should be jailed,'" Seymour teased.

"Give me a break," Hank grumbled, and then he retrieved the exact quotation from his tablet. "To be exact, what he said was,

> 'I do, however, believe that corporations which deliberately, purposefully, maliciously, and systematically sponsor climate lies should be given the death penalty. This can be accomplished through an existing legal proceeding known as *charter revocation*. State Attorneys General can invoke this remedy whenever corporations put their profit-making before the public welfare.'"

"It's a pretty radical statement," Noble interjected. "It characterizes differing opinions as lies on the premise that what he believes is God's truth."

Hank had no retort but dug in his heels anyway. Taking a slightly different tack, he said, "It's a fact that the CO_2 levels that cause greenhouse-gas emissions continue to rise and have surpassed monthly averages for the first time in our history. The former chief of the World Meteorological Organization himself said, 'Time is running out,' referring to the constant rise in the levels. The U.N. has stated that reaching these high levels holds 'symbolic and scientific significance.'"

"You make it sound so apocalyptic," Seymour chided. "In fact, there are other scientific reports that show the earth is cooling, as evidenced by the increased ice in the Antarctic."

"That's just not true. CO_2 emissions are responsible for the warming effect and it has been steadily increasing over the past decade."

"Excuse me, Hank, but for the past decade, there has only been a marginal increase in CO_2. In fact, there is also scientific proof that CO_2 emissions have a lesser effect on global temperatures than previously thought," Seymour persisted.

"It's a quixotic notion that humans alone influence the climate," Noble prefaced, and then he asked in jest, "Hank, what do you suppose ended the Ice Age? It can't be blamed on humans, factories, or autos."

Hank cleared his throat, ignoring Noble's ridiculous question and took a defensive stance. "The Intergovernmental Panel on Climate Change refers to it as a pause or hiatus. They also speculate that the slowdown is another indicator and when the average global temperatures begin to rise again—which they will—it will be at a faster rate."

"Hank, the IPCC is not a scientific body. It's a political arm of the United Nations. And in the past, the IPCC has had to backtrack many of its findings, ultimately admitting that their models may have been faulty," Paolo challenged. "And by the way, the global warming hiatus as you call it, will be twenty-one years old this October."

Chase could see that Hank was gearing up for another round and quickly cut in. "Paolo is correct. After much backlash, the lead author of one of the U.N.'s reports honestly conveyed that the temperatures have remained flat for the past fifteen years. He even went so far as to acknowledge that the computer models couldn't replicate the prolonged pause that you refer to in the recent slowdown. Let's not forget; it's the IPCC that's been promulgating the rules, based on faulty scientific models. The U.N. relies on them to push their agenda—to develop a sustainable global environment."

"This is starting to sound like the same old case for global governance wearing a different disguise," Noble revealed.

"In my personal opinion that's the ultimate goal of the UN, a threat we should not ignore," Paolo warned. "Their goal is to spend one-hundred-billion dollars a year to fight global warming as part of their agenda. As you would expect, the money comes by way of pledges from countries and private donations. Having said that, they have never been able to establish a coalition among world leaders to reduce the CO_2 emissions. As former House Speaker Tip O'Neill said, 'All politics are local.' That includes nations and continents looking after their self-interest. It doesn't require a huge leap in conjecture to understand that unless everyone jumps on the global warming bandwagon—it will have little to no effect. They set the deadline for 2015 to establish that binding agreement. 2015 has come and gone."

Hank didn't react and continued to listen as he mentally armed his defense. Everyone else was active on the playing field.

"To Paolo's point," Noble was quick to submit, "you may recall that in 2014 the leaders from the largest polluting countries didn't even attend the U.N. Climate Summit held in New York. The leaders from China, Russia, India, and Australia, to name a few, were absent. Even today, their support continues to be lukewarm, in a manner of speaking, finding domestic issues more prominent."

"Leonardo DiCaprio attended the summit," Seymour mocked.

Chase thought it time to throw in the towel. "We can debate the existence of global warming or climate change, or whatever you want to call it, until the ice caps melt—but it's not helping us determine the effect it has on jobs." He repositioned in his chair and directed his attention toward Seymour once again. "You, sir, created the firestorm when you started off the debate referring to the administration's policies as being revolutionary. Would you care to elaborate?"

"Of course." Seymour, noting that Hank was temporarily subdued, continued. "Undeniably, there is science on both ends of the spectrum. It's widely agreed that climate change exists, but the rate at which it's changing is inconclusive. The majority of citizens are in agreement that we should take steps to move toward renewable energy sources. And no one would deny that we must become energy-independent as a country. However, to reach that goal we must utilize all sources of energy and carefully transition to renewable energy over time." Seymour paused before upping his tone a notch. Then he added, "Instead, during the recession, the Congress passed a stimulus bill committing seven-hundred-eighty-seven-billion dollars, out of which ninety billion dollars were allocated to green-job programs funded by government investments and tax incentives."

Hank, not sure of Seymour's point, stated, "The Department of Energy said the green job programs were 'to lay the foundation for the clean energy economy of the future.'"

Chase took issue straightaway. "That's what they said. But the administration never factored into the equation the hundreds of billions of dollars the local and state governments were forced to spend to transition to green energy using renewable energy resources. It was a heavy burden then and the numbers continue to climb."

"The precise point," Seymour stated. "The attempt to revolutionize renewable energy resources became a formula for disaster—which we are now experiencing in the early stages."

Chase furthered the point, redirecting his attention to the entire group. "It's undeniable that when the former president ordered the head of the Environmental Protection Agency to impose a thirty-percent cut in carbon-dioxide emissions from existing coal-fired plants, it was devastating for those coal-producing states. Granted, they had until 2016 to implement them, but the prediction in the loss of jobs from several organizations, including the U.S. Chamber of Commerce, proved to be accurate. Over seven-hundred-thousand jobs have already been lost, resulting in a loss in GDP of fifty-one-billion dollars."

"Whoa, Chase, you've been doing your homework. But most of those jobs were absorbed by *green jobs*. In the energy-efficiency sector alone, there's an emergence of jobs," Hank retaliated, stepping back into the game.

"What are green jobs anyway?" Seymour asked, shrugging his shoulders. "It's become a catchphrase for any job that's somehow, even remotely, connected to renewable energy. A large number of those jobs fall in the administrative, clerical, and bureaucratic positions. Most of which do not produce goods or services. The only green is the greenbacks we're spending."

Hank ignored his humor and countered, "According to a study by the Economic Policy Institute, twenty-six percent of all clean-energy jobs fall into the manufacturing sector and those jobs are more accessible to workers without a college education. It's also projected that those jobs will come with higher wages, producing a positive effect. Seymour, how can you argue that point?"

"It's a false premise, because the manufacturing sector has been converting to more efficient technology for years, requiring fewer skilled workers. Ultimately, they force the unemployed skilled workers to settle for low-wage positions. Chase alluded to that earlier when he spoke about the STEM jobs."

"Another study," Chase pointed out, "coincidently from Baari's alma mater, concurs with Seymour's premise that green jobs are not synonymous with productivity. In fact, the University of Illinois School of Law and Economics go so far as to say that 'economic growth cannot be ordered by Congress or by the United Nations.' Hold on—let me read this:

'By promoting more jobs instead of more productivity... encourage low-paying jobs in less desirable conditions... Government interference—such as restricting successful technologies in favor of speculative technologies favored by special interests—will generate stagnation.'

Which is the situation we are tackling now. They also highlight that,

'Some technologies preferred by the green jobs studies are not capable of efficiently reaching the scale necessary to meet today's demands and could be counterproductive to environmental quality.'"

Paolo, who had also examined the report, retrieved it from his tablet and added, "The University of Illinois study specifically stated that,

'Government mandates are not a substitute for free markets. Companies react more swiftly and efficiently to the demands of their customers and markets, than to cumbersome government mandates. Also imposing technological progress by regulation is not desirable."'

"I agree; companies are not suicidal," Hank admitted. "They want to perpetuate their enterprise."

"Then let's focus our attention on industry-specific jobs. Thus far, we have touched on the effects of eliminating coal," Chase noted. "What about oil and natural gas?"

"I'd like to take that question," Noble volunteered. "I recently worked on a case where I became rather educated on the subject."

He noted their look of surprise as they tried to figure out how the subject matter fit into his bailiwick. He gave them a moment to gather their attention. Then he explained that coal production at that time provided about twenty-four percent of the energy consumption and that today, oil and natural gas provide approximately sixty-five percent of the energy.

"You saw what the impact was on the industry," he noted and then clarified, "This market, however, is a tad more complicated and volatile. In fact, in the past few years, job loss is less of a problem than job creation."

"Even with the backlash from the environmental groups?" Seymour asked.

"Surprisingly, there have been periodic surges. To date, there are nine million people employed in this industry, many in positions that only require a high school education, yet they receive above average wages. But it's unpredictable. What's not—is our need to become energy-independent, as you highlighted.

"We all agree. So what's the point?" Hank asked, eager to move the discussion.

"My point is that there are policies in play that retard that need," Noble replied.

Hank appeared to be coming around to the realities, but Noble continued to press the point. "We already possess proven technologies that provide for clean production of oil and gas that can be produced right here in the U.S. Hydraulic fracturing, or 'fracking' as many call it, is a safe, effective means to extract oil and gas from below the earth's surface. But it continues to meet resistance, despite study after study to support its safety. There are over two-point-six-million miles of pipeline traversing the country. But when the Keystone pipeline required eight-hundred-fifty-two miles of new pipeline, the environmentalists protested. Fortunately, Canada resisted the Chinese and local options. Now the pipeline is underway. But the political bickering caused delays and cost thousands of jobs at a crucial time."

"So we need to be smarter in all realms of energy production," Hank conceded. "It's evident that in the foreseeable future we cannot rely exclusively on solar and wind."

For fear of losing their attention, especially Hank's, Noble brought his point to a quick close. "Precisely, because those renewable energy sources lack the technology for long-term energy storage. When the wind doesn't blow—and the sun doesn't shine—energy is not being produced. We'd be at the mercy of elements we can't control, even with environmentalist voodoo," Noble concluded, hoping he had made his case.

As the others had sat back and listened, Seymour became restless with all the dogma. The wannabe stand-up needed a mood changer. Now he had the perfect opening. He couldn't resist. "By the way, anybody ever find out how much it cost the taxpayers to install solar panels in the White House? All that expense, so twenty-two energy-saving one-hundred-watt light bulbs could shine brightly for twenty hours a day." Then, lacing his jest with sarcasm, he suggested, "That's like putting stained-glass windows on the outhouse door. Does anyone ever recall roaming around the White House without lighting? There was a lot of fog, but no darkness." Seymour was aware that Hank initiated the project and tried to egg him on.

"So how many taxpayers does it take to screw in a light bulb?" Hank quipped, not taking the bait.

While the others laughed, Seymour's own light bulb lit up.

"Brilliant, Hank. You gave me a great idea for the infomercial to articulate the energy policies!"

Paolo was also aware of Hank's role in the project and appreciated the humor, but he was eager to get back on point. "All kidding aside," he redirected, "The U.S. has continued to lead the pack in reducing CO_2 emissions, while at the same time emissions have increased worldwide. As the U.S. works to reduce emissions from coal plants by the required thirty percent, China and India continue to build new coal-fired power plants. At the same time, Europe returned to coal energy and gave up on solar and wind as its main power source, finding it too costly. Are we sharing the same world?"

As Chase listened to Paolo's point, his interest suddenly piqued. He jumped in. "I remember Germany's situation in particular. They tried the same approach, shutting down their nuclear power reactors and dismantling coal-fired plants to encourage renewable energy. As a result, the Germans coined a new term, *energy poverty*. Their energy costs spiked over thirty percent in a five-year period as costs rose during the rapid transition."

"Rapid as in *revolutionary*?" Seymour goaded in the form of a question.

"Yes, and as a consequence they found themselves once again firing up the coal plants. Then it soon fell to the United Kingdom as they began to roll back the green costs on their utility bills. The most notable reversal of policy was Australia. As one of the largest polluters of greenhouse gases, they ended up repealing their carbon tax." Eyeing his tablet, Chase read, "Their prime minister said it was, 'a useless destructive tax which damaged jobs, which hurt families' cost of living, and which didn't actually help the environment...'" Looking up at the group to catch their expression, he grinned, "And while I'm on a roll, the Canadian Prime Minister Harper said, 'No matter what they say, no country is going to take actions that are going to deliberately destroy jobs and growth in their country.'"

"Well said, Chase. That's exactly why I referred to the climate initiatives as revolutionary. And those policies caused hundreds of thousands of people to lose their jobs." Seymour stressed.

Chase acknowledged his point and then quoted a term used by another luminary: "Jobs lost due to the anti-carbon regulations are considered 'collateral damage.'"

They all smarted at the statement by the former head of the Climate Action Project, a well-funded partisan environmental group. They also knew Chase was stressing his point, by purposely making reference to the insensitive phrase that referred to hard-working Americans who lost their jobs caught in the political crosshairs.

"Throughout this debate, we've once again proved that there's science on both sides of the global warming issue," Noble contended. "Debating whose science is correct will continue until hell freezes over or, I guess in this case, it would be the other way around. But the realities we face are the current policies in place that are singularly driven to push for renewable energy at the expense of economic growth. Without a consensus, it will be a hard sell to change any legislation for the sake of jobs."

"I agree, but we're still dealing with a false premise," Seymour insisted. "Let's deal with the fact that there's no conclusive evidence that climate change is as dire as the proponents say or that we can do anything about the outcome! I agree with the move toward renewable energy—I disagree with the herculean push. Humans have little influence on an established historic trend."

Chase took Seymour's declaration as a resounding conclusion to the global-warming debate and reentered the conversation. "No one can negate that this hasn't been a lively exercise, but once again, after a week of examination, we have arrived at no immediate measures for relieving the job crisis."

Paolo interrupted. "Let's not throw in the towel so soon! I say we give it another crack, but focus on the tax implications and see if we can find any relief for businesses to inspire them to expand."

"Paolo has a point; what say you?" Chase asked, tossing the idea out to the group.

The slow, reluctant nod of the heads made it unanimous.

"I guess we have our homework cut out for us," Seymour announced, "but first I need some sustenance," he yawned.

On that note, they agreed without hesitation. They collected their paraphernalia, dropped it off at their assigned workstations, and then retired to their suites to freshen up for dinner.

30
A TAXING DEBATE

The embroiled group had spent several days dissecting the various taxes that had been imposed in the name of climate change. The one that captured the most focus was the proposed and unpopular carbon tax. The tax that would be levied on all coal, petroleum, and natural-gas producers. It appeared to be the sticky wicket. Emotions ran high on the issue and they once again operated at a fever pitch.

Chase started the discussion with an assertion. "Baari failed to have his sweeping Climate Change bill pass. Ever since, the Congress has been sitting uncomfortably on the issue, never being able to come to a consensus. But it's never been tossed in the dustbin either."

"In this instance, the Congress understands," Noble stated. "Imposing such a tax would increase energy costs and place a greater burden on our less privileged citizens."

"I've heard the same reasoning from former colleagues," Paolo agreed. "The economic consequence on the middle and lower classes is precisely the stumbling block that brought the Congress to an impasse."

"We have already discussed the negative effect it brought down, down under in Australia, until they repealed the carbon tax. However, Sweden and British Columbia are two shining examples where the carbon tax has enjoyed success." Noble acknowledged.

"You're correct. Sweden returned the tax revenue to the government's treasury," Seymour said. "Although, it's interesting to note, there's no mention of how it's being used to promote renewable energy, now that they have their mitts on the money." Applying a touch of sarcasm, he added, "It may sound familiar to a number of U.S. government programs. Those with no accounting for how the funds are disposed or if they had even been transferred."

"British Columbia, on the other hand, created an exemplary revenue-neutral tax that returned the revenue back to its citizen by way of tax cuts," Paolo cited.

"Bingo! And in both cases, the tax decreased the greenhouse gases and fuel consumption. And there was no negative impact on their GDP," Hank proclaimed, as though he had a personal hand in its success.

Seymour shot up in his chair.

It was apparent that the devil in Hank had pushed a hot button.

The others sat back and watched the specter as Seymour spewed.

"This entire discussion is based on the false assumption that humans can prevent global warming. Imposing a tax on the U.S. to reduce CO_2 would be negligible in the rest of the world, where they are not restricted. To make matters worse, imposing a tax on energy companies would compound the negative effect, either in the loss of jobs, reduction of manufactured goods, or in the possibility of companies relocating overseas."

"What I find of greater concern," Chase interjected, "is the question of how the revenue would be spent. We don't need to bloat the government coffers further, only to have the revenue dissipate into the netherworld. Seymour, you even pointed out that there's no evidence that Sweden is using the revenue in any way to foster renewable energy."

Hank, in a good-humored mood, stated, "All of you—are fighting the tide." Then, reverting to form, he claimed, "A carbon tax could provide a positive outcome. There's talk among economic luminaries, from all political factions, about mirroring something similar to British Columbia's carbon tax. The tax would be revenue-neutral by offsetting existing taxes. It could show up in a reduction of corporate taxes or personal income taxes."

Seymour looked up to the ceiling and moved his head about as if he was sniffing the air.

"What's your problem now?" Hank asked, annoyed at the distraction.

"I smell a commodity coming on," Seymour cajoled. "We all remember the Chicago Climate Exchange, the brainchild of Richard Sandor, Al Gore, and George Soros. The brilliant scheme to trade carbon credits on the commodities exchange. It doesn't look like a hard asset to me."

"I remember it didn't turn out so well for some of the largest shareholders in the exchange. Waste Management, International Paper, and Ford Motor Company were among the embattled," Chase relayed.

"I remember it as well," Paolo added. "The investors were banking on Baari to pass the cap-and-trade legislation. When he failed, the unholy trio, among other insiders, managed to sell the company to the Intercontinental Exchange in London for a hefty profit."

"Had they just held on a while longer," Hank speculated, as though recalling fonder times. "In the end, Baari found a way to push cap-and-trade through. In retrospect, his use of a loophole and the EPA to accomplish his goal ended up evading the will of the people. But it readied him for the next step, the carbon tax." Hank eyed Noble before making his parting shot: "Then, his administration abruptly disintegrated."

Noble ignored the inference.

Seymour didn't. He lashed out, "Why are we rehashing history? Bottom line—climate change has gone from a science to a political agenda. Clearly, it's a tool to empower governments, using climate change as the justification for further taxation."

"You seem rather defensive," Hank goaded. "Perhaps it has to do with your role when we worked together in the White House."

"Nice try, Hank." Seymour was not swayed and continued to make his case. "Either way, the actions of our government will have little effect. Some years back, Derrick Morgan, from the Heritage Foundation, released a study that proved the carbon tax would hurt U.S. competitiveness. According to my notes, he argued that the carbon tax would:

> '(1) do next to nothing to lower global temperature, (2) harm American manufacturing competitiveness, (3) create a new revenue stream based on behavior modification, and (4) harm low-income Americans. Energy supplies can be delivered and new supplies created through the private sector rather than through mandates, regulations, taxes, and subsidies ordered by government.'"

Seymour looked up from his tablet and persisted. "Many today still endorse his theory. I know you're all familiar with the old *consensus of theory of truth*. We banked on it during Baari's campaigns. It's when people tend to take statements to be true simply because there is a general consensus. Without scientific proof there's a widespread belief the world is undergoing a human-induced major climate change. To date, we have no true consensus as to the effects of global warming—climate change—okay, Hank! But whatever the name, the issue of the planet heating up because of humans is not a proven fact."

Noble took the opportunity to weigh in with some specifics. "A poll conducted some years ago by Pew Research indicated a third of the respondents believed government action was not warranted. Less than thirty percent felt global warming was a priority, and forty percent believed measures to reduce greenhouse gases could be delayed until the economy improved. I believe that if a similar poll were conducted today, it would reflect similar sentiment. The consensus of theory of truth on this issue is embedded in the minds of people."

"It's evident that we can't even arrive at our own consensus," Hank stated. "But it's also clear that there's no way to calculate the number of jobs that would be affected if the carbon tax were eventually imposed."

Hank seemed to have uttered his closing statement. And, with all arguments having been aired on both sides, the group concluded that the tax might end up becoming a necessary evil and possibly prove to be positive for the economy.

In the end, Hank was correct.

They also agreed that one possible measure to preserve jobs, if the carbon tax passed in Congress, would be to reduce corporate taxes, which were the highest in the industrial world. That point would be shelved for another discussion.

By unanimous vote, inspired by fatigue and hunger, they agreed to adjourn.

Until Noble happened to clear his throat to retain their attention. "Before you take off, give me a minute," he asked.

It had not gone unnoticed that, despite another long day and a working lunch that somehow had worked its way into the daily routine, no one had complained. In fact, the group seemed to thrive on the heated intellectual exercises over a variety of subjects, and continued to manage their virtual isolation deep below the earth's surface, with a minimum of gripes. They ate properly, utilized the fitness room when time permitted, and spent the rest of the time working diligently, many times pulling late-nighters to conduct the research necessary for the next day's topics.

Noble concluded it was time to give them a night to let their hair down, metaphorically speaking, for they were all due for a serious haircut. Hank and Seymour had forgone the daily shave, sporting incipient beards. Paolo managed to find four sides to every T-shirt. And Chase ditched his bowtie weeks ago. Noble smiled inwardly, as he noticed how they were beginning to resemble the young bucks from Harvard that he remembered from all those years ago. It pleased him that everything was gelling—but then again, they were only at the halfway mark. They still were committed to present a proposal to the president in twenty-six days. And although everybody's spirits were high, he reasoned that they could use a break. And, feeling like their nursemaid at times, he needed one as well. He reckoned that it was worth the risk.

"Listen up. We've all been working incredibly hard these past few weeks and I say it's time for a night out, so to speak."

Hank wasted no time and shined a mischievous grin.

"No Hank—no lap dancers."

Noble brought down the house; it was a rare occurrence. *I really do need a break,* he thought as he ushered them off to their suites. "Go clean up and meet me back here in a half-hour."

31
BOYS' NIGHT OUT

As the eight o'clock hour arrived, the gang returned to the reception area, looking refreshed and ready to party.

"*Fantastico!*" Paolo cheered as he walked into the room, followed by the others.

Spread before their eyes lay a feast fit for a bunch of frat boys from their halcyon days. In the last half-hour, with the help of Jax, the table had been transformed into their table of old. The piles of papers, tablets, and coffee cups had been replaced with pitchers of beer filled to the brim, stacks of pizza boxes, and a large tray of hot, spicy Buffalo chicken wings.

"Dig in," Noble beckoned. "Oh, Chase, the green pitcher is gluten-free, but not alcohol-free, of course."

"Ah, Noble, me boy, you think of everything," he replied, with a relaxed smile.

"Except, the low-fat, low-carb," Hank teased. "Oh, what the hell? It's boys' night out."

"Hey, we're missing someone," Noble noted, as he counted heads.

All of a sudden, 70s music came blaring out of the lounge.

"What's a party with no music?" Seymour declared, as he danced his way back to the table and poured himself a mug of beer.

Without missing a beat, they engaged in effortless conversation covering a host of subjects and the entire gamut of sports known to man. Their debate topics were verboten. It was a welcome relief that was clearly expressed on their grinning faces. The teasing and cajoling continued for hours, as they reminisced about the years together, until the inevitable topic arose—Simon.

"Noble, any more word on the investigation?" Chase asked with unusual composure.

The others suspected the beer had a welcomed effect.

Noble replied with equal calm. "As you know, there have been no other intrusions on any of your lives, other than the first occurrences. Max checks in with your families on a regular basis. But trust me—I'll keep you posted should anything change."

"I trust nobody's been screwing around with my life?" Hank inquired, as he crossed both fingers on both hands.

"Max checked with your foundation and your credit rating. There have been no breaches to report. I guess you dodged the bullet, my man."

"So maybe it is a coincidence. Each attack on our families was different. Besides, if it were Simon, he would have targeted Hank first," Chase conjectured, with a bit of hope and a prayer on his part.

"I promise I'll keep you posted. For now, count yourselves lucky; it appears to have ended."

Hank, picking up on Chase's comment, broke the momentum, and changed the subject. "Noble, how come you never joined our group?" he probed, with a playful grin. "You could have been a renowned member of La Fratellanza."

"I told you guys at the time; I'm not a groupie. It's that simple," Noble reiterated.

"There has to be more to it than that, considering your profession," Seymour noted. "You must work with teams of people. Besides, you did hang out with us on campus from time to time."

"I admit it! I enjoyed having dinner with all of you. But that's different from studying together every day, sharing ideas, working together to solve problems—not my cup of tea. As it turned out, it was one of the smartest decisions I ever made."

"Excuse me, Noble; then what are you doing in this godforsaken place? Is it retribution?" Hank persisted.

"Drinking beer." That was his second quip of the day. A novelty for Noble.

They all had a good chuckle, and then Chase reverted to the killjoy.

"Noble, did you ever consider that had you joined our group, most likely you would have talked us out of playing Simon's insane game? You could have changed history."

"Chase, let's not go there," Paolo pleaded.

"Things could have been a lot different for all of us."

"Look, by the time we even figured out what Simon had planned, it was too late," Hank admitted.

"I'll answer your question as best I can." Noble hoped to end the interchange. "Simon was a master manipulator. I'd like to think that I would have been able to figure him out sooner and stop the game before it began—but I didn't. It took me years to get into his complex mind, to be able to predict his next move. So answering your question with complete honesty—I don't know. We'll never know. On that note, I'm going to go refill the pitchers. Thanks to Jax we have an entire keg to consume."

Noble stood up and poured out the remaining beer and then headed to the kitchen. Even out of earshot, he could hear the din of the conversation. The subject matter was predictable. "Baring my soul to a bunch of guys. This is why I'm not a groupie," he muttered to himself.

By the time he returned to the table, the table had been turned on Hank.

"Do you think Simon was working alone?" Paolo asked. "We know Baari was influenced by the Godfather and the Financier, but never thought about the possible connection to Simon at first."

"You knew about the Godfather and the Financier?" Noble asked Paolo, while tossing a raised brow in Hank's direction.

"It was clear toward the end that Baari was taking his purported policies too far. Hank told Seymour and me that Baari started to ignore his advice and thought he was getting his instructions elsewhere."

"What about the former first lady?" Seymour asked.

"Maryann Townsend!" Hank exclaimed, and then quickly adjusted his tone. "Ah, she hadn't a clue at the time. She found out about Baari's past after Noble gave Baari the ultimatum and forced him to resign." Catching Noble's glare, he stopped short. Then with the utmost seriousness, he stated, "I'm positive she has no idea about La Fratellanza."

"I meant about Maryann and Simon," Seymour persisted, nosily looking for confirmation.

Hank eased into a smile, relieved at the redirect. "Okay, so we all figured out that she was the reason Simon's bedroom was off-limits. It was obvious that Simon's choice for a mate for the junior senator was a bit too convenient. But trust me; Simon also used her; she was a pawn just as we were."

Chase, still focused on an imaginary scene in the bedroom, blurted out, "No way! I agree his choice was too easy, but never thought of him—her—no way!"

The other members of La Fratellanza could not hold back their snickers.

Seymour ribbed, "Chase, at times you are so naïve. But that is part of your charm, Bro."

Paolo continued to probe. "Hank, you never answered my question. Do you think Simon was working alone?"

Hank, with some discomfort, confessed, "I thought there was a possibility that Simon was working indirectly with the Godfather and the Financier. I could see my sphere of influence continue to ebb."

"So we were *all* puppets," Seymour underscored.

"But Baari was clearly *Pinocchio*," Paolo insisted, using his proper Italian enunciation.

Noble set his beer mug down with a thump, causing everyone to look his way. At that moment, he decided to voice the gnawing thought that had dogged him throughout their discussions. "Curious, we just spent weeks debating crucial policies that Baari pushed and no one in this room ever mentioned Simon's possible influence—until now."

The others remained silent, not sure if Noble was asking a question or making a statement—or fishing.

Chase surprised everyone and spoke up, although rather reticently. "As we discussed the various topics, there were elements in our shadow thesis that reared their ugly heads. I admit, at times, I wondered whether it was possible that Simon had direct control over the policies in the White House. I just tried not to let it be a distraction."

"Of course, there were similarities! What do you think we were doing there?" Hank blurted out. "Our thesis was not just about getting an illegal immigrant elected!" He inhaled to regain his composure. Then in a more relaxed manner, he apologized. "Chase, old boy, sorry about the outburst. I know your involvement was on the periphery during the campaign and you had no way of knowing what the rest of us were assigned to perform."

"But it's clear now that Simon had his own vision and planned a different outcome from the start," Chase replied.

"This is old news, guys. Let's change the subject," Hank pleaded, quick to steer away from his direct, sometimes willing, sometimes unwilling, involvement. "Hey, Paolo, when did you become such a conservative?"

"I mutated into a reasonable thinking person," Paolo replied with a fake jab to Hank's shoulder.

"I think his brother-in-law had something to do with it," Seymour jested.

"As a matter of fact, it was my gorgeous wife who taught me about the beauties of small government—and giving people more control over their lives."

"You know what Julia Roberts says: "Republican' comes in the dictionary just after 'reptile' and just above 'repugnant,'" Hank quipped, basking in his rejoinder.

"And 'Democrat' comes in the dictionary just after 'demented' and just before 'demonic,'" Paolo countered, deflating Hank's moment.

"And who said that?" Hank challenged.

"Me!"

They all laughed in good spirits. Then Seymour broke out into a comedic skit.

"Did you hear Jimmy Fallon the other day? He announced that Chicago reversed its plan to name a high school after Baari because it received multiple complaints from people in the community. He guessed the parents were afraid their kids would spend eight years at the school and still not get anything done."

That brought down the house, but mostly because of Seymour's perfect mimicry of Fallon.

As the late evening hours rolled on, there didn't seem to be any letup in the conversation that continued to flow from topic to topic. Until Noble took the opportunity to rally their attention.

He raised his mug, as though he was about to make a toast, and said, "Guys, I want to thank you for the sacrifices you've made and commend you for more or less leaving your partisanship at the doorstep. Frankly, I wasn't sure you had it in you. If only Congress could adopt the same attitude for the sake of the country. Here's to you."

"Ugh! This is getting too heavy. I thought it was a night to let our hair down," Hank complained in a kidding manner.

Hank's right, Noble thought, and as he brushed away his serious demeanor. "Anybody up for a game?"

"One problem: the last game's over," Paolo announced, as he pointed to the wall clock.

Noble let out a big grin. It was obvious to the others that he had an endless number of tricks up his sleeve. "How about the Giants versus the Phillies?"

"Now we're talkin'," Hank answered, making a high-five gesture in the air. "Don't forget the chips!"

It took a matter of seconds for the guys, with refilled pitchers of beer and the last of the wings, to head to the lounge. Noble stopped off at the kitchen to pick up the prearranged snacks Jax had left behind when he made his evening delivery. By the time he returned to the lounge, the party was in full swing.

In a flash Noble grabbed the remote, turned off the music station, and switched the TV setting over to the built-in DVR. As he deftly scrolled down to select the prerecorded game played earlier that day, he announced, "It's time for *baseball*," in his best sports-announcer voice. He quickly joined the others, who had already spread out in a variety of comfortable sprawls on the sofas. They all sat back, sipped on their beers, and rooted for their chosen teams.

Three for San Francisco, two for Philadelphia.

32
THE SELF-STIMULUS

Their virtual night out ended up being akin to a revisit to Jake's Pub, their off-campus haunt, where many a drink had been downed. Although their capacity had diminished over the years, all survived the frat party—if one didn't count the fuzzy heads and the slow start the following morning. Notwithstanding, it didn't delay them from hightailing it out of their suites and into the kitchen.

"Good morning fellas. Looks like y'all had a dandy time last night," Jax teased, while he cleaned up the rest of the debris from their table in the center of the room.

Hank, trailing behind the others, commented, "We're a little worse for the wear."

"Hey, Mr. H., how'd you like those chicken wings?" Jax grinned.

Hank rubbed his paunch, and replied, "They went down just fine, as you can see."

"I have a fresh pot of java brewing. It should fix y'all up just fine—for whatever it is you do in here," Jax announced, and then he continued to tend to his duties.

Once they returned to their spotless table, with breakfast plates and cups filled to capacity, they began to put away their food, surprising themselves at how famished they were. Minutes later, Jax reappeared from Paolo's and Seymour's suite, carrying their laundry.

"Little light on the undies, boys." He chuckled as he held up the half-empty bags.

"No spouses around. Great opportunity to take a little leeway," Seymour answered back, as he noshed on his bagel.

"You boys are looking a little shaggy around the ears as well."

"You don't happen to provide spa services?" Seymour asked.

"You'd trust me with clippers?"

"On second thought," Seymour uttered, and then, before popping the last bite of bagel into his mouth, he replied, "I don't think so."

Noble had finished his breakfast long before the others, but continued to sit back and enjoy the repartee as he sipped his remaining coffee.

Jax continued his banter with Seymour as he sauntered in and out of the other suites, collecting the other laundry bags. "You gentlemen enjoy your day now," he offered, as he finally departed.

At five minutes to nine, the last of the plates had been returned to the kitchen and the cups had been refilled. Then, all seated and accounted for, the group picked up momentum. With less than a month to go and heavily armed with solutions to offer the president—there was still no silver bullet in sight. The traces of frustration that had crept in were apparent. It was time to regroup intellectually and emotionally. All agreed to devote the first hour of their session that day to recap. They went around the table taking turns, with each member pinpointing what he saw to be the major issues—until it was Paolo's turn.

"Perhaps our approach is all wrong," he conjectured. "Eight years have passed since the Great Recession and still more than forty million Americans either are out of work or can't find full-time jobs. Those statistics added to the momentous increase in anti-poverty spending that has surged fifty percent. Food stamps alone have tripled. Our immigration policies have added new burdens, thrusting millions of immigrants into government subsidy programs since amnesty was imposed."

"What are you suggesting?" Hank asked. "We've already dissected most of the policies that directly impede job growth or cause job losses. Eighteen new or increased taxes imposed by the Universal Healthcare Act have been identified. Those taxes alone attribute to approximately three million jobs being lost and, at the same time, the inflated mandatory spending stoked the fires with another forty percent increase."

Seymour added to Hank's assessment. "We've also hashed out the various renewable energy policies and taxes, including the carbon tax. And we've haggled over the pros and cons of the minimum-wage hike. All of which place heavy burdens on the taxpayers. No wonder there is such unrest in the country."

"Let's not forget the corporate taxes levied on American businesses," Chase reminded them, primed to enter the discussion.

"Which have not only perpetuated the problem, but magnified the issue by discouraging corporate investment. The culmination of taxes from whatever source, whether they are from healthcare or renewable-energy compliance, has driven U.S. companies to relocate to other countries to take advantage of a lower tax base. A countless number of lost jobs have been left in its wake. The Big Whopper was the beginning." He quickly retrieved some notes from his tablet. "Listen to this. Stephen Moore at the Heritage Foundation referred to the process as inversion. Moore, quoting from the Congressional Research Service, said, '...roughly 50 major companies have relocated abroad to lower their U.S. corporate tax burden over the last 10 years—and the trend is accelerating.'" Chase looked up at the group and finished paraphrasing the quote. Pfizer, the pharmaceutical firm has been talking about moving its headquarters to Europe. Medtronic, a medical firm, has toyed with the same idea. Even Walgreens is exploring a move overseas. Moore goes on to make the argument that supports our prior assessment that the U.S. corporate income-tax rate is the highest in the industrial world."

At the mention of "tax rate," Paolo couldn't resist adding a little humor to breakup Chase's pontification. "Hey, guys, you know the word 'rate' in Italian is *tasso*. Amusingly, *tasso* also means 'badger.' Pointing to the fact that the corporate tax rate has become a real hassle."

The others chuckled until Paolo recaptured their attention. "Seriously, to Chase's point, Mort Zuckerman, of *U.S. News and World Report*, summed it up best when he highlighted the three main components of the country's plight." Paolo read from his tablet, "'The faith in the American dream is eroding fast... The lack of breadwinners working full-time is a burgeoning disaster...' and 'The great American job machine is sputtering.' In my view, Zuckerman's observations are spot on. But whether it's the Universal Healthcare Act, the Climate Change Initiative, or the numerous other areas we have scoured, we still have not come up with concrete answers to solve the problem. We must find a way to renew corporate investment."

Seymour, an avid history buff, was quick to proclaim, "One reason is the administration had returned to the mistakes of the past, following in the footsteps of FDR. Santayana was right about repeating history. Raising taxes, raising the minimum wage, and increasing government-revenue-intensive programs are nonstarters to stimulate an economy. The temporary stimulus jumpstarts are merely hiccups that only prolonged the recession."

"In my view, the billions of dollars that were spent in stimulus spending missed the mark, only adding salt to an already festering wound," Chase attested. "They proved to be political forays dressed to look like economic solutions."

Paolo took a deep breath and then seized the conversation once again. "Look, despite our mental gymnastics, we haven't delved sufficiently into the heavily bloated spending programs. There is little doubt that until the government gets spending under control they will continue to have a voracious appetite for taxes. It's not molecular physics; it's simple arithmetic. You can't spend more than you have. The only way Uncle Sam can pay for these spending programs is to tax or borrow— neither sound solutions to an expiring economy. And turning on the printing presses to create money that is increasingly devalued is not a winning formula. Our massive entitlement programs alone make up forty-four percent of the economy thanks to Social Security, Medicare, and Medicaid—all of which have outgrown inflation."

"I couldn't agree more," Hank submitted. "Too much emphasis is placed on the validity of the programs. But in addition to spending *per se*, we also need to identify the enormous waste and abuse within the various federal government departments. To date, there's no real evidence that this fraud pandemic is being seriously tackled. Medicare fraud alone is estimated to be about sixty billion dollars a year. That would pay for close to half of the UHA!" They were surprisingly angry words from a man who played a significant role in the former administration. An administration that produced programs never funded at inception.

The others at the table took note, including Noble, who, up to that point, had sat back jotting down notes on his tablet while he listened. Startling the others, he abruptly spoke up. "Government cannot spend its way to prosperity. Attempting to do so only increases the burden on the taxpayers, placing them in a catch-22 death loop."

"Speaking of a death loop, don't forget the Estate Tax," Chase pointed out, and then he backed up his point by citing Rachel Greszler, also at the Heritage Foundation. "A while back she reported the results of an analysis conducted by their Center for Data Analysis. They found that repealing the federal death tax would 'increase economic growth by forty-six-billion dollars over the next ten years and add an average of eighteen thousand jobs per year throughout that period.'"

"That's just another example of helping the rich—I won't repeat myself—you get my drift." Hank's point was clear.

"What you don't get," Chase countered, "is that the wealthy will continue to spend their money in ways to avoid the tax versus investing their capital, which is not the most efficient use of capital. Besides, forget the rich. It sets a horrible example for a country that taxes the property of the dead, which already had been taxed before. Maybe that's where the expression 'taxed to death' started."

Hank quickly veered off the issue. "That's why we've been looking at all the policies and tax burdens that are stifling the job market. Let's not lose our focus—the real impediments to job growth…"

"Hank, hold that thought. I need a potty break, so I can be fully engaged," Chase requested.

The others noted how Hank had engaged in the conversation with more gusto and wondered whether his conscience was driven by his past indiscretions. Indeed, they were eager to see more of the reformatted Hank in action. Sensing the next round would also require full focus, they were happy to take a break.

33
WASTE NOT, WANT NOT

"Okay, guys, listen up," Hank announced loudly to gather their attention. He even remained standing to ensure all eyes were on him. "Paolo is correct. Perhaps we have put the proverbial cart before the horse. If we focus on the spending that perpetuated the increase in taxes, we might get closer to exactly what is slowing the economy. We have spent weeks debating the policies that are stymying job creation—and we're only inching along to a finished resolution the president can impose without delay."

"Granted, we've come up with numerous valid solutions to consider," Seymour interjected, "but as you yourself said, they all require, either repeal of legislation or new legislation. It would take Congress an eternity to effect change."

"Hear me out. I suggest we all step back and reexamine each of the long-term solutions we've bounced around thus far. We still need a vehicle to implement the changes we've exposed—but we're missing something. We should go over the areas we highlighted again. This time look back at the spending abuses as the generator of overspending. It doesn't happen in a vacuum."

Hank sat down and waited for a counterargument. Much to his surprise, it didn't surface.

"I agree, in principle, with both you and Paolo," Chase admitted. "You've hit on a salient point. But the president still won't be able to make changes in a timely manner. The snail's-pace Congress would have the final say. We need a diversionary tactic. A rope-a-dope."

Noble picked up on Chase's unambiguous expression. "So—what are you suggesting?"

"We have another option," he replied, as he fingered his horn-rimmed glasses down to the tip of his nose, giving him a professorial air.

"And?" Hank inquired, with impatient curiosity.

"I took another go at studying the CBO projections for revenues and outlays for 2017—they were spot on—and it's not pretty. But it presents a possible solution. I've given this a lot of thought." He paused and then spoke more deliberately. "It's time for another sweeping tax reform. It's been over thirty years since Reagan's Tax Reform Act. Once enacted, it simplified the tax code, instituting two tax brackets, and removing various deductions. Now there are six income brackets with many more complexities. Is this what we call progress? It's a creaky system of spare parts held together with baling wire and chewing gum."

"You're not talking flat tax again," Hank grunted.

"Whether it's a flat tax, a modified tax, or marginal tax, the debate must include both individuals and corporations." Anticipating Hank's next move, Chase quickly added, "A major component must also be to remove many of the allowable deductions, providing a direct benefit to the corporations. The so-called corporate welfare. But that will all have to be worked out." He held up his hand to hold off further debate for the moment. Then, glancing at his tablet, he said, "You may find these statistics quite interesting. They are a few years old, but in 2013 there were 73,954 pages in the Internal Revenue Tax code. Six thousand changes have been made in a ten-year period. The most extensive tax reduction in tax revenue comes from the Healthcare exclusions, costing seven-hundred-sixty-billion dollars over a five-year period." Chase looked up and announced, "My favorite, can you believe—six-point-one-billion hours a year are spent on tax preparation by individuals and businesses."

"The numbers are staggering, but to an even greater point," Noble added, "is the collection of taxes. The Internal Revenue Service is a problem unto itself, but not for the obvious reasons." He caught the mild chuckles, but continued. "The IRS has eighty-thousand employees who are responsible for collecting more that ninety percent of the revenue. But they are also saddled with administering various health, education, and retirement policies, including the Earned Income Tax Credit. The tax collector ain't what he used to be. It's no wonder they overpay individuals on average of fourteen billion dollars a year. It's unsustainable and makes Chase's case for reform."

"Also to your point, about the death loop," Seymour joined in, "the government habitually spends more than they recoup in tax revenue. Unquestionably, the current structure of taxation is self-destructive. And in our anemic economic state, more families have joined the ranks of the low-income, causing government subsidies to rise. That means the base from which the government derives the tax is shrinking— There's no doubt we are spiraling out of control."

"It sounds more like the country's caught in a maelstrom," Paolo interjected.

"We can reverse the trend. Here are two other steps I'd like to propose," Chase stated, and then looked carefully at each of the others before completing his statement. "First, a spending moratorium to be imposed for one year. Second, new short-term tax reforms to be retroactive to January of this year, providing some immediate relief in the way of a tax holiday. A tax rebate will be allowed on all individual and corporate 2018 tax forms to compensate for the overpayment of 2017 taxes—It could pave the way for the solution we are seeking."

"What don't you get—The government is broke!" Hank blurted out. "We can't afford the loss of revenue. I might be able to buy in on a modified version of a tax rebate for individuals, but I fail to see how helping corporations get richer will have any positive impact. You're barking; excuse me, *banking* up the wrong tree."

"I couldn't help but agree with Hank, save his last comment," Seymour retorted.

Hank appreciated the endorsement, but he had already handed over the last straw to Chase.

"Who cares? The myth about corporations being given a free ride must be abolished. It just constrains our progress!" Chase, in a raised voice, insisted. "I'm so tired of that argument. And Hank, you're forgetting about the small-business owners. They are a vital part of the business community and offer the best opportunity for job growth."

The others were taken aback by Chase's unusual outburst. The issue had obviously touched a raw nerve.

In a more calm tone, he asked, "May I continue? When corporations have more disposable income, it's likely they will apply capital to expand and create more jobs. When wealthy people have more disposable income—their spending stimulates our consumer-driven economy. The Estate Tax was one example. But if our taxing policies don't unlock capital to produce hard assets, the only choice will be to continue to print money, which debases our currency. Don't fret, Hank; those corporations and wealthy individuals will still pay a disproportionate share of the taxes as they have historically. They may be taxed at a lesser percentage, but we have proposed eliminating many of the current allowable deductions. A point I attempted to make earlier. The net result can only be positive for the country and, especially, for those who are impoverished."

"Chase is right." Paolo fell in step. "As long as they are forced to play by the rules, we shouldn't be influenced by the financial success of any given company or individual. Remember free cash flow produces the liquidity for companies and individuals to invest, benefiting the overall economy. How many jobs do entitlements create—I ask you?"

Ignoring his rhetorical question, Hank challenged, "Not if they use technology to expand. They will only displace workers."

"Hank, you're starting to sound like a Luddite," Paolo chided, and then he continued to chastise. "If they had their choice, the Luddites would have ended the Industrial Revolution. We can't stand still while the rest of the world embraces technology; otherwise the U.S. will wind up in the technological garbage heap. It's a natural cycle of business— an area where government doesn't have to be involved."

Hank chose to back off and take a different approach. "Okay, so the carbon tax is presumably to encourage companies not to pollute by affecting their bottom line. Now you want to relieve companies of paying a high corporate tax. Won't that, in essence, be a wash and obfuscate the purpose behind the carbon tax? Are we going to forget the environment? There will be no incentive not to pollute."

"What I am proposing is for a rigid twelve-month period, giving the administration time to launch our longer-term proposals," Chase stressed. "Hear me out, please. I suggest a freeze be placed on all new spending and any recent appropriations for select projects to help offset the loss of revenue. And we can't give in to special-interest groups, despite public reaction."

"Remind us again of the total revenue we're talking about?" Noble asked.

"Revenue from income is currently two-point-eight trillion dollars. It will depend on the tax-reform components, but if we revert back to the two bracket system of the nineties—I'd say the loss of revenue would be closer to roughly one trillion."

"What! Did I hear you correctly?" Hank bellowed. "You want us to find close to one trillion dollars of proposed expenditures that will be considered cuts, even if they are *temporary*?" he asked, underscoring the word *temporary*. "Congress never met an expenditure cut that they liked."

"Look upon it as a temporary shortfall and not a loss, *per se*," Chase explained. "It may not cover the loss completely, but for the short period the payback will be realized in other ways. If Congress reforms the tax code, it will provide an opportunity for the private sector to free up capital to expand their operations, increase their profits, and boost their taxes. The promise of a rebate would, in essence, provide families with a windfall to stimulate the economy further. It could be just the self-imposed stimulus we need to increase consumer spending, which, don't forget, counts for over seventy percent of the economy. We're delving into the tax bases and not relying on an artificial so-called stimulus."

"We'd leave the state and local governments alone?" Hank asked, in a manner that sounded more like an ultimatum than a query.

"Yes, we're talking only federal taxes. Now here's how I suggest we approach it. The Congress reviews twelve groups of legislation comprised of the cabinet-level and a few sub-level departments, which constitute the annual appropriations requests. I say we focus on the specific departments responsible for the areas we've identified. Our challenge will be to find savings where outlays can be suspended for one year, with an eye to a possible permanent suspension. This is a time for drastic actions; no half steps or platitudes will do. The goal is to right the economic ship so we can sail into the future."

"You mean focus on the same areas where the Congress consistently shirks its responsibility to make the hard decisions," Seymour carped. "They've been slavishly churning the government wheels on a month-by-month basis, very much like the indebted consumer."

"I have to agree. Passing the *Continuing Resolution* has become an unending *non-solution*," Paolo observed. "It's a convenient way for Congress to evade its responsibility by hiding behind the resolution.

"More importantly," Seymour added, "this is the same do-nothing Congress we need to approve our proposal. Are they up to the challenge?"

"Remember, this time President Post has the necessary margin in Congress," Noble added. "It looks like the time is ripe to make a radical move. It's now or never."

"The American public would also have to buy in. It's not going to be unanimous, but their support is essential," Chase stated, and then he added, "In some ways they are just as much to blame, blinded by

Congress' overspending and easy-money policies. It fed right into their habit."

"I guess I'll have my hands full trying to convince the American public to put their trust in their government again." Seymour imparted, half-jokingly, for he knew his task would be an enormous challenge—in particular, selling the corporate tax relief.

"Convince them and the Congress will have no choice. They are lily-livered and only respond to the vote," Chase declared. "Now back on point. We need to focus primarily on discretionary spending, but don't forget to look between the lines of the non-discretionary items as well."

"'Non-discretionary' is such a loose term, other than to mean *do not touch*," Hank noted.

"That's why I said look between the lines. There are many areas of duplication and waste. Let's look for any type of spending that can be suspended. Even if it will be a tough sell. Are we all in agreement?" Chase asked with slight trepidation.

Surprisingly, after such a heated exchange the nods were not hesitant, but eager. He had his answer.

"Great; now here's how I'd like to proceed. Obviously, any spending bills associated with climate change must be addressed?"

"The bull's-eye is obvious," Seymour quipped.

"Just look for the red flags."

Chase turned and looked toward Hank with an arched eyebrow.

He quickly replied, "What—you don't think I can be objective?"

"Of course, I do," Chase indulged, and then continued. "As we also look at the various healthcare bills we'll find there's a lot of crossover, which complicates the issue. They've been chopped up and diced to fall under the Departments of the Treasury, Labor, Health and Human Services, and Education. And who knows where else."

"Such fun! I'm glad you left out the Department of Sanitation," Hank grinned. He was becoming more ebullient, as he had shifted to tacit support.

"There's more to this mixed bag," Chase said, "including the Department of Housing and Urban Development, Transportation, the Small Business Administration, and the Social Security Administration, not forgetting SSI, SSDI, and Medicare, programs that fall under Social Security."

"Tackle the Holy Grail? The grand bargain to reform entitlement spending," Hank teased in response.

"How can we touch entitlements?" Seymour asked hesitatingly.

"We may have to touch some entitlements; it's unavoidable. They're everywhere," Chase cautioned. "Bear in mind; some cuts have already been made to Medicare."

"Yeah, but that was to help offset the cost of the healthcare program," Hank shot back, adding, "I know, we're robbing Peter to pay Paul," not wanting to give the others time to reply to the obvious.

"This time around, any cuts, especially to the safety net, must be prudent, humane, and thoughtful," Chase cautioned. "This is not a chop-happy exercise to wield axes.

Noting Noble's unusual silence during the conversation, all heads moved in his direction.

"I'm just waiting for my assignment," he acknowledged passively. In reality, he was rolling over in his mind their overall strategy.

"In that case, we also need to tackle immigration and national security," Chase pointed out. "You would know best where to look within the Departments of Homeland Security and Defense spending."

Again Noble remained pensive and silent.

The others sat back awaiting his response, as Noble appeared lost in thought.

Then he bolted upright.

"I like it," he replied, responding to the plan in totality. "I think it could work. It should instill consumer confidence. Small businesses may become less fearful of expanding and restore the full-time worker to its historic level. It could even stop the bleeding of companies moving abroad to reduce expenses, and could even lure some back. It also holds the promise of stimulating confidence in our new president. We don't have the luxury of ignoring opportunities to save our country." Noble stopped short, once more retreating to his inner thoughts.

The others waited for the anticipated *but*.

"But—I have one question. When the tax holiday is over—what prevents everything from reverting back to the old normal?"

Everyone's attention shifted again back to Chase, eager for the answer.

"I'm glad you asked. Here comes the next step in my proposal. Congress would be required to establish bipartisan commissions to study our long-term proposals and implement our solutions to stimulate the job market. They would have one year to pass the bills or propose legislation. A non-government commission should be established to revamp the tax code. This process would afford us some breathing room to implement change. Everything will be fast-tracked to avoid the bureaucratic morass."

"It would be easier to find solutions when the economic ship is on even keel and not sinking," Paolo concluded. Then, noticing Seymour brandishing a huge grin, he inquired, "What's with you?"

"The optics will be great! Describing some of the spending programs that will be frozen for a year. Once the voters tune in to my infomercials, those programs might even end up in the permanent deep freeze—I love it."

"Then we're all on board. I'll forward each of you the plan in the next few minutes; you'll find it on your tablet in the Renaissance Project folder," Chase instructed. "Tomorrow, we get to work."

Noting that they still had an hour before Jax would arrive with dinner, Hank, Seymour, and Paolo scurried to their workstations.

"Don't forget the president will be calling in at the end of the week," Noble shouted out, and then he asked, "Can we be ready?"

"We'll be prepared," Chase assured as he followed close behind the others.

34
THE GIFT THAT KEEPS ON GIVING

"What's the matter? You've been talking to yourself more than usual," Doris asked, as she entered Max's office.

"Nothing!" she snapped and hurriedly got off the subject. "What's that?"

"One of the guards dropped this off. It was left at the front gate with your name on it. Nice gift," Doris remarked with a mischievous look on her face. "You'll notice it's already gone through security." She handed Max the two-by-three-foot painting, loosely draped in plain brown paper.

Max carefully peeled away the wrapping as Doris explained, "The guard apologized for having to open it, but said he was just following protocol."

"Thanks, Doris."

Her secretary took the cue to leave.

Left alone, Max grumbled, "All I need is another mystery to solve—now a secret admirer."

After placing the paper gently on her desk in forensic style, she rested the painting on the arms of the nearby-overstuffed chair. Then, stepping back, she studied the canvas. The oil painting was of three clowns sitting around a table drinking tea. There appeared to be a signature in the upper-left-hand corner, but it was indecipherable. She continued to admire her new acquisition for several minutes more, until an odd sensation struck her.

"Doris!" she called out. "Please get the Georgetown police chief on the phone."

Seconds later, she saw the flashing light, but skipped the intercom button and went straight to line one.

∽

"Chief, Natalie Salvatore, the director's sister, filed a police report sometime last month reporting a break-in. All that was reported stolen was an art collection."

"Yes, Deputy Director, it's been given top priority. Although I did inform Mrs. Salvatore that, given the value of the collection, the chances of tracing it to a fence would be highly unlikely."

"Thank you, Chief; I appreciate that you're handling the case. Would you please email me a copy of the list of stolen items?"

"I'll get right on it. I'll have it to you in a few minutes. Is there anything else I can help you with?"

"Not for now, thank you. I'll wait for the report. Enjoy your day."

Almost as soon as she hung up the phone, her computer screen beeped with the incoming email. In a flash, she retrieved it and eyed the list of stolen items. Halfway down the list was the description of one of the paintings; it read: Three clowns drinking tea.

Max was bowled over. *Why would the thief, Natalie's thief, be sending this to me? Whoever is doing this must be somehow connected to Simon. This person has to be carrying out Simon's last wish. But what's the endgame?* She continued to deliberate a bit longer, until she decided it was time to become an art enthusiast.

∽

It took her about an hour plodding through the Internet, looking for anything that resembled clowns drinking tea—What she discovered was incredible. She texted Noble immediately. No sooner did she hit *send,* Doris stuck her head back in the office.

"The Buffalo police chief is now on the phone. What's with all the chiefs today?"

"Thank you, Doris."

"This is Deputy Director Ford."

"Yes, Deputy Director, I thought your office would like to know that we've recovered a body near the Long Point National Wildlife area in Norfolk County, Ontario. It's about ninety-four miles down the Niagara River from the Peace Bridge."

Max tried to hold back all hopes. "Have you identified the body?"

"According to the coroner, it's pretty badly decomposed. However, the height, hair color, and clothing they salvaged would suggest that we found your Simon Hall."

Max still wasn't going to allow herself to believe he was dead until she saw the corpse for herself. "Chief, I want you to seal the body and send it to our forensic lab in D.C. without delay. I want our coroner to conduct another forensic autopsy."

"It's already been sent to..."

She cut him off. "Stop it now. Whatever the destination, please redirect the body to Washington. It's an essential part of our overall federal investigation that's still open. I want it here by tonight, if at all possible."

"Yes, ma'am. It's not been closed on our end either. But I'll follow the protocols we've established with the SIA."

I hate it when they call me "ma'am." "I'll report back our findings. Thank you for your cooperation, Chief." She hung up the phone and texted Noble again. *Damn you, Noble; call me.*

She fixated a while longer on the painting until she looked up at the wall clock; it was 6:58 p.m. In two minutes, Stanton would place his daily call and ask her to meet him at the Blackfinn. But tonight, she would repeat what was becoming a blanket excuse; she had "had an exhausting day and was heading home." It had been a couple of days since she had been out with him, but, all told, they had spent an unusual amount of time together in the last month. Of course, it was always dependent on the president's travel schedule, but Max started to wonder if POTUS spending so much time in house was best for her relationship. *Too much of a good thing, kind of thing*, she thought. On cue, her cell rang.

"Hi."

"Hi yourself. How about a nice cold beer to soothe your nerves?"

"Not tonight." She kept the conversation brief, but did inform him about the painting and the body that was recovered.

"Let's pray it's Simon."

"I'm sitting in on the autopsy tomorrow morning. It will be grisly, but our coroner is the best in his field. I personally need to be sure it's him."

"You sound frustrated. What's the matter, babe?"

"It's Noble! He should be the one officially to identify Simon's body. Not being able to reach him at a time like this is inexcusable. Something's going on with him. It could be personal or professional; either way he's not confiding in me."

"Your concern sounds personal. What's going on between you two?"

"Piss off."

"I repeat: What the hell is going on with you? Your mouth is starting to sound like one of my agents."

"I am an agent. Stop looking at me through your rose-colored glasses."

"Max, can't I be concerned about you? It's obvious the job is getting to you. Talk to me."

"I can't talk about it tonight. I'm tired and you're right, frustrated. I'll call you tomorrow after we confirm the autopsy results."

"Max, chillax. And I love you."

After a slight hesitation, she muttered, "Love you too. Gotta go."

He's right. I'm not myself. She tried to convince herself that she wasn't avoiding Stanton, just creating a little space between them. With Noble away to parts unknown, La Fratellanza missing, Simon possibly resurfacing, and Stanton overly available—it was becoming more than she could bear. The only thing for certain was that she wanted to avoid the mysterious person in the hoodie. Max was positive that if her stalker appeared again, Stanton would insist on protection and she would lose the battle—one more thing she was not prepared to face.

35
UP IN SMOKE

Max arrived back in her office early the next morning after a restless night's sleep. Something was bugging her. The crimes against the families of her suspected members of La Fratellanza were too clean. She reviewed the case files again. Since the first series of crimes, nothing else had occurred. "I'm missing something," she uttered and then thought, *Could it really be Simon playing around with them? Could he be planning something on a larger scale?* Max clasped her ears and shook her head, as though somehow it would rid her mind of such crazy thoughts. Then, as she reached for the forensic reports from Natalie's break-in, Doris buzzed her.

"Hank Kramer's secretary is on the line. She asked to speak with Noble."

"Thanks; I'll take it."

"This is Deputy Director Ford."

"I'm in terrible mess," said the frantic voice on the other end of the line.

"What can I do to help you?"

"I assumed Director Bishop was a friend of Mr. Kramer, having visited him many times at the White House. And I was hoping he could help me."

Max explained that she was filling in for Noble while he was traveling and assured her that she would be happy to assist her in his absence.

The secretary appeared to calm down, having solicited Max's support. "Mr. Kramer's office was raided by the local police and they found narcotics hidden behind a file cabinet." She swore that Kramer had never been involved with drugs of any kind.

"I'll promise to investigate the matter thoroughly. It is essential that you don't discuss this with anyone other than the local authorities, if you want to help Mr. Kramer," she instructed, all the while thinking, *Is this the missing piece to the puzzle?* She ended the call, having reassured Kramer's secretary that she'd investigate and keep her informed.

Now, I'm convinced someone is targeting the members of La Fratellanza and their families. Max scurried out of her office with the pile of case files and headed to the conference room. As she breezed past Doris, "Hold my calls" was all she had to say.

Then, in her usual analytical style, she began to lay out each element of the cases. She used the virtual keyboard and rapidly typed each of the criminal events as they occurred, along with gnawing questions—questions only Noble would be able to answer. After completing the list, she sat back and began to analyze the data, looking for a verifiable clue.

<u>Paolo Salvatore</u>	Stolen Art
Who knew the importance of the art?	
<u>Amanda Ridge (Noble Bishop)</u>	Identity Theft
Who would have access to her SSN?	
<u>Chase Worthington</u>	Money Siphoning
Why siphon money from his bank?	
<u>Seymour Lynx</u>	Obscene phone calls
Why obscene phone calls?	
<u>Hank Kramer</u>	Narcotics possession
Any record of him using/selling drugs?	

Max studied the display screen intently for a period of time. Then, her mouth gaped open as though she had just been punched in the solar plexus. The clue to the mysterious crimes was right in front of her. "*Somebody's definitely messing with us. But it can't be...*"

In mid-thought, she hastily used the mouse pad to underline a series of letters. Again, she stared in disbelief. *This is too easy, Simon wouldn't make it so obvious,* she reasoned. Then she admonished herself. *Simon is dead. But maybe the crimes aren't sheer coincidences.* Without hesitation, she grabbed her xPhad and texted Noble. "This is a ridiculous way to communicate," she complained aloud. Then, in exasperation, she tossed the smartphone down on table.

36
BEYOND THE GRAVE

It was late in the evening when the secure phone rang in the reception hall, but the group appeared to take little note of the intrusion as they continued to tap away at their keyboards at their workstations. After all, Noble was the only one allowed to answer the phone. But it didn't stop them from being curious as to whether it was the president on the other end of the line.

Noble unobtrusively left his workstation to take the call.

"Yes," he responded to the caller.

"Director, you need to call Max. She's sent you several text messages, and she needs to talk with you now."

"Can't it wait?"

"No, sir."

"Thank you."

The guys were engrossed in their research and tallying the numbers. An opportunity presented itself. "I'll be back shortly," Noble shouted from the opposite end of the room, and then he left the facility.

Standing on the other side of the metal doors, he inserted his xPhad into the secure sleeve and placed the call.

"Max, what's up? I just received your text messages."

"Noble, I hate this means of communicating with you. You're being as elusive as Simon was. I need you to be more available!"

"Max, relax. What's going on?"

"Why does everyone tell me to relax? It could be that I'm dealing with a dead body and a stolen painting!"

In an attempt to calm her down, he replied, "One at a time, please. What do you mean a dead body?"

Max inhaled deeply before explaining the call she had received from the police chief in Buffalo. "Based on the description, it could be Simon. I've arranged for our coroner to conduct the autopsy. It's scheduled for tomorrow morning."

"Good call, Max. We need to control the situation and we need confirmation. Please, God, let it be him."

She heard his last comment and assumed it was not meant for her ears, but directed to the man upstairs.

"Now, what's this about a painting?"

"I received a gift today that was dropped off at the front gate."

Odd means of delivery, he thought, but coaxed her to continue. "And…"

"It's an oil painting," she hesitated, and then said, "of three clowns sitting around a table having tea."

"We had a painting like…" He stopped short. He dreaded where this was heading.

"Yes, I'm sure it's the painting from your parents' collection that was stolen."

"It had very little value, if any. Why would someone steal it in the first place and then send it to you?"

"You'll have to wait a moment for that answer. First, you're wrong." Max loved to take the rare moment to stump Noble. "The painting is titled *The Unwrit Dogma*. It's an original oil by Newell Convers Wyeth, the great American painter and illustrator, and the father of the famed Andrew Wyeth."

Noble was stunned. "Are you sure it's an original?"

"I'm not an art expert, but I think I was able to detect Wyeth's signature in the upper-left-hand corner of the painting. By the way, I haven't told Natalie. I didn't want to freak her out. But there's more."

Noble sat back and listened, fretting over what could be next. He knew that when Max got into her sleuthing mode—anything was possible.

"Some of Wyeth's paintings sell for over one million dollars. But wait, before you get too excited—the painting is also listed in the National Stolen Art File at the FBI."

"What?" Noble let the shock settle in before he proceeded. He remembered when and where his parents had purchased the art. "I went home for spring break during my first year at Harvard. Soon after I arrived, my parents returned from the county fair. That's where they purchased that painting for some measly sum. I can't remember how much, but they never paid more than a hundred dollars for any of their art. They simply liked collecting."

Out of nowhere, Noble had a flashback to the time he learned that Hamilton had purchased a painting for two hundred and fifty euros in a flea market in Florence. Later he discovered that he owned a fifteenth-century masterpiece painted by a Venetian named Andrea Mantegna. Noble felt a slight quiver as he recalled that Hamilton ended up selling the painting at a Sotheby's auction for close to twenty-nine million dollars.

"Perhaps we should try to get back the rest of the collection," Max suggested.

Noble had the same fleeting thought, but wisdom prevailed. "Be careful; I'm not sure I want a stash of stolen goods on my hands."

"Did Simon have any way of learning about your parents' art collection?"

"I fail to see the connection." He was befuddled by the question, until the words passed his lips. Another memory resurrected. It happened after the death of his parents, when he returned to Harvard. Simon was the first person he spotted when he returned to campus.

"After my parents' death," he explained, "Simon offered his help. I thanked him, but said there was nothing to do. I told him Natalie and I had decided to hold on to everything, until such time we were ready to sell the house and most of their possessions."

"Did you mention the art collection?"

"Yes," he divulged with a hint of ire, more directed at himself than anyone else. "Now, where are you going with all this?" He was eager to hear her conclusions.

"Noble, first there was the stolen art, then the identity theft, the money siphoning, the obscene phone calls, and wait—I saved the best for last—the Chicago police chief is looking to bring Kramer up on narcotics possession."

"When did that happen?" He was shocked.

"I received a call the other day from Kramer's secretary. It appears the local authorities received an anonymous tip that led them to conduct a raid at his office. That's when they found the drugs."

"I can't believe Hank's into drugs."

"Listen to me—S as in 'stolen'—I as in 'identity'—M as in 'money'—O as in 'obscene'—and N as in 'narcotics.' Voila!"

"Spells 'Simon.'" He was in disbelief, but at the same time amazed at Max's mental agility. "Nice work, Max. Therefore, the plausible explanation is that he orchestrated his petty revenge crimes before his demise. Perhaps his ultimate revenge all along was aimed at his fraternity brothers and he strived to accomplish his goal from beyond the grave, which only adds luster to his triumph."

"I agree. He most likely prearranged his retribution in the case of his death. That's why I have Stanton reviewing the interrogation reports from Dugway. Maybe one of his recruits is the guy carrying out his wishes."

"Good call. You might even discover the secret admirer who sent you the painting."

"Cute. There's still something that puzzles me. You've explained how Simon would know about the art collection. So he went after Natalie to get to Paolo. But why would he go after you and Amanda for identity theft?"

"I suppose, in a way, I stole his identity. When Hamilton and I first discovered that Simon Hall and Mohammed al-Fadl were one and the same, we placed both names on the Terrorist Watch list. From that moment on, Simon was no longer a free man and was forced to go undercover."

"And siphoning Chase's account?"

"During the interrogation, Chase admitted giving Simon the password to his bank's online banking system. He swore at the time, he had no idea it was to siphon money for Simon's slush fund he affectionately named 'Uncle Rob.' Chase said he trusted Simon when he told him he was going to set up several untraceable accounts to transfer the funds. He admitted to letting his guard down because of their close relationship."

"This is far too interesting and typically ingenious on Simon's part. I can't wait to hear about the obscene phone calls."

"Simple. It was part of Seymour's smear campaign tactics he used on Baari's opponents in the U.S. senatorial race. When his wife discovered he was behind the reported calls, she almost divorced him."

Max chuckled. "And Kramer a drug dealer. I don't buy it either. But why did he go after Kramer at his Chestnut Foundation and not mess around with someone close to him, like Simon did with the others?"

"I'm not sure where that's coming from, other than Hank had exhausted his list of close companions because of his perfidy. Perhaps, because he was so engrossed in his foundation, that's where Simon could inflict the greatest pain. Hank's betrayal would have given Simon the ultimate axe to grind."

"Or perhaps, he needed an 'N,'" she quipped.

"Aside from being gifted a painting of mine, anything else strange happening with you?"

Max wasn't sure if she should level with Noble, sensing he would take Stanton's side and order protection. She couldn't lie to him either, so she used one of his tactics and downplayed her concern. "Just this weird guy in a hoodie that keeps showing up at the Blackfinn. Thus far, he's been just creepy and harmless."

"Did you tell Stanton?"

"Yeah, he's been with me every time the hoodie appears on the scene. I've got it covered. What about you? Are you still climbing summits, studying your navel, and contemplating life?"

Ignoring any prolonged personal discussion, Noble bypassed the question and cautioned, "Stay vigilant—Simon's ghost may have a plan for you."

"Comforting thought, but I hear you." She appreciated his concern, but not enough to let him off the hook. She groused, "Noble, answer my text messages! Otherwise I can't keep you posted."

"I'll do my best. Gotta go."

37
MEET THE SPENDTHRIFTS

On the forty-sixth day, Noble entered the reception area ready to run the numbers, until he discovered five empty chairs around the table. At the same time, he picked up on the chatter emanating from the lounge.

"Anyone working today?" he asked the group seated among the sofas.

Hank was the first to speak. "I told them," he replied, in a solemn tone.

Chase most annoyed, blurted out, "That proves Simon is still out there. Out of all of us, Hank's confession had to have been the final nail in the coffin."

Noble was starting to come to the same conclusion, but he didn't let on. "There has been no other activity since the initial crime to your families, but Max is still heading up the investigation."

"Be straight with us. Who else could have known about Hank's dalliances with drugs except Simon?" Chase questioned with a tone of apprehension.

Noble glanced at Hank, surprised he had been forthcoming.

Hank apparently had no problem, confessing to his brethren that Simon had caught him once using recreational drugs. It was during a time on the campaign trail when the pressure was immense. All it took was a veiled threat from Simon to spur Hank toward other means of legal recreation. He chose the female variety.

"Simon could have shared that knowledge with anyone," Noble opined.

"You mean like the senator?" Seymour quipped, tossing aside his actual concern.

"Hey guys, you're blowing this out of portion. It's probably some sick prank. You have my word that my agency will get to the bottom of it. In the meantime, we have work to do." Noble let out a deep breath, curtailing any further discussion on the subject. "I'm going to grab another cup of coffee. I'll meet all of you in a second."

The others dragged themselves out of the lounge and headed to the table, preparing themselves to gear up for another round.

✑

For the next several hours, the members of group relayed all they had exposed after days of diving deep into the spending budget. Now it was time to untangle the veritable web of obfuscation they had uncovered.

"As a starting point," Chase opened, "federal spending is over four trillion dollars. Healthcare, including Medicare and Medicaid, has surpassed Social Security as the most expensive entitlement program. Welfare-spending programs constitute a trillion dollars. One-point-five trillion dollars are appropriated to discretionary spending. Without addressing the recklessness, it's abundantly clear that the greatest negative effect will fall squarely on the low-to-middle-income families."

"Why not just raise taxes on the rich?" Hank asked, more than satisfied to belabor the point.

"Let me say it another way. A *millionaire's tax* is a gimmick and it won't fix out-of-control spending and waste. You could tax the wealthy a hundred percent of their income; it won't bring us any closer to paying for the entitlement programs. We need to tackle the core issue—recklessness," Chase stated. He quickly deferred to Noble.

"The recklessness you referred to stems in part from the disorganization of the governmental departments and the massive redundancy. It's an unfathomable labyrinth that defies all sensibilities," Noble stated sternly.

Chase scratched his head and then asked, "I thought that was Gore's pet project back in the early nineties?"

"Correct; the National Partnership for Reinventing Government was set up under Clinton. Gore was tasked with heading up the project. Nothing came out of it. Ten years later the Senate submitted a bill and tried to establish the Government Transformation Commission." Reading from his tablet, Noble quoted, "Their charter would have been, 'to help Congress and the president improve government performance, reduce duplication and wasteful redundancies, achieve fiscal sustainability, and enhance credibility with the American people.' Sadly, it's still sitting on the Senate's mountainous prorogue pile. The public knows it as kicking the can down the road, which explains one of the central issues."

Paolo added in disgust, "While government talks a good game, the ordure of redundancy is piling high."

The others let out a chuckle at Paolo's phraseology, but continued to listen to him carefully.

"Each year the Government Accountability Office submits a report to the president and to the Congress. The detailed report identifies areas of overlap and duplication, along with highlighting opportunities to achieve financial benefits, in the way of savings. The Congress has addressed less than half of the proposed suggestions, and they continue to squander billions of dollars each year. Here are just a few examples identified by Congressman McMichael of Texas." Paolo swiped his tablet and then read them, one by one, as the others followed along on the large monitor.

FEDERAL AGENCY DUPLICATION OF SERVICES

- 100 economic development programs spread across five agencies within the Department of Transportation.

- 20 programs addressing homelessness are spread across seven federal agencies, including the Departments of Education, Health and Human Services, and Housing and Urban Development.

- 44 employment and training programs are spread throughout the Departments of Education, Health and Human Services, and Labor.

- 82 teacher quality programs run through the Departments of Defense, Education, and Energy, as well as NASA and the National Science Foundation.

- 15 federal agencies are involved in administering 30 food safety laws.

"Also, there appears to be duplication in the appropriation process itself. Here's a prime example," Seymour highlighted. "The Senate, as ordered by the Committee on Environment and Public Works, requested fifty-five-million dollars a year until 2019 for programs to be carried out under the North American Wetlands Conservation Act. The NAWCA would then appropriate that money to the U.S. Fish and Wildlife Service. Hmmm," he said, as he scrolled down the screen on his tablet and continued to read. "Interestingly, the House of Representatives, as ordered by the Committee on Natural Resources, requested thirty-five-million dollars a year through 2018 for programs to be carried out under, none other than the NAWCA, that would in turn appropriate that money to the U.S. Fish and Wildlife Service. It appears all is fair in appropriations. They're all swimming together in the same pool—Unfortunately, it's our pool of money." He snickered.

"Smells a little fishy to me," Chase added, as he wrinkled his nose.

"It smells worse than that. I found similar bills," Hank stated, "but with an interesting twist. You guys remember when we put through the Statutory Pay-As-You-Go Act in 2010?"

"Of course," Paolo answered. "It resurrected a bill that was kicking around in the nineties, which was supposed to ensure that new spending was offset by revenue, whether through cuts or newly added revenue. It was contrived to be a zero-sum exercise. However, I recall there were some exemptions."

"Over one-hundred-fifty programs, to be more or less exact. Naturally, Social Security was among them. But what's interesting, is Pay-As-You-Go has become a euphemism for Pay-As-Much-As-You-Can. By way of example, I came across nine separate bills that fit the definition, all from the House of Representatives, requesting changes to the Internal Revenue Code." Hank swiped his tablet and a list appeared on the monitor.

COST OF 9 AMENDMENTS TO THE IRS CODE

Permanent S Corporation Built-in Gains Recognition	$ 287,000,000
Permanent S Corporation Charitable Contribution	56,000,000
Charitable Giving Extension Act	80,000,000
Permanent Active Financing Exception Act	5,563,000,000
America's Small Business Tax Relief Act	8,579,000,000
Student and Family Tax Simplification Act	936,000,000
Child Tax Credit Improvement Act	7,799,000,000
Private Foundation Excise Tax Simplification Act	174,000,000
Amend IRS Code of 1986 for bonus depreciation	39,831,000,000
Total Net Increase in the Deficit for 2017:	**$63,305 BILLION**

"Almost sixty-four-billion dollars. Nice number, huh? They were all subject to the PAYGO rules and in a few cases, there is presumed revenue to offset the outlays, but only partially. What you see on the monitor is the net increase to the deficit."

"And that's just nine of hundreds of spending bills that have been put forth before the House and the Senate," Chase stated, and then showing signs of frustration, he added, "We could spend a lifetime listing all of the abuses, duplications, and instances of milking the system. We must find the means to bring the government-spending mill to a complete halt. It will provide time to seriously reduce spending and install stopgaps to eliminate the fraud. Remember the KISS principle—Keep It Simple, Stupid. The government works best when its policies are kept simple and not made unnecessarily complicated."

"What is most disturbing," Noble pointed out, "is while the government chants the 'tax and spend controls' mantra, all taxpayer dollars are channeled straight to the Federal Reserve to pay the interest on the national debt—Did you hear me gentlemen?—The interest on the national debt! Not one penny goes to pay for a spending program. We keep digging a deeper, debt-interest hole to devour our tax receipts."

"I thought the purpose of taxation is to take care of the health and well-being of Americans?" Seymour remarked; it was more of a statement than a question. "They must think we are all a bunch of pishers."

"Now you know why the government is so keen on taxing corporations," Chase expanded. Then, with a bit more petulance in his tone, he elaborated. "Those dollars, in addition to revenue generated through excise taxes on alcohol, tobacco, and firearms, *et cetera*—are all the money available to pay for the bloated spending programs. At this rate the government will never catch up with itself and will spend an eternity in servitude, requiring the Fed to cover their losses by distributing Monopoly money printed by the Treasury—in essence, continue to pile on the irresponsible deficits to the national debt."

"You've just given me some more optics." Seymour chuckled.

"How do you have so much fun with such depressing information?" Paolo asked.

"It's all about the message and the recipient. Remember, I have plans for Julia. This time not to ignore the facts."

"You are such a cynic."

"May we get back to the point at hand?" Hank prodded, and then continued, "Not only is the spending out of control, so are the billions of wasted taxpayers' dollars, whether through improper payments, incompetence, or outright fraud. In a report released by the Heritage Foundation, pages and pages of governmental waste were identified. Here—I've listed a few for your viewing pleasure." He swiped his tablet and again read them aloud.

U.S. GOVERNMENT WASTE

- Federal Communications Commission spent $2.2 billion in phones for low-income Americans. 41% (6 million) participants found ineligible.

- National Endowment of the Arts spent $100,000 to fund a video game depicting a female superhero saving planet Earth from climate change.

- Department of Energy's Savannah River Facility spent $7.7 million on severance packages for 526 temporarily hired contract workers, in lieu of layoff notices.

- Taxpayers paid $51 million a year to maintain and operate 3.5 million square feet of unused office space.

- Transportation Security Administration spends $3.5 million annually to lease/manage a warehouse in Dallas, Texas to store $184 million worth of unused security equipment. An additional $23 million in depreciation costs were lost because 472 carry-on baggage-screening machines had been housed there for nine months or more.

"If that doesn't get your head spinning, check these out." Hank replaced the graphic with another equally incredulous one on the monitor. He rattled off the bullet points:

AND THE WASTE WASTES ON

- The Defense Advanced Research Projects Agency held a $6 million convention on the science of storytelling.

- Social Security Administration overpaid benefits by $2.11 billion and $850 million in cash benefits by double dipping into disability insurance and federal unemployment insurance.

- The Conservation Reserve Program pays farmers $2.1 billion annually not to farm their land for a period of at least ten years.

- The Department of Agriculture endorsed the "Meatless Monday" initiative and then a few weeks later announced plans to purchase $170 million worth of meat from drought-stricken livestock producers.

"These are only a few choice examples but the list is endless," he fumed.

"I appreciate your frustration, Hank, but you were there when all this was going on," Chase remarked.

"Enough of your reproof! Haven't you heard of changing your stripes? With the exception of Noble, we all had a part in what's playing out today. Even you Chase. You may have been in the background crunching numbers and filing campaign forms—but you were on the team."

"I'm humbled," Chase avowed, trying to sound convivial. "What's done is done. Now it's our opportunity to erase the record."

"May we continue?" Noble asked, trying to curb another distraction.

Paolo did not hesitate and jumped in. "Let's not forget the annual September Spending Spree, called the 'use it or lose it' season," he joked.

He was referring to the federal government's fiscal year that ended on September 30, whereby all government departments were obligated to forfeit unused appropriated funds to the Treasury by October 1.

"According to an article in RealClearMarkets by Furchtgott-Roth," Paolo continued, "for the departments to justify their current spending level and avoid future spending cuts—they simply race to spend every last dollar, without regard to the merits of any expenditures. We all remember the four-point-one million-dollar conference the IRS treated themselves to in 2010. Well, Furchtgott-Roth reported that in 2014 they also spent $2,410,000 on toner products in a single purchase. Other examples cited included the Department of Veterans Affairs spending over $1.8 on artwork, the State Department spending $24,868 for a 50 inch LED HD TV for the embassy in Kabul, Afghanistan, and $20,362 for alcohol in New Delhi, India. The year before the State Department spent $5 million on crystal glassware for several embassies."

It was apparent to everyone in the room that before they had conducted their infinitesimal research on spending, they had no idea the extent of either the direct or the indirect abuse that was eating up the taxpayer dollars. While sharing looks of despair, Chase had one last point to make on the spending abuse.

"Santayana might be proven right again," he said. "A similar fiasco to the financial crisis of 2008 appears to be brewing on the horizon. The student-loan debt now exceeds a trillion dollars and outstrips credit-card debt and auto loans combined, as pointed out by Rana Foroohar of *Time Magazine*."

"You're absolutely correct," Hank granted, although it was evident he was, in part, still trying to make amends. He continued. "When Baari extended the pay-as-you-earn program, creating a student-loan forgiveness system, he created another bubble that is destined to burst. Qualifying college graduates only have to pay ten percent of their annual income for up to twenty years; then the balance of the loan is forgiven. Whoosh! The debt vanishes, but reappears in our tax burden. However, Baari threw in a nice inducement. If a college grad works for the government, the loan will be written off after ten years. A classic example of double-dipping."

"Worse yet," Chase added, "he then had the audacity to offer two years of free community college to those who have completed the first two years and had maintained a grade point average of two-point-five or above. A nice gift from the taxpayers, wouldn't you say?"

"Baari should have taken remedial courses in constitutional law," Seymour challenged. "I'm not so sure it would pass muster if it had ever made its way to the top of the heap of constitutional challenges."

"Rightly so," Chase stated. "But herein lies the problem. There are many variables, such as the graduate's annual income, where they work, and even which school they attended; all determine the cost of their loan. It's like trying to understand your telephone bill. But once again, the American taxpayers would be the ones to absorb a high percent of the loan, and by many taxpayers who were never privileged to attend college."

"Certainly, one for the list," Hank volunteered.

"It's evident that the massive tax-and-spend policies have paralyzed businesses from risking their capital to expand in the U.S. and to create more job opportunities." Noble summed up further. "Available capital is put on hold, rather than being injected into the economy. Excessive tax burdens, increased healthcare, and energy costs continue to starve the economy of needed seed money. Families are caught in the crosshairs."

Seymour lamented, "At one time, America was the greatest, debt-free nation spurred on by self-determining—self-sufficient people. Today, one-third of our population receives a government paycheck and fifty percent of the population receives some form of government subsidy."

"What is it?" Noble questioned, noting Seymour's sober expression.

"We're trying to solve a problem in a vacuum. Again, maybe there is no silver bullet. Perhaps the quick fix we've been looking for is a simple promise to the American people—one the government must keep."

"That's a tall order considering the malaise in the country. The wounds the prior administration inflicted are still raw and the Congress is considered the culprit," Paolo postured.

"Remember, I know how to get things done. I'm the *King Macher*. I'm ashamed that I once used my abilities to convince millions of voters to follow blindly, a misbegotten leader. But I still have the old stuff to influence. This time around—we'll give the people the straight skinny. No more smoke and mirrors."

"Seymour, it was your message that drove America into this mess," Paolo chided, and then he retreated. "Sorry pal, that was unfair. Maybe you're right. Perhaps an honest straight-to-the-point message could be the tipping point. The country's mental state is such that they may be receptive to ideas formerly considered extreme."

From Chase's expression, he was already on board. "It might be our viable option to calm the waters after they've been roiled and allow for real positive reform to take place. In the end, sadly, it was the government that perpetrated the crisis—but it's also the government that must lead the rebound."

"We must jumpstart the process by enlisting the public's trust," Paolo opined. Then, sounding slightly more skeptical, he added, "Seymour, my friend, we can supply the ammunition, but you're going to need a larger hat and more bunnies. Maybe they'll solve the problem, while they're in the hat together."

"Leave it up to me, the Bunnymeister!" he pronounced with great self-confidence.

"I thought you were the King Macher?" Hank ribbed.

"I wear many hats," Seymour replied with pizzazz.

It took a few moments, but then Noble came through. "I'm sold. Let's get together first thing tomorrow. The moment of truth has arrived. It's time to lay out a cohesive plan and communications blitz for the president."

38
THE AUTOPSY

"Max, I hear you're sitting in on this one?"

"Yes, Doc. I'm a glutton for punishment. What have you found so far?"

"Well, based on the height, bone structure, and natural hair color, along with the clothing and the bullet hole, described in the crime scene report—I'd say it's your guy—I'd say it's Simon Hall."

"C'mon Doc," she said suspiciously. "You'd never settle for such skimpy evidence."

"You've been hanging out with the stiffs and me too long, Max," he teased. "As you can see, there's been a lot of decomp, especially in the facial region. A few animals certainly left with their bellies full."

"But why the face? What animal is smart enough to only attack that part of the body?"

"Glad you asked. I was curious as well and scaled off whatever skin sample I could locate. It showed high traces of rabbit urine."

"Rabbit urine?"

"Yes, it's the major attraction for coyotes and is often used to bait them."

"Coyotes? The corpse was found in the lake region."

"You and I seem to be on the same wavelength. I checked it out. Evidently, in southern Ontario, they're having a huge problem with coyotes coming out of the forest and into the towns looking for food. Coyotes normally have a keen sense of smell and the faint human scent doesn't alarm them. They tend not to engage."

"Except for this poor guy. So you're telling me he died somehow. Then a rabbit pissed on him, and then a coyote ate him. What a way to go."

"Max, I would say, based on the urine content of my samples, some human sprayed this guy deliberately."

"You think to destroy his identity?"

"You got it. The fact that there is no water or other fluids present in the lungs also proves he didn't drown. Most likely he was killed and left where he was found."

"So if this is Simon's corpse, it happened weeks ago. Therefore, he would have been exposed to the external elements for a period of time."

"And being dehydrated it also made the dactyloscopy difficult."

"The what?" Max winced.

"Fingerprint analysis, my dear."

"Okay, but not impossible." She didn't like the expression on his face, with or without his use of a fancy word. And without the corpse's face, she needed a fingerprint.

"I was able to rehydrate the right thumb and retrieve a fairly usable print, but it's useless."

"I don't understand."

"Our corpse had a severe case of pitted keratolysis. It's a bacterial virus that attacks various extremities, but primarily affects the feet. However, in extreme cases, it can affect the fingertips, rendering them useless for identification."

"I'm still confused. There would be some pattern to go by."

"They're useless because the pitting of the skin changes the circular and longitudinal patterns on the fingertips over time. Therefore, there is no consistent pattern. I'd say this guy worked in a profession that required rubber gloves. They're usually responsible for providing a breeding ground as the hands sweat. Not exactly Simon's sort of profession."

Her heart sank as she let out a huge breath and asked, "Doc, are you sure? What about dental records?"

"You're grasping, Max—look for yourself; they're all destroyed. The only hope we have is to run a DNA test. But we'll need a sample of Simon's DNA for comparison. Can you get me the DNA samples they took from him when he was processed at the Draper Prison?"

Max was becoming more distressed by the moment. "Forget it..."

The coroner cut in. "What's the problem?"

"The warden was ordered to place Simon in maximum security

immediately upon arrival and to bypass the indoctrination process, until Noble had an opportunity to interrogate him. That would have included fingerprint and DNA evidence, except he escaped the next day."

"Oops," the coroner replied. "In that case, Max—there's even more troubling news."

"Don't do this to me."

"It's the gunshot wound that doesn't make sense. Look here." The coroner pointed to the bullet hole a few inches above the left kneecap.

"That's where Simon was shot."

"I know—according to the crime scene report. Noble stated that he saw Simon limp on his left leg as he headed to the side of the bridge, leaving a blood trail along the way."

"Exactly, right after he was shot."

"If he was shot by the agent as described in the report, the trajectory of the bullet would have entered in this direction." The coroner held up his pen horizontally.

Max was confused as to where he was heading, but she listened with great interest.

"The bullet in this corpse entered in this direction, upward." He once again held up his pen, but that time vertically and at a ten-degree angle. "The bullet that entered this guy pierced his femoral artery. He bled out instantly. There's no way he could have limped anywhere."

"So you are saying you're a hundred percent sure this is not Simon?"

"I'm not saying Simon is not dead; I'm just saying this is not your guy."

Max looked over toward the grotesque remains of what once was a man. His distorted body stretched out immodestly on the metal table pushed her mind into overdrive. "Hey Doc, isn't it possible that the bullet didn't hit the artery at first, but the impact of hitting the water caused the bullet to dislodge and that's when it severed the artery?"

"Highly improbable."

"But possible! Come on; after a hundred-foot drop?"

"It's possible," he allowed, "but I have grave doubts." He smiled, knowing she would catch the double entendre.

"Cute, Doc, but we have the bullet and the one you pulled out of Abner Baari's skull. See if they match."

Only a select group of people had knowledge of how the former president Abner Baari died, including Max and the coroner. Even President Post was not informed, in order to protect him should the truth ever leak. The public was told that Baari had died of a heart attack shortly after returning to the States to visit his wife and daughter. The former First Lady and senator, Maryann Townsend, knowing the full story, agreed to the deception. She had no choice, as it was tacked onto her own immunity agreement. Fortunately, La Fratellanza had not suspected that the senator had aided and abetted Simon and Baari in their escape. One fact that the insiders did know was that it was Simon who shot Baari in the car before he fled and jumped. There was no doubt that the sound of a gunshot had prompted the agent on the bridge to shoot Simon. It was a reaction to the sound.

"This is not your day, kiddo. The bullet shattered the bone, which is why I suspect it deflected and then hit the artery instantly—not after a fall. Sorry, I recovered only bullet fragments, not enough for testing."

Max was disappointed, but not yet willing to give up. "If this isn't Simon, could Simon have survived the fall?"

"After he jumped, he would have had to place himself perfectly in a seated chair position. The slightest change in position would smash his spine and damage internal organs. Most likely, he'd ruptured his spleen. With a gunshot wound in the upper leg—it's improbable he could maintain that position in the fall."

"Okay, so if it's not Simon, then who the hell is he?" she huffed in frustration.

"That, my dear—will be your job to find out. And with no clear means of identification, I'll have to list him as 'John Doe.' Time to sew him up and ship him out."

"Doc, don't close this case yet. Keep the body in the drawer. I'm not convinced. But if isn't Simon, perhaps there's a family out there looking for this guy."

"Will do. But find them soon; he is taking up valuable space." The coroner patted her on the back. "Go get 'em, Max."

She had hoped beyond hope for a different outcome. *But what if the Doc is correct, and it's not Simon?* she pondered.

⌒∽⌒

As Max headed back to the White House, she reviewed in her mind the events of an autopsy she had supervised in another case. At the time, she was shocked to learn that Noble had considered cremation to let the whole sordid affair disappear. She was thankful that the intelligent side of his brain had prevailed. After all, Baari was a U.S. president and, even if he was disgraced, the American people still had the right to mourn. The true cause of death, however, would never be revealed. The chosen course of action was to maintain a slight distortion of the facts. Having to explain why a U.S. president and a terrorist were taking a road trip together certainly would have created a very messy scandal in a time of an extreme national crisis.

39
WHO IS JOHN DOE?

Max arrived back at her office flustered and frustrated. She was not ready to accept the possibility that Simon had not committed the crimes against the members of La Fratellanza, even if the facts suggested otherwise. One thing for sure was that she was positive the corpse had something to do with Simon. She had to identify the body. In her usual style, she zoomed past Doris and called out, "Get the Buffalo police chief back on the line."

The intercom light flashed and she went straight to line one. "Chief, can you check to see if a white male was reported missing or found dead, during the week of April third?"

"Hold on Max; let me pull it up on the screen." He retrieved the names straightaway. "Yes, there are three, all reported suicides. Typical around this time of the year. The Falls are a lure for the desperate and despondent. We call it the *Spring Cleaning* season," he chuckled.

"I fail to see the humor."

"Sorry, ma'am. But after doing this job as long as I have—you become a little cynical."

"Chief, male or female, please!"

"Right. All males."

"Email me their descriptions."

"Who are you looking for?"

She didn't think it wise to announce the autopsy results quite yet. "Thank you Chief; just playing out a hunch. Enjoy your day."

∽

Max heard the beep signaling the incoming mail. Flashed across the screen in bright yellow letters were the initials BPDNY. She retrieved the email and quickly scanned the files. None of the male descriptions came even close to that of the corpse. She had hoped the missing person was from Buffalo, making her job easier. Now she would have to tackle Interpol's FASTID system to widen her search, a search that would now have to include Canada. The Fast and Efficient International Disaster Victim Identification system was the only police database that identified missing persons on an international level.

She tapped furiously at the keyboard and expanded the search radius beyond the Buffalo area to encompass all counties surrounding Lake Erie and the Niagara River. Then narrowing down the search, she focused on persons reported missing within the specific time frame and typed "04/03/2017" and "04/30/2017" in the date range fields. Within seconds, one of twelve pages popped up on the screen. The entire list contained over one hundred names and photos. *The chief was right*, she thought; *the spring cleaning season is upon us.* Max knew that in New York State, in the prior year alone, over eight thousand adults had been reported missing. The unspeakable number of missing children was a staggering three-fold.

The screen displayed a photo and a name for each of the missing. For the moment, the photo served no purpose, except to give Max pause each time she saw the face of another child. Her heart wrenched as she thought, *I can't imagine how their families must feel.* Skillfully, she tapered her search further by entering the data for the height, hair color, eye color, and sex in the appropriate fields. Then she hit the *Enter* key. The list was rapidly reduced to seventeen missing persons. She scanned face after face for several pages until one made her flinch. The photo looked eerily familiar, and so was the name printed alongside it.

Without wasting a second, she split the screen on her display. On the right side, she retrieved the case file for Simon Hall. Then after scrolling through several pages, she finally located the report that was made on the day of his infamous jump. It was the testimony from the desk clerk at the Super 8 Motel in Defiance, Ohio. He had testified that a man fitting

Simon's description had checked in the night before. He had registered as Leon Miller. The name Max was viewing on the left side of the screen was the same name. *It could be a coincidence* was her momentary thought until she clicked on the name and retrieved the Missing Person report. Above the name was printed "April 3, 2017, Port Dover, Ontario." Below was a photo and description. Max studied the report.

DESCRIPTION

Date(s) of Birth Used:	December 21, 1976	Hair: Black
Place of Birth:	New York	Eyes: Dark Brown
Height:	6'5"	Sex: Male
Weight:	230 pounds	Race: White

Remarks: Leon Miller was last seen wearing ripped jeans and a gray "Abercrombie" brand shirt. He usually wears his hair just below the ears, parted to the left. There is a scar on his left knee from prior surgery. There are no other distinguishable marks.

THE DETAILS

Leon Miller was last seen leaving his home during the early morning hours of April 3, 2017. He is a commercial fisherman from Port Dover, Ontario. His family reported that his boat was missing from the nearby marina. He has not been seen or heard from since that time.

"Astonishing!" Max exclaimed. "Aside from the slight age difference, Simon and Leon could have been twins from their facial features alone."

Max reached for the phone.

"Hey, Doc, did you find any evidence of an old knee injury?"

"There was some boney scar tissue on the left femur a few inches above the patella, reminiscent of a football injury. It didn't seem important to my findings based on the other evidence. Where are you going with this, Max?"

"Would a commercial fisherman be a likely candidate for pitted keratolysis?"

"That would be one of the pitfalls, sorry, occupational hazard. What's the signif…"

Max cut him off. "The corpse's name was Leon Miller."

"Good work. What do you suspect happened?"

"Leon Miller was an alias of Simon's. And they look like they could be twins. Simon must have switched clothing with him, so there's definitely a connection between the two. The way I see it—Simon searched long and hard before he found the perfect candidate to help him escape."

"You think Simon shot him in the same location as his own gunshot wound, except pointed it upward to kill this Miller guy instantly? Huh, interesting theory."

"Exactly, an attempt to fake his own death. He must have sunk the boat, and with Miller inside. It's taken this long for the body to resurface and dry out."

"So Simon is still out there?"

Max didn't want to contemplate the answer. "I'll send you the specifics so you can contact the family. Call me after they claim the body."

"Will do."

Max sat back, all of a sudden feeling spent. It was late, her head was spinning, and she was more than ready to call it a night. But first, she had to let Stanton know what she had discovered.

cゐ

"Hey, how are you doing?" she asked, trying to seem lively.

"I'm fine, but you sound tired."

"I've been able to identify the body—It's not Simon."

He could tell from her voice that she was distraught, but her statement was resounding. Despite this fact, his trained mind needed verification. He had to ask, "Are you sure?"

Max filled Stanton in on the gruesome details of the autopsy and her discovery that the corpse belonged to a man named Leon Miller. "So Simon is still out there somewhere!" she bellowed.

"Hey Max, I thought there was no connection between the petty crimes and the possibility the corpse was Simon."

"I still have to consider the possibility!" she shouted again, unable to control her frustration.

"This is only a case. It's a bad idea to make it so personal. Why is it so upsetting to you anyway?"

"Simon's making it personal!"

"Whoa! Take a deep breath."

"I'm sorry, but I'm afraid that until we know Simon is dead, it will consume my thoughts like it has Noble's. I'm being pulled into the same mindset—like it or not."

"There's something more going on with you, Max. Level with me."

"Dammit! I'm angry that he dumped this case on me! Simon was Noble's nemesis. He was never supposed to be mine!" she blurted out.

"Feel better?"

Max didn't respond. Having just juggled her own reality and having answered her own gnawing question, she had nothing more to say on the subject.

Stanton wasn't sure his timing was right, but he took a shot. "Honey, why don't I come over?"

"Not tonight. This has been a bitch of a day," she answered, making no attempt to hide her mood any longer.

"I'll cook while you take a nice, long, hot bath and sip on a nice cool glass of Prosecco. There might even be a backrub available," was his final plea.

Stanton's right. I need to chillax. Besides how could I refuse such an offer? Maybe it's just what I need. "Okay," she relented, "Give me about an hour and then I'll meet you at my place."

"Hey, Max, I love you."

"Love you too."

40
THE FINAL SOLUTION

Ever since the president conferenced in the week before, one message had resonated loud and clear. It was delivered in the president's last words before he signed off: *I've placed the future of the nation in your hands. The only option is to succeed.* Although the words were unsettling, they had an all-encompassing effect on the group. Now they faced the ultimate challenge.

All the members of La Fratellanza were stressed to the limit. They were desperate to return to their families and to resume their normal lives, but it was not in the cards for at least another month. In four days' time, the president would arrive at the facility and the group would lay out their plan in its entirety. With a few more days of fine-tuning, the president would then deliver his speech. For the remaining weeks, they would continue to operate behind the scenes, literally below ground.

With military precision, Seymour would continuously spin out his infomercials. Chase would conduct the weekly surveys and ensure the media received the polling results. Noble would post the latest results on the website and share them with all social media networks. Hank and Paolo would monitor all the activities of the appointed commissions and draft statements for the president's weekly addresses. If Seymour's predictions were correct, and they most always were, positive signs would appear within weeks. Eventually, the day would come when La Fratellanza would resurface, but by then their lives will have changed forever, especially as they would continue to monitor the results of their master plan—albeit from the sidelines.

Noble sat back and watched as the group members shuffled their papers and scanned the data on their tablets. He fully recognized the sacrifices they had made and admired their determination. They doggedly trudged on with an honest desire to save their country. Now it was time to pool the results of their collective contributions into a cohesive plan and implement the Renaissance 2017 Project.

"Let's get started," Noble sounded off, garnering everyone's attention.

Chase stepped to the fore. "I've identified the key points from our discussions. Let's review each step to make sure we've covered all our bases. Hold on a moment—Let me pull them up." He swiped his tablet and the culmination of over two months' work was summarized by six bullet points on the monitor.

<u>RENAISSANCE 2017 PROJECT</u>

- SPENDING MORATORIUM
- REPEAL UNIVERSAL HEALTHCARE MANDATES and FINES
- SIMPLIFY INCOME TAX STRUCTURE
- REFORM ENTITLEMENT PROGRAMS
- MODIFY RENEWABLE ENERGY POLICIES
- ESTABLISH PRIVATE COMMSSIONS

Chase began to recap. "Starting with the first bullet, Congress will immediately freeze appropriations for all new spending bills until July 1, 2018. Also appropriations for all Pay-As-You-Go Programs that are not fully funded will be suspended for the same time period."

"Congress also needs to enforce the PAYGO guidelines," Hank insisted, and then strengthened his point by asserting, "Certainly, they need to differentiate between policies and politics and stop being sycophants to the special-interest groups."

Paolo, pleasantly surprised by Hank's apparent bipartisan declaration, agreed. "*Bravo*, Hank. They can't be allowed to punt anymore. Congress has to start running the ball."

"You two just gave me a great idea!" Seymour exclaimed, as his mind conjured up another image for an infomercial.

"I've included the PAYGO component on the website, showcasing all the programs that operate under a deficit," Noble informed.

Chase motioned back to the monitor, highlighting the second bullet point by running his finger across the sentence on his tablet. "According to my numbers, if the UHA mandates and fines are repealed, the loss in revenue can mostly be reclaimed by eliminating the fraud within Medicare and from the Earned Income Tax Credit claims. This also includes removing all ineligible applicants who signed up for the healthcare plan."

"And now comes a potentially problematic situation," Paolo noted, as he gestured to the next point.

Chase picked up and stated, "Personal income and corporate tax rates must be restored to Reagan Era percentages. By further reducing the number of advantageous corporate tax deductions, it will offset the proposed carbon tax and remove companies from the ranks of corporate welfare."

Seymour chimed in. "We also determined that any reductions in personal income taxes resulting from rate changes will be retroactive to January 1, 2017. The impact will be felt immediately by the American public."

"I have it noted," Chase indicated and continued to the next point. "Without a doubt, the greatest drain on government spending is entitlements. The programs must be reformed, particularly with the anti-poverty subsidies. It will also help to identify the illegal immigrants who are on the roster, placing further burdens on the system. Actions to legitimize or deport illegal immigrants must take place, no longer leaving them in limbo at taxpayer expense."

"Equally destructive to the economy and job growth is the next bullet." Seymour noted. "All Environmental Protection Agency policies must be reviewed for cost effectiveness, benefits, and timing. The EPA has been placed in a choice position, allowing policies to be imposed without scrutiny."

Noble agreed. "Thanks to the Baari administration, the clever use of the Clear Act provision gave a non-cabinet post *carte blanche* to impose regulations, allowing the EPA to become not only the enforcer but the judge."

"Wearing my nonpartisan suit, at the very least, all timeframes placed on companies to conform to renewable energy standards must be extended," Seymour inserted, and then threw it back to Noble. "Ta-da! The next and last issue is your brainchild."

"Not mine alone. Privatization of government functions that belong in the private sector is nothing new, but having been kicked around over the years, the idea has never passed muster. There's no denying that it's proved to be a successful option for many state and local governments. And let's not ignore the numerous countries that have privatized activities with great success. But first and foremost, a commission will be established to sort out the likely activities and the associated cost impact."

"I'm in agreement," Hank stepped in, somewhat surprising the others once again, revealing his new magnanimity. "Neutral commissions should be established for each of the areas we've targeted. I've been giving this some thought," he announced. "I know this has been a formula for failure in the past, but by imposing rigid controls and strict timetables, it could prove successful. I'd suggest each commission be comprised of eight senators and eight congresspersons, divided equally between the two parties. Then each party would enlist four retired CEOs from a Fortune 500 company. It would provide a bipartisan commission with private-sector input."

Noble sat still a moment and then, with an arched eyebrow, he stated, "That could work. I can add a tab to the website for each of the commissions and then publish their mission statements, timetables, *et cetera*. I'll design it so the minutes from the meetings can easily be published online. Transparency must underlie all that we do."

"I'd like to add one more member to each commission—a lobbyist," Paolo suggested with a little added gusto, knowing he'd get some backlash.

"You can't be serious," Chase stated. "You're inviting the fox into the henhouse."

"Strange as it may seem, Paolo has a point," Hank submitted. "Lobbyists are probably the most singularly expert on a specific subject. They tend to focus on a cause or two and grasp the specifics in minute detail." Directing his question back to Paolo, he reiterated, "Many of whom are your clients. Would you be able to put together a list of names by the industry they represent? People you believe have the integrity to shed their biases, and the capacity to serve objectively on a committee with members of Congress?"

"We're only suggesting six commissions be established. There's a wide assortment of competent, scrupulous lobbyists to select from. It will require some fine-grain screening, but it can be done."

"Chase?" Paolo asked, attempting to solicit his support.

"You don't have to convince me. But you will have to convince the president and gain the confidence of the American public."

"Now that it all appears amenable to everyone, I also have a suggestion, rather an exception," Seymour added, and then he proposed, "She's not exactly a CEO, but I think that Maryann Townsend would be an asset on the Universal Healthcare Commission. She's worked on the Act from inception in her role as the First Lady, and will bring a unique perspective, now that she has spent time in the private sector. It will be her act of redemption."

The others couldn't hold back their smiles at the prospect.

Paolo particularly liked the idea. "I'll add that to the president's speech. It will allow him to toss out an olive branch, even if she throws it back at him."

The time finally arrived for Noble to ask the trillion-dollar question. "Seymour, can you make a cogent argument to convince the American people that this is their way to salvation?"

Seymour didn't react immediately, which was unusual for him, making it all the more a nail-biter. Then, with characteristic ease, he boasted, "Piece of cake. I told you from the start—In the end it will all be about the message."

They knew from his tone of voice that his piece of cake could be more than any of them could chew. But surprisingly it didn't have a negative impact, especially on Chase.

"We're gonna make this happen!" he broadcasted loudly, as if he were a coach in the locker room.

"Looks like I've got my work cut out for me as well," Paolo acknowledged with an unexpected sigh of relief.

"The dynamic speech should be short and to the point, without a lot of fanfare," Noble cautioned. "I know this president, and he doesn't mince words." Noble glanced at Hank and noted the naughty-boy look on his face, and asked, "Yes, Mr. Kramer?"

Maintaining his mischievous expression, Hank replied, "There's nothing in the constitution that states the vice president and the speaker of the house must sit behind the president when he is at the podium speaking to the Congress."

The others listened curiously trying to figure out what Hank had up his sleeve.

"During the president's speech, they should sit in the chamber with the rest of the members of Congress. The president could emphasize that he's speaking to all Americans, including everyone present before him. He might even want to add that on this occasion he doesn't require a cheerleader behind him, nor does the opposition."

The others chuckled while Paolo exclaimed, "*Buon idea!*" He was falling back on his Italian in a moment of elation.

"Nice touch," Noble admitted, and then on a more serious note, he warned, "We have just three more days to wrap this up. I'll have the website ready; what say all of you?"

"I'm just polishing off the speech, with a few additional lines," Paolo noted, as he winked at Hank.

Seymour raised his right hand. "All the infomercials are about ninety percent complete. Hank and I will have them ready for your viewing the day after tomorrow. We'll still have time for some final editing."

"I'll need a little time tomorrow to work on the surveys I've created for polling purposes," Chase indicated, and then asked, "Seymour, can you make time to review them?"

"No sweat. But Noble, are you going to have the secure feed ready by the time we start blasting the airwaves?"

"It will be ready. There will be no trace back. Also the links into the Civic Analytics' and Catalist's databases will be operational."

"Noble, doesn't that border on illegal?" Hank asked with his hallmark grin.

La Fratellanza were familiar with both companies having heavily used their services to promote the election of Baari. The data-mining techniques proved invaluable to create the appropriate voter-information databases for a miniscule of targeted segments of the population.

"They'll earn their reward when the country is back on course," Noble replied. As if on cue, he was saved by the flashing red light that momentarily distracted the group.

They were all startled, having not realized the late hour. It was eight o'clock and Jax was his usual prompt self, arriving with their dinner.

"Anything else we need to review?" Noble asked as he gave Hank the evil eye.

"We've got it covered," Chase stated with confidence, also eager to end the discussion.

"Then you guys go freshen up. I'll help Jax set up in here," Noble volunteered.

They gladly obliged.

41
COUNTDOWN

For the past sixty-one days, the group had dissected, debated, and deliberated the issues they found responsible for the country's woes. And after the last seventy-two exhaustive hours, which blended into seamless days and nights, with few breaks—they had finalized all the necessary steps to implement the Renaissance 2017 Project.

Now the moment of reckoning had arrived. As the members of La Fratellanza sat around the table, and fixated on the empty, newly placed regal chair, memories quickly resurfaced, as each, in his own way, brought to mind another time when they took on the impossible—and succeeded.

Noble bore witness as he watched them, apparently absorbed, reflecting on their past accomplishment. He also reflected, but on more recent events—those encompassing Simon. He wrestled with the reality that once again, he was anointed to lead the charge to save the country from a national disaster. This time there was not a single face to place on the hydra-headed enemy.

Watching the time, Noble said, "The president will be here in fifteen minutes." Then he urged them to get up and loosen their bodies and minds. "You're all looking a wee bit uptight."

"I'll go brew some fresh coffee," Chase offered, "my eye-opener special."

The others kicked into motion.

On schedule the red light flashed above the chamber entrance. They knew this time it was not Jax and quickly headed to stand next to their chairs. Suddenly, the doors parted.

"Welcome, Mr. President," Noble greeted, as he clasped the outstretched hand.

The president then proceeded to greet the others in a similar fashion. After making his way around the table he pointed to the attention-getting chair, and asked, "May I sit here?"

"Yes, sir," Hank replied. Being the closest, he summarily pulled the chair out as a show of respect.

Once the president was seated, the others followed suit.

As scripted, Chase began. "Mr. President, in our last conference meeting we identified several overall areas that must be addressed, either by a change in policy or remedial legislation. But you'll note up on the monitor we've pared it down to the top six most far-reaching issues that will have the greatest impact. We're convinced that job creation and a strong economy will provide the impetus we need for sustained growth."

He gave the president a moment to review the bullet points on the monitor. Then Chase reviewed each point supported by tangible evidence to support their recommendations for restructuring.

"You're asking for drastic reforms," he observed. "First off, I find it highly improbable that I'll be able to convince Congress to invoke a spending freeze—and I will not resort to using the executive pen. The weapon of choice for my predecessor."

"Sir, I'd like to hold off on the process for the moment."

"Continue."

Chase looked in Hank's direction, who picked up on the cue.

"Mr. President, we recommend that commissions be established for each of the issues identified. It's our strong belief that spending must be tackled first and foremost to reduce the tax burden on individuals and corporations—the major impediment to job growth and economic stability."

"Hank, commissions take excessive time and in the end they tend to become political fora bearing little tangible results."

Hank gave a nod to the president and then proceeded to explain the makeup of the commissions, along with the stringent guidelines and strict timetables that would be imposed.

The president seemed unconvinced.

"Granted, you've zeroed in on the target problems that plague the economy, but I'm still unclear as to how this will stop the downward spiraling. The first bullet point is indeed a start, but I only have a razor-slim majority. I know with certainty that a handful of my own guys might not endorse an across-the-board spending freeze." The president appeared even more dubious.

"Sir, if I may?" Seymour asked.

"Go on, Mr. Lynx; your ideas are usually scintillating."

"We need to unbutton the shirt collar on conservatism. Quite honestly, sir, your administration's message should have been more strident. With all due respect, you did win the election, but not the popular vote. To reach the American public this time around in a moment of crisis, we believe they'll be more receptive to a positive message that offers them genuine hope. We're in a battle to win their hearts and minds. The past failures have conditioned them for a message of honesty and competence. This time around the message needs to be cool to be convincing."

Seymour was in his stride—He had the president's attention. He moved in with his fastball pitch.

"With a successful campaign the American people may be swayed to support programs that offer them a glimmer of realistic hope. History shows that revolutions are based on hope, not hopelessness, and our ideas are revolutionary. But in the end, we are confident Congress will be forced to act."

"Seymour, along with the rest of your brethren, you do not carry the reputation of being impractical. But how can you be so certain?"

"With much chagrin, sir—We've done it before."

For the first time, the president softened his expression. "I'm well aware of your accomplishments, although it's the results that will keep me in the Oval Office."

Seymour, feeling he was back in the game, said, "Sir, if you will indulge me for a moment longer." He quickly placed the first of his infomercials on the monitor and then flashed through each one of them in succession.

The president sat back and watched intently.

The others watched the president.

"How many taxpayers' dollars does it cost to screw in a light bulb? Clever," the president stated with a pained expression, and then he acknowledged, "Although I do like the way you revamped *The Life of*

Julia." He paused. "Okay—I understand your micro-granulated market analysis that leaves no person untagged. And I understand you'll bombard the airwaves as you did in the past in an attempt to garner the support of our citizens. But how does that translate in to forcing Congress to act?"

Chase tackled the answer. "Mr. President, that goes back to your original question as to how the Congress can be convinced to invoke a spending freeze." Noting the receptiveness on the president's face, he explained in detail how he would personally conduct full-cycle surveys weekly to plumb the mood of the public. "I will then feed the polling results to the media outlets selectively. I'm confident that, with our laser-like questions targeting the appropriate population segments, we can convey a clear and honest message that will reveal support for our approach. The polls will prove to Congress that their best recourse is to join in the reforms. Sir, we believe the American public will give you the year you need to implement the necessary legislative changes."

Hank ventured back into the conversation. "Think of this as more than a political campaign, but a formula for success based on transparency and reality."

"Hank, the campaign trail is hardly cold. Yet, there are some residual sores that haven't healed." The president smiled for the second time and then nodded to encourage Hank to continue.

"Speaking from experience, sir, we need to marshal forces, just as we did during our get-out-the-vote campaign. No question, we need to target the *Jon Stewart* followers—the Milleniums and Gen-Xers. Representatives from your administration must appear on the major news segments to sell the various reforms. Communities must be organized to get out the message. I can use my Chestnut Foundation to initiate some of the drives. We'll pass out T-shirts scrawled with 'Renaissance 2017' and create walking billboards. We must generate a wave—a movement."

"Hank, if I may," Seymour interjected. "Sir, this is a movement—a cause to restore America's greatness. In addition to our other tools, we will utilize Thunderclap, the best crowd-speaking platform on the Internet. We'll create a campaign with a compelling message about the rebirth of America. Our citizens will be inspired to share the message with millions of people around the globe. World economies are inextricably intertwined. This could possibly establish a model for other countries and will demonstrate our strength as a nation."

The president took note of both Hank's and Seymour's exuberance, but admitted, "In all honesty, I find marketing the future of country rather distasteful, as though it was the latest iPhone release."

Hank took the opportunity to respond. "We assure you, Mr. President; this is not purely economics and unfortunately it will come down to politics—that calls for a full-court press of communication tactics, using every media. We need to appeal to the young, the minorities, and the female voters, the ones who have given up. I wish I could say it's just the sign of our times, but this method of getting out the message is here to stay. It's how business is conducted."

Noble sensed the president found the realities uninviting and cut Hank off. "Sir, tactics are a necessary means to accomplish the goal, but you have our word there will be no obfuscation. The message will be truthful and straightforward." He swiped his tablet and the home page of the website appeared on the monitor. "This is the Renaissance 2017 website that will provide all the information on the purpose, the method, and the expected results that will be derived from the reforms. The infomercials, social networking sites, and other means of messaging will point the public to this valuable resource, where they can learn and understand the issues in an honest concise format."

The president watched the various web pages on the large display as Noble ran through their features. The others spent the time studying the president's various expressions. All appeared to signal a mild acceptance.

"Sir, your speech will trigger the campaign. At that moment, everything will move into high gear," Paolo stated. "I've taken the liberty of emailing a copy of the speech to your private email address. You possess the only other copy."

"Ah yes, I must not forget you, Mr. Salvatore. Give me the gist of the message, Paolo, and we'll review it in detail later."

"Sir, the speech will be short and succinct. I've timed it to take approximately twenty minutes. Primarily, you appeal to the American people for their support to help you reform their government. It speaks to how we must learn from historic mistakes and how we can't spend our way to prosperity. You single out the overspending, fraud, and abuse and how it stands in the way of any future tax relief. The overriding message will ring loud—to restore jobs and the economy. You will implore Congress to do their job and follow through on the people's wishes." Paolo continued to elaborate on a few other points and then stopped, noting that the president appeared nonplussed. Even after mentioning the symbolic revamped seating arrangement for the vice president and majority leader, the president remained expressionless.

Uneasiness prevailed at the table.

"Mr. President." Seymour stepped forward, willing to brave a potential storm. "You may recall that we asked you in our prior meeting to enlist your press secretary to leak information to the media. This will broaden the reach of the message by giving the news outlets a heads-up on the speech. This should also induce viewers to tune in. Immediately following your speech, everyone with an electronic message device, be it a TV, computer, handheld device or whatever, will receive the first infomercial I showed about the Renaissance being the rebirth of America. That will be the start of the massive communications campaign we have planned—a plan to create a movement that Hank and I alluded to earlier."

All remained silent, sitting on edge, awaiting the president's response.

After moments of contemplation and still burdened somewhat with doubt, the president spoke out. "Despite all your hocus-pocus, you're asking me to make a promise to the American people that I can keep. That's a formidable task by any measure." Then, shifting his direction, he looked directly at Noble. "How can I be sure all of this will happen just as you say and with the intended results?"

"Sir, I don't mean to make light of your question, but Seymour is correct. It's all about getting out a valid message that is supported by honesty and transparency. You recognize this group as having the tools and a proven record." Noble realized he was going for broke in what may have been the last opportunity he'd have to give the president advice on this matter. He paused briefly before making his next statement. Then with great sincerity, he declared, "I've spent two months in solitude with these gifted men. I have full confidence the plan will succeed, notwithstanding the headwinds we face."

The others were blown away by Noble's compliments, but refrained from acting.

The president stood up.

Instinctively, the others rose from their chairs eagerly, awaiting his closing words.

"You have my blessing," the president said, "but you might consider soliciting some additional support and ask God to join forces to help you save the country."

The president shook their hands warmly and walked out of the chamber. The group remained in a paralytic stance as the reality set in—They had just received the green light.

42
THE ART OF FUGUE

The days seemed to be getting longer to Max with each new discovery, adding to her concern about flying solo. But as soon as she entered her apartment she began to relax. As part of her normal routine, she first kicked off her shoes and then tossed the day's mail onto the ever-increasing stack. *Odd*, she thought, as she noticed that the pile had been moved. She glanced toward the kitchen and spotted it on the counter. *Hmm, Stanton must have moved the mail when he was here last night. Oh well*, she thought, and thrust the envelopes onto the pile.

Retreating into the bedroom, she changed into a pair of sweats and pinned her hair up off her neck. Magically, the stress began to recede further. "One last gesture and I'll be totally at ease," she said, thinking aloud, a frequent occurrence when at home alone. She walked into the kitchen and uncorked a bottle of Capannelle Chianti. Then she poured herself a glass of wine and moved into the living room. Once curled up on the sofa, she began the arduous task of sorting through the mail, hoping that the majority was the usual junk. Then, just as she ripped open the second envelope her smartphone rang.

"Hey you, what a pleasant *not-so* surprise."

"Wow, you sound in a good mood. That is a pleasant surprise."

"Sorry, I've been so on edge. But last night was wonderful."

"Just what your secret agent man ordered. Like another backrub?"

"It's so tempting, but I have to do some boring *life stuff* tonight. Like get rid of a couple weeks of mail. By the way, did you move the pile that was on the table in the foyer?"

"No, why would I?"

"Duh! I guess I moved it and didn't remember. I'm really losing it."

"Go pour yourself a glass of wine and I'll catch you tomorrow."

"Already did. Thanks for being so understanding."

"Love you."

"Love you too."

Max took a few more sips of wine and enjoyed the warm soothing feeling in her throat, along with the sensation in her relaxed neck muscles. And after discovering the majority of the mail was junk, she was in heaven. "Just a few more pieces of mail to go!" she spoke out again with glee. The next one she happened to pick up was a brown CD jacket with no markings. Inside was a CD with no label. "You slippery devil, you did move the mail, making sure I'd find the CD." Max smiled as she thought about her rough, tough, ex-military, and now-secret-agent man. At times, he could be a real romantic. "What's my problem?" she asked herself as she walked over to the stereo. She inserted the CD and hit the *Play* button. Curled up back on the sofa, she poured herself another glass of wine and prepared herself to be wooed.

As she listened, she found the melody quite pleasant. But halfway through the track, there was a repetition of cacophony she found intrusive. At times, it sounded like the music score from a Bela Lugosi movie, not what one would consider romantic. "What was he thinking?" Max questioned, as she continued to listen, waiting for his hidden message. "Surely, it's there somewhere. It can't be that subliminal." But by the last track, Max had become restive. "This sounds so familiar."

She used the remote to select the *Repeat* option and listened to the CD several more times, almost obsessively, as though it were an intoxicant. It wasn't the wine consumption; that had ceased some time ago.

Then on the fourth go-around, she sprang up from her sofa. "Oh, no!" she called out and raced to the CD cabinet. She tossed case after case onto the floor until she found the CD she was searching for. By that time she was frantic. Hastily, she exchanged the CD for the one playing. Then seated, that time on the floor, she slowed down her breathing and listened one more time.

"Oh my God. It's Bach's *Art of Fugue.*"

A sudden flashback of her interview with Simon's mother came to the fore. She grabbed her phone instinctively to call Noble, until she realized he was unavailable. "Damn you!" she shouted, and then hit the speed dial for Stanton.

∽

"Hi hon, change your mind?" he asked coyly, knowing it was a long shot.

"Yes! Come over right away!"

"Are you okay? You sound upset."

"Please, come as quickly as you can."

∽

Max remained seated on the floor, frozen in place while her mind spun like a top. She could hear Simon's mother's voice describing his obsession with Bach as a child. It was the crucial clue that led Noble to locate Simon's failsafe code, which he had buried in the operating system of several of the nation's electrical grids. It allowed Noble to foil Simon's plot and to avert a national disaster. She replayed it in her mind, recalling the day Noble explained how he had used Bach's combinatorial permutation to break the failsafe code. The CD for Bach's *Art of Fugue* was also found in Simon's car on the bridge.

"This can't be happening. Stanton, where the hell are you?" she pleaded aloud. Still seated on the floor, now clutching her knees, she rocked back and forth. All of a sudden, weird thoughts began racing through her mind: Greek philosophers, Pythagoras's *Table of Opposites*, and Bach's use of the Pythagorean philosophical principles in his compositions, largely in the *Art of Fugue*. She remembered at the time it was pretty wild stuff, but Noble described how the premise behind comparing opposites, such as right and left, or odd and even, led him to decipher Simon's code.

Suddenly, the sound of the doorbell interrupted her thoughts. Her heart rate began to recede. She pulled herself up off the floor and rushed toward the door. "Forgot your key, Agent?" she called out.

43
A MESSAGE FROM THE GRAVE

La Fratellanza were pleased with themselves. Once again, they pulled off the impossible, knowing they had a wall of colossal challenges facing them. The president had signed on to their plan and the theme of his speech to the nation. Paolo, with the help of the others, had written the most inspiring speech of his lifetime. And without grandeur, they would return home having had their own experience of a lifetime that could never be shared, but a grateful nation would be their reward. However they were not heading home quite yet.

"Finish up; we only have a few hours before lift-off," Noble rallied. "We'll be watching the televised speech on our monitors. So the moment the president ends his speech, you'll all move into action."

"The first infomercial is ready for prime time," Seymour signaled.

"Chase, are you all set?"

"The target audience is selected and the poll is ready to roll."

Noble had been pretty tough throughout trying to keep them focused, especially during the last stretch. He thought now was an appropriate time to compliment the group on all they had accomplished. "You've all worked hard for this moment. And you should all be proud."

"Aw, gee, Noble, thanks," Paolo kidded.

The other members of La Fratellanza broke out in a cheer, patting one another on the back. Noble sensed they were beginning to feel redeemed.

In the course of their victory lap, the secure phone rang.

Noble excused himself and took the call.

∽

"Max is gone!"

"What?" he reacted, hiding his alarm that mirrored the shock in Stanton's voice.

Stanton explained the phone call from Max. "Something spooked her and she asked me to come right over. When I arrived, she was gone. And she's not answering her smartphone." Stanton recognized that Noble was not free to react, so he continued to explain that the lights were left on, a wine glass had been tipped over, and a CD was still playing. He hesitated. "Noble, it was the *Art of Fugue.*"

Noble gulped, loud enough for Stanton to detect.

"I know what you're thinking—Simon's alive. Max believed the same. I told her she was becoming paranoid. Did she tell you about the stalker?"

"Yes."

"I saw the face, what little was exposed—It wasn't Simon."

"I'm leaving the facility now; I'll take the copter. Meet me in my office in thirty minutes."

"I have to leave," Noble shouted out to the others.

"You'll miss the crescendo," Seymour shouted back.

Noble, not responding, dashed out of the facility leaving the others only to speculate.

∽

Once outside the facility, he placed his xPhad in the secure sleeve. It began to vibrate rapidly as it downloaded a series of messages and notifications—all that had piled up waiting for the signal. It took him a moment to weed through all of them looking for one from Max. "There it is." He hit the envelope. The message read **MAX IS WAITING FOR YOU** ☾. Operating in high gear, Noble used the same App tracking device he used to locate Simon in Salt Lake City. He hurriedly sent a message, replying to the original SMS text. It read **SEE YOU SOON!** As the message was sent to the receiver, the tracking device would be able to locate the exact location of the sender's smartphone. It was in the process of receiving the message. Literally nanoseconds later, the following coordinates appeared on his device: **LATITUDE 38° 51' 55.6445 LONGITUDE 77° 4' 26.6484**. With record speed, he converted it to an address. "Son of a bitch." He called Stanton immediately. "Simon has Max. I want you and two of your best sharpshooters to meet me at this location. I'm sending it to you now."

Stanton picked up the address on his cell. "I'll be damned! That's down the street from the Pentagon."

"Stand down until I arrive."

44
THE KILLSHOT

Using their thermal imaging riflescopes, the SWAT team was able to determine that only two figures were in the home, both in the front room and positioned near each other. The SWAT team had already gingerly walked across the roof of the ranch-style home to confirm there were no other inhabitants. Once they signaled the all clear they moved in stealthily.

The front door was left ajar. They assumed it was intentional, presumably by Simon. Stanton was the first to enter, brandishing his sidearm. Noble followed closely behind, unarmed. The SWAT team remained stationed outside the windows facing into the front and side of the living room, each with a clear shot. No one was taking chances with Max's life.

Noble hid the tension he felt as he stared at Max bound and gagged in the chair nestled in the corner. A light had been purposely placed over her head to illuminate the scene. Off to the side was a shadowy figure, and although it was difficult to identify the silhouette, Noble surmised who it was.

"Simon, step out into the light where we can see you," Noble ordered.

Everyone stood in place with tensions rising, as the figure came out of the shadow and moved slowly toward Max.

What the hell, he thought, completely dumbfounded. Noble immediately ordered, "Step away from Max, and put your hands out where I can see them."

"In due time, Director," came the cunning reply from a surprising voice.

"I don't understand. Why you?" Noble questioned, still baffled by the scene.

"For starters, you killed the former president. You ordered them to kill Abner Baari!"

"You're wrong. We have the shell casing to prove the bullet did not come from any of the agents or Canadian Mounties on the bridge. That left only one person who could have fired the shot. Let's quit the idle talk—Where's Simon?" Noble demanded, but in a controlled manner.

"He survived the fall, after having brilliantly planned every step down to the second. Simon estimated the height, the angle to jump, and which way the currents would drift him toward the boat he had waiting for him."

"You mean Leon Miller's boat?" he asked cautiously, watching for the slightest movement.

"Yes, he couldn't believe his fortune in finding the perfect lookalike to help him escape. It was a flawless backup plan if he couldn't make his way into Canada. What he hadn't counted on—was to be shot."

"He wouldn't have been shot had he not shot Baari first. Again—step away from Max."

"Director, aren't you curious as to where Simon is?"

Noble remained silent, negotiating the situation skillfully. He allowed the conversation to flow calmly for the moment. He couldn't afford a rush act with Max's life still in imminent danger. He stood up straighter and his voice took on a calmer edge. "So where is Simon?"

Stanton took his cue. He knew Noble was going to take it slow and easy.

"He's dead!" shouted the half-shadowy figure. "He broke his back in the fall and suffered internal damage. But he lived long enough to help me set the stage, so I could carry out his ultimate revenge. True to Simon's M.O., he had planned it long before that day on the bridge."

Simon is really dead. It took Noble a moment to let it sink in. Then he thought, *Is that what he meant by Act Three?* But for the moment, there was a more pressing question. "Why are you involved? I don't understand why you'd get mixed up in this."

"Because you ruined my life, just as you destroyed Simon's. First, you forced the president to resign in disgrace and then you destroyed my political career. That alone caused a firestorm in the press, plastering my face everywhere. You may recall a certain car salesmen in Salt Lake City. Well, he finally connected the dots and started to blackmail me to add to my woes. The day Simon died I swore I would carry out his plan, with a few added steps."

"Is that why you went after Natalie and Amanda?"

"They were just for sport." A callous smile surfaced and then out of nowhere a gun appeared at Max's head.

"You didn't lure me here to kill Max. I'm the one who destroyed your life. Let her go!"

Noble made no headway.

Without warning, an index finger emerged on the trigger. "This is for the man I loved. This is for Simon."

Max's eyes widened in a pleading stare.

Pop was the only sound from the single shot that pierced through the menacing assassin's forehead.

The former First Lady and senator—Maryann Townsend—was dead.

Stanton, with his unmistakable accuracy, had fired the fatal shot.

Not missing a beat, the SWAT team immediately moved in to secure the crime scene.

Noble heaved a sigh of relief as he looked over toward Max unharmed. "It's finally over," he said, as he rushed to her side. It was apparent, as she sat gagged and bound in the chair next to the corpse, that shock had begun to set in. Hurriedly, he released Max from her bonds and wiped the blood spatter from her face. On impulse, Noble pulled her to her feet and held her tightly in an attempt to keep her calm. Max's arms responded in kind.

At the same time, he ordered Stanton to go to the Capitol. "In forty-five minutes, the president will speak to the nation. You must inform him about the senator's death before he begins." He knew that the planned statement referring to Senator Townsend must be stricken from the president's speech.

With the SWAT team swirling around the scene, Noble had yet to release Max from his embrace. He could still feel her body tremble as she clung to him. Suddenly, overcome with an unexpected emotion, he whispered, "Thank God; I thought I had lost you forever."

In that instant, Stanton turned and looked at her. Their eyes met. His expression reflected no trace of shock or anger, only sorrow. Much to his dismay he realized that at that moment, she was no longer his.

45
THE PRESIDENT'S SPEECH

Stanton, still dealing with his inner fog generated by the traumatic crime scene he had just left, managed to work his way through the Secret Service detail. He reached the president, only minutes before he was slated to speak to the nation.

"Mr. President, Senator Townsend has been shot and killed," he reported, in a hushed voice.

"Oh my God, how can you be sure?"

"Sir—I fired the fatal shot." In a rapid pace, he updated the president on the circumstances.

Then, placing the horrific news aside, the president had no choice but to enter the congressional chambers and face the nation. He took a few moments to brace himself. Then he squared his shoulders and walked to the podium with a firm resolve.

He was instantly greeted by traditional applause, as only Congress could muster.

Now, standing at the podium, the president waited for the crowd to settle down. Then he began.

"Mr. Speaker, Mr. Vice President, Members of Congress, my fellow Americans."

As the president delivered his opening greeting, the empty chairs behind him did not go unnoticed. Nor did the sight of the vice president and majority leader squirming uncomfortably in their seats next to the Supreme Court justices—not in their usual exalted perch.

He dismissed the questioning stares and looked over a sea of skeptical faces and spoke.

"For those seated in the rear of the chamber, rest assured the
vice president and the majority speaker are in attendance.
However, throughout the duration of my presidency when I
am speaking in these chambers, the usual cheerleaders will
not be seated behind me, but will be seated among their
fellow members of Congress."

There were slight chuckles among the crowd, but it was obvious
from the expression on the faces of the vice president and the majority
speaker that they were discomfited.

"When I address the Congress and the nation, the focus
must be placed on my words, not on any choreographed
reactions."

[CIVIL APPLAUSE]

"Tonight, I come to the podium with a heavy heart
as I speak to the citizens of our great nation who are
suffering. Whether it be from the lack of jobs, unaffordable
healthcare, or government mismanagement, we have suffered
unprecedented hardships. We all know our country is sadly
divided on these issues.

There are several root causes, some obvious, others more
insidious. Part of the division stems from special interests that
have segmented our population. I won't deny the fact that the
mere existence of the prevailing disagreements in our society
are no more than an expression of the freedoms and liberties
we enjoy in our great nation. To challenge issues is one of our
basic freedoms. But when power and influence overshadow
the will of the people, they ignore the common good—the
foundation on which our government was designed. The
freedoms we cherish are threatened by our unstable economy,
staggering national debt, and the lack of jobs for our citizens,
all of which are untenable and have created unrest. Our
national security continues to face undue risk, as exemplified
by our failure to thwart terrorism and infectious disease
pandemics, giving rise to fears. We have not achieved energy
independence despite abundant oil and coal resources. All of
these issues add to the conflicting points of public view.

We are a weakened nation that has lost her stature in the
eyes of our friends and enemies throughout the world. They
have come to believe we are unable to stand strong and firm,

as we have historically. Our image as the world leader has
faded. If we are to regain our place as a world leader, the days
of vacillating on crucial issues are now declared over. The
do-nothing Congress will be brought back to life. The spending
beyond our means will be replaced by common sense."

[MILD APPLAUSE]

"Since I have taken office, I've met with congressional
leaders of both parties in the White House to adopt a more
partisan approach to problem-solving, one that does not cater
to special interests. There have been some sharp disagreements
in these meetings, but thus far, no bloodshed. Make no
mistake; my allegiance is to one special interest group—to the
citizens of the United States of America. As President, I govern
for all of our citizens—that is non-debatable.

[POLITE APPLAUSE]

"Tonight, I pledge to the American people—a pledge your
government will keep."

The president noted the shuffling of seats, absent of any ovation,
as though the audience were preparing itself for the customary "Trust
Me" riposte.

He continued.

"I'll work with Congress to send to pasture the infamous
pen used to issue executive orders. I will insist elected
representatives represent the will of the people. I will
dedicate myself to push for sweeping reforms to eliminate
the malfunctioning of the past government and to return our
nation to her greatness. Together in concert with Congress, I
will execute plans to stop wasteful spending and to put into
place tax simplification to provide relief to individuals and
corporations. Past insincere promises and their attendant
failures are being replaced by plans of action.

There was no applause, but the muffled gasps and constant shuffling
about were noticeable. The president suspected the crowd's mental
calculators were in overdrive trying to determine the feasibility of such
a strategy. He gave them time to ponder briefly.

"I am sitting on a parcel of specific remedial proposals

to attack the major issues. Over the next few weeks, there will be a series of infomercials to reach out to enlist the support of all our fellow citizens for the positive approaches on which we are embarking. Our goal is to provide clarity and understanding of our programs so everyone will have adequate information to form an opinion. All of us must share a common cause. It is the cornerstone of an open government that operates close to the people."

[MILD APPLAUSE]

"I will establish bipartisan commissions to review the policies regarding healthcare, climate change, and energy, to execute my action plans objectively, and to play a major role in the introduction of major reforms. Status quo is not acceptable. The members of the commissions will be selected in conjunction with both the minority and majority leaders in both Houses. I will personally appoint business leaders from the private sector in consultation with congressional leaders. Strict guidelines and timetables will be enforced and all actions will be fast-tracked. These proceedings will not be televised, but the transcripts will be made available online to the public."

[UNENTHUSIASTIC APPLAUSE]

"Many listening tonight experienced the Great Depression. All of us have been through its progeny, the Great Recession. We must learn from our mistakes. It's unfortunate that we did not respect the old axiom that we can't spend our way to prosperity. It is my responsibility to serve as the executive branch leader. This is where the buck stops. But I can't do it alone. Congress must fulfill its legislative responsibilities delegated to them. Both houses must work together to put our fiscal house in order.

We must stop the government wheels from spinning before the treads tatter. With the promise of tax relief, it will begin to help pave the surface for a smoother future."

The president noticeably looked down away from the head-on camera. Staring directly at the members of Congress, he admonished,

"For those of you in the chamber, this is not a time to showboat, but a time to carry out your responsibilities, as you were elected to do by your constituents. You'll have one year from today to pass the appropriate legislation. This is your opportunity to recapture the respect for your government. This is your opportunity to restore American's standing throughout the word with friends and foe alike. Don't squander this moment in history."

[STONE SILENCE]

Looking once again, straight up into the camera, he continued to address the nation.

"Let's work together to usher in a new era to restore our nation's greatness. Together, let's usher in the era of the Renaissance of America. Let's resolve to match our actions with our resources. We can look back one day and proclaim this is the time we picked ourselves up by the bootstraps to regain our niche in the world. All of us will benefit, but especially our children and grandchildren."

"God bless you, and God bless the United States of America."

[STANDING OVATION]

The president's speech was short and succinct. It lasted exactly 24 minutes, including the rather modest applause. Now the applause in the chamber was deafening.

Then it stopped.

The hand clapping had been replaced by the vibrating hums coming from the smartphone in the crowd, signaling an incoming message. It had all but dissipated as the president walked down the center aisle and headed for the exit. When he went to eye the crowd to offer a smile of gratitude, he instead encountered something quite astonishing.

The entire audience appeared to be glued to their individual handheld devices in unison, as they watched the first 30-second infomercial introducing Renaissance 2017. The president, deeply gratified by the sight, envisioned people all across the U.S. viewing the same message simultaneously. Now able to avoid the anticipated line of handshakes, he quickly maneuvered out of the congressional chamber with the secret service entourage in tow.

∽

As they scurried out of the building, Stanton was the first to commend the president on his performance. "Congratulations, Sir, on the standing ovation. Especially from the other side of the aisle."

The president smiled. "Don't be fooled; it wasn't so much for me as it was for their constituents who were tuned in."

Within minutes, they approached the motorcade waiting to drive them back to the White House. Both had noticed that the night's warm, sticky air had remained from the earlier hours. It was 8:37 p.m.

Then for some inexplicable reason, as the president was about to enter the limo, he glanced back at the monumental structure from where they had just departed. He was thunderstruck. At that very moment, he observed one of God's most glorious canvasses. The Capitol radiated in a spectacular golden hue as the skies opened up and the sun melted slowly into the horizon. Totally overwhelmed, the president pointed toward the sky and declared, "There's a message there for all of us."

"Yes, Mr. President," Stanton replied, equally awestruck by the specter.

Maintaining his gaze, the president pronounced, "Our country's future shines bright."

EPILOGUE

Six weeks had passed and there were signs of a slight improvement in the economic momentum as the markets stabilized. La Fratellanza had been finally escorted back to their home cities to resume their never-to-be-again "normal lives."

Chase Worthington returned to his home in Connecticut with spirits high and his depression at bay. His wife was in awe at the obvious salutary effect his three-month rehab had this time around.

Seymour Lynx returned to Hollywood, exhilarated by a brilliant idea for a new TV series.

Paolo Salvatore returned to his family in Georgetown. Within days, he reopened his office doors and worked closely with his lobbyist clients, pushing the president's agenda.

Hank Kramer returned to his office of old, not at the Chestnut Foundation, but as the Chief of Staff to President Randall Post.

The president's initiatives and his promise for reform met with an initial 64 percent approval rating in recent polls. It was a welcome message from the American people, who were willing to give him the yearlong breathing room he requested.

Congress cancelled its August recess to remain in session, which falls into the "miracles" category.

As for Noble and Max—Well, that's another story.

ACKNOWLEDGMENTS

As always, I offer my deep appreciation and gratitude to my publisher, David Dunham, for his continued confidence in me as a novelist. And for giving of his own time to see my projects to fruition. But I know David couldn't do it without his amazing colleagues, Managing Editor Crystal Flores and Associate Publisher Joel Dunham. Thanks to all of you.

My profound thanks go to my special inner circle of talented readers whose suggestions and insights continue to help enrich my stories: Ann Howells, Donna Post, Maestro Debra Cheverino, and Alfredo Vedro.

A special thanks goes to those who have allowed me to use them as real life characters in my story to add to the realism: to Alessandro Galli and Elena Salvicchi, the restaurateurs of Birreria Centrale and Osteria da Ganino. To Simone Galli my appointed tourist guide. To Andrea Prestani, Moreno Chiarantini, and the rest of the incredible team at the Perini Gastronomia in the Mercato Centrale. And to Giovanni Righi, who not only opened the doors to the wonders of the Republic of San Marino, but gave of his generosity during each of our frequent visits.

Lastly, how does one begin to thank family members and friends who continue to support my efforts and forgive my more-than-frequent absences?

ABOUT THE AUTHOR

 Sally Fernandez, a novelist of provocative political thrillers, wasn't always twisting facts with fiction. Heavily endowed with skills acquired in banking, she embarked on her writing career. Fernandez' focus on computer technology, business consulting, and project management, enhanced by business and technical writing, proved to be a boon. Her works of fiction reflect the knowledge garnered from her business experiences, while living in New York City, San Francisco, and Hong Kong.

Fernandez' foray into writing fiction officially began in 2007 when the presidential election cycle was in full swing. The overwhelming political spin by the media compelled her to question the frightening possibilities. As a confirmed political junkie, she took to the keyboard armed with unwinding events and discovered a new and exciting career.

Redemption: Aftermath of The Simon Trilogy is her fourth and final novel in a series, following *Brotherhood Beyond the Yard*, *Noble's Quest*, and *The Ultimate Revenge*. Each book provides an exhilarating platform for *Redemption*, with a gripping narrative that challenges the reader to put the book down. The ever-elusive Simon's daring escapes allow him to add unheard-of dimensions to the classic cat-and mouse-game. Her development of the other characters is destined to create a lasting bond between them and the reader. Despair not; Fernandez already has a new series in progress.

A world traveler, Ms. Fernandez and her husband, also editor-in-residence, split time between their homes in the United States and Italy.

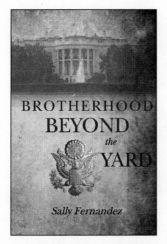

In 1990, an extraordinarily talented young man was discovered on the streets of Florence, Italy. His gifts are readily apparent, his ability to lead unmatched, and the possibilities for his future endless. Several years later, a group of scholars at Harvard known as La Fratellanza devise a brilliant thesis in the form of an intellectual game. When the game morphs into a real-life experience with the election of President Abner Baari, no one could have foreseen the consequences—or ramifications.

Director Hamilton Scott of the States Intelligence Agency is dispatched to Florence to coordinate a sting operation with Interpol to trap a terrorist, but as he digs deeper, he finds himself in a complicated mystery that has the fate of the United States, even that of the president himself, on his shoulders. As Hamilton drives the investigation forward with clear-headed integrity, Brotherhood Beyond the Yard provides an array of disturbing possibilities while delivering a rush of thrills.

Sally Fernandez's crackerjack international thriller expertly weaves seemingly disparate events into a cohesive whole leading to a shocking, shattering climax; a classic blend of character study and well-plotted action sequences keeps the pages turning faster and faster. There are no sacred cows here as Fernandez drives straight to the highest seats of Washington and questions anyone—and everything. A hair-raising page-turner from start to finish, Brotherhood Beyond the Yard examines political ideology, the international banking crisis, the role of Internet technology, and international terrorism with ferocious insight.

www.sallyfernandez.com

Fresh on the heels of her acclaimed first novel, *Brotherhood Beyond the Yard*, Sally Fernandez has penned a sequel that will add more sparkling thrills to the trilogy she is authoring. Major earth-shaking events in Europe and the USA converge to fuel Interpol and the States Intelligence Agency to join forces.

Although seemingly detached, the threats prompt Noble Bishop, Director of the SIA, and Enzo Borgini, Executive Director of Police Services for Interpol, to conduct joint investigations. Leading-edge technology is used to unravel the labyrinth of connections. The events are not coincidental. The enormous risks facing the USA and the world eventually draw the newly-elected president into the picture.

Land grabs, political manipulation, and a terrorist camp—along with sea changes in the American psyche—are skillfully woven to form a tapestry of intrigue. Readers of *Brotherhood Beyond the Yard* will renew their acquaintanceship with some of the characters in the sequel. This time their roles are more expansive and transparent, adding to the lingering intrigue. The widely sought mastermind of the global terrorist threat adds a breathtaking twist that lends even more intrigue to the narrative.

Written in the author's patent style, readers will be beguiled by the artistic marriage of established facts with a storyline that lifts creativity to new heights. Readers are challenged to separate fact from fiction, in the true Fernandez style.

www.sallyfernandz

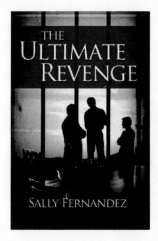

The Ultimate Revenge is the explosive conclusion to "The Simon Trilogy" that has held political thriller readers tightly in its grasp. The author's earlier books, *Brotherhood Beyond the Yard* and *Noble's Quest*, provide an exhilarating platform for the launch of this final chapter of a gripping narrative that challenges the reader to put the book down.

The ever-elusive Simon's daring escape from a high security prison allows him to add unheard of dimensions to the classic cat and mouse game he has played with Noble, the SIA Director. The manhunt for Simon engages two geniuses and a collection of talented operatives, all immersed in a chase with more twists and turns than a rodeo bull. In the process chicanery and double-dealing unfold at the highest levels, continuing some of the manipulations of the earlier books. Max, Noble's trusted partner, comes into her own, as she uncovers startling evidence and suggestive connections that reveal the nation's power grids are at risk.

Of greater significance are the hidden agendas of some of the world's most powerful recognized leaders to pursue their goals toward a supra-national one-world government under the guise of global warming. Simon, the deposed President Baari, and the jihadists find themselves sharing the same boat, each driven by separate motives but all resulting in a potential disastrous national emergency of huge proportions. The future of the United States is precipitously at stake. The capture of Simon becomes the highest priority as he continues to elude his captors with his usual bag of tricks. Meanwhile, Noble staves off a massive national emergency with his technical prowess. Simon, finally cornered, provides an explosive ending to a fast-paced trilogy that is not for the faint of heart.

Fernandez has proved once again that she has mastered the art of blending fact with fiction, leaving the readers to make their own judgments. Whatever the outcome, it raises the inviting question, "What if?"

www.sallyfernandez.com